The House Beneath the Oak Trees

by

Faye   Belle

The characters and places in this story
are fictitious. Any resemblance to actual
persons, living or dead, or actual events
is purely coincidental.

This book is dedicated to my mother
and father, for always encouraging me to
follow my dreams.

One

'Let's get this party started!' Anita cheered as she pulled open the door without Penny having to press the bell.

Penny squeezed past her excitable aunt who was waving her arms and matching each step she took, trying to catch Penny into an embrace against her will. Penny giggled and managed to duck past her, dumping her bags in the hallway and searching for the items she had packed which she knew would divert Anita's attention away from herself.

'Are we ready for this party, then?' Anita asked, moving towards her again, the same way she did every time she saw her youngest niece.

'Obviously,' Penny turned around, waving the two bottles of champagne she had nearly forgotten to bring as she left her flat earlier that morning.

'Whoohooo,' Anita took a bottle from Penny's hands, examining the label.

'Right, so the house is about twenty minutes away from the train station,' her mother said as she entered the hallway, 'I'm just checking we know the route. Oh, hello love,' she looked at Penny, noticing her arrival. She had a large map spread out in her hands and her small reading glasses perched on the end of her nose. She leant forward, creasing the paper as she gave Penny a kiss on the cheek. 'All ready to go? Have you packed your coat and your sunscreen?'

Penny's mother, Maggie, was a kind and generous woman. Short and round in appearance, she was every inch the typical maternal figure, with a gentle laugh and warm, welcoming eyes. Most people who met her wanted to embrace her in a hug as soon as they saw her, getting the impression just by looking at her that she would gladly return the gesture.

'Yes, Mother!' Penny said in a sarcastic tone, mocking her mother's cautiousness and her obsessive need to always be prepared.

Penny was excited about this trip away, organised for her sister's thirtieth birthday to a remote countryside location. They had booked to stay in an apartment in the countryside in Oakdene, a small town near the larger city of Charterville. Penny's mother had found the place after spending hours researching the perfect getaway location for them. They wanted to go somewhere peaceful and quiet, yet somewhere that was close enough to a city centre if they fancied something livelier. Her mother had told Penny that Charterville was a vibrant city which hosted several bars, restaurants and local unique shops. Having never been to that part of the country before, Penny was looking forward to the long list of events her mother had planned.

'Oh, hang on, I don't think I've remembered my coat!' her mother scurried back into the room.

Although she had given Penny strict instructions to arrive at her house on time, her mother was late, fussing about something as usual. Knowing it would be a while until they would end up leaving, Penny made her way to the kitchen. The walk was instinctive and she headed straight to the fridge to see what there was to eat. Penny opened the door and peered inside before reluctantly deciding to push it shut. Having less hours at home, due to her busy law career in the city, had caused her to lead a somewhat unhealthy lifestyle, grabbing food as and when she could and having a glass of wine each evening to relax from the stressful day at the office. She had noticed she was slowing gaining weight and in an attempt to take better care of herself, decided to go on a diet. Eating more healthily and exercising at lunchtime, Penny had thought that she was making progress, until the last couple of weeks when she noticed she had slowly gained the odd pound here and there which she could only attribute to the extra glasses of wine at the weekend.

'Are we ready yet? Look, I'm out here on my own waiting for you!' Anita yelled from the hallway and Penny shut the fridge, grateful for the interruption.

Penny couldn't help but laugh when she saw her, sitting on her packed suitcase, coat wrapped across her round frame impatiently. Anita was Penny's only aunt and was like a second mother to Penny and her sister Fiona. Penny's father had left them when the girls were very young, forcing her mother to quit her own successful job to look after her two daughters. Anita saw her sister's struggle and decided to move away from her home where she was living alone to help raise the children. Penny's mother had not remarried which suited Anita perfectly as she had never found anyone to settle down with either. Growing up it had only ever been the four women together and Penny couldn't have imagined going on a trip like this without Anita joining in.

'So, you're planning on leaving without me then are you?' Fiona strode into the hallway.

Penny jumped when she saw her sister and ran towards her, 'Happy birthday! I'm so excited to get away.'

'Me too! I'm planning on going shopping, going to the spa, do some shopping and erm… oh yeah more shopping,' she laughed.

Fiona hugged her sister and although she tried to push the feeling away, Penny felt a stab of jealousy when she saw how she looked; dressed effortlessly in a casual but sleek black dress, looking as though she had just stepped out of a

—

movie. She did not envy her sister, but Penny always thought she paled in comparison when standing beside her. Her mother had always told Penny that she was pretty, although Penny never quite believed her, especially when standing next to her gorgeous, model-like sister. She knew she was plain-looking, with her average shoulder-length brown hair and freckles that were sporadically scattered across her otherwise pale face.

'Right, I think I have everything,' her mother had entered the hallway, dragging three heavy cases behind her.

'Mum, we're only going for a week. You're worse than Fiona!' Penny laughed, 'What on earth have you packed?'

'Well I want to be prepared. You never know what will happen. Is that all you have?' she looked with concern at Penny's compact weekend case.

'We're only going for a week,' Penny shrugged, convincing herself she had packed appropriately.

Although to some a week away with your mother and aunt would seem like the last thing you would want to do, Penny couldn't deny that she was looking forward to it. It had been a while since the four relations had spent time on their own and although they were all incredibly close, Penny thought it would be nice for them to reconnect and make new memories.

They heard the beep of a car from outside and excitedly rushed through the doorway, clambering into the taxi that had arrived to pick them up to take them to the station. Having four people with luggage crammed into a small hatchback made the short distance to the train station rather uncomfortable, however they refused to allow it to dampen their spirits. Penny was squeezed into the back seat next to Anita and the way she was positioned meant she had no choice but to look out of the window, listening to the conversation of the women behind her, all giggling at the terrible jokes the driver was making after noticing their excitable mood.

As they reached the station, Penny's mother marched them straight through the ticket machines and onto the designated platform where they would catch their train. Predictably, when the train lazily rolled into the station, Penny's mother ensured that they were the first ones on, her and Anita storming forward to secure the best seats. Penny nestled beside her sister and took a bottle of champagne out of her bag.

'Let's start as we mean to go on!' Penny said, popping the cork.

'Yay. Happy Birthday to ME!' Fiona grabbed the first plastic glass that Penny took from her bag and held it under her nose, indicating that her glass should be filled first.

Penny laughed at her sister's excitement. She realised that to her, this trip was a pretty big deal. Fiona had met her husband Paul when she was still at school and they married when they were twenty-one. Although Penny had big dreams to pursue a corporate law career, Fiona was the opposite. All Fiona ever wanted to do was to follow her passion, which was beauty. She was lucky that she had inherited all the good genes that existed within the family which made this easy for her to pursue, working in salons until she had finally saved enough money to open her own.

'So, let's talk about what outfits you've brought with you; I think we'll have time to hit the shops when we're there, don't you?' Fiona snuggled into Penny's shoulder.

Their mother leant forward and interrupted their chance to gossip, 'So, the first thing we are going to do is collect the keys for the apartment and then head out for a walk around the area…'

'And buy tea bags, we cannot forget the tea bags!' Anita

—

chirped in, pointing at her handbag, 'I don't think the ones I brought with me will last us all week!'

'Well yes, we will look in the local shops and pick up some provisions,' her mother said, bringing out one of, what seemed like, a million maps from her handbag. 'Then I thought we could go out for a nice dinner, I have researched some nice restaurants to choose from.'

'Then we need to find out about the ghost and ghouls in the town. I was doing a bit of research and there are…' Anita said, leaning into the group.

'Oh, stop it Anita!' Penny laughed, accustomed to her aunt trying to scare them all everywhere they went.

'You know, I had the weirdest dream last night. We arrived at the apartment and then really weird things started happening,' Anita continued.

'What things?' Fiona asked, mild panic in her voice. She had always thought their aunt was psychic.

'Well, first we heard noises and then we saw things wandering around. You Fiona,' Anita stopped to point, 'I think they were after you, they started visiting us in our sleep, their restless bodies…'

Penny looked at her sister and saw her eyes had turned into two wide circles, clearly buying into the usual hocus pocus Anita spread whenever they were together. Everywhere they went Anita ensured they always had enough teabags to last them a lifetime and an array of different ghost stories to scare them before they went to sleep.

'Yeah, then we all start to disappear and things get weirder, and then we sleepwalk, oh and then we hear crying, oh and then our heads blow up!' Penny laughed, rolling her eyes. 'We've heard all the stories Anita, they're getting old, you're going to have to conjure up a new one if you want to convince us!'

'Okay if you don't want to take me seriously...' Anita replied, turning her face to the side, pretending to be offended. 'Don't come running to me when they take you first.'

They laughed at the typical conversation they always had and spent the remainder of the two-hour train journey looking through the guidebooks and making plans for the week ahead, excitedly choosing where to go on what day and what was on the 'must do' list for each person. Penny decided that for her, the activity she was most looking forward to was the visit to the spa. She had been silently noticing that her joints were aching when she went to sleep and her neck was sore from the countless hours she spent crouched over her computer screen. A full day of relaxation would be exactly what she needed before she returned to the grind of the city.

When the train pulled into the station, they jumped up out of their seats so enthusiastically that Anita knocked over the second bottle of champagne they had opened and they watched as it trickled onto the seats they had just pushed themselves out of.

'Oh no, the champagne, quick, pick it up before we lose it all,' Anita turned back to get the spilled drink as the others paid no attention to her, more concerned with not missing their stop.

Looking through the train window, Penny could see that the platform for Oakdene station was small and as soon as they stood up from their seats, the warning sounds began buzzing telling them they didn't have long to depart from the train before it headed to its next destination. Quickly, they gathered their possessions and made their way towards the exit. Anita jumped off at the last second before the doors closed, clutching onto the bottle of champagne she had carelessly tipped over just moments before, a wide smile across her face at her achievement of saving some of the drink.

They were the only ones who had got off the train and the only people, it seemed, to be standing in the station. The silence was almost deafening, if that was even possible. Penny wasn't used to being somewhere so quiet and still that the silence made her nervous, and she checked around to ensure they had got off at the correct stop.

As they made their way to the exit, Penny noted that there were no staff around either; no guard to check their tickets and no one to ask for directions. She looked to see if she could spot anyone waiting to board a train but there was no one to be seen. Glancing up, she was surprised to see that there wasn't even a board overhead which told passengers when the next train would be. It was as though the train station had been abandoned, completely forgotten about in a world of modernisation, giving the illusion that they had stepped back in time. Penny laughed, instantly attracted to the solitude which was so different to the chaotic, bustling city she was used to.

They left the station and walked onto the street where they noticed a single vehicle waiting under a Taxi sign. Penny wondered why the driver would bother coming to pick up fares in a place like this; even on the street there was not one person to be seen. They walked up to the car and Fiona rattled on the window to get the driver's attention. The man was surprised by the noise which seemed to have awoken him from a deep sleep and he jumped quickly out of the car to put their luggage into the boot.

They climbed in as Penny's mother shouted the address to the driver. Penny could tell by her high-pitched tone and by the way she had omitted to say 'please' that she was over excited, her usual good manners seemingly having been left on the train.

The driver eyed the women in his rear-view mirror for a moment before saying, 'Erm, are you sure that is the right address?'

Penny's mother looked down at her piece of paper, a look of annoyance on her face at the possibility that she may not have been as organised as she had thought she had been. A smile quickly resurfaced as she clarified that yes, that was indeed the correct address.

'Are you sure?' he asked.

'Yes, I'm looking at the address in front of me. Here,' she pushed the printed confirmation into the man's hand.

The man looked at the piece of paper and then back up at the group in his mirror and then back down at the paper.

'Is there a problem?' her mother asked nervously.

'Erm. No there's no problem, not really... but... well... I haven't taken anyone there for some time.'

'The advertisement says the building has been converted into holiday apartments?'

'Well yes I see this, it's just that... Well are you sure you want to?' He continued to stare at the paper before shaking his head. 'Okay then. We'll be there in ten minutes. What are you here for, people don't often come this far to stay in that house since...'

'Since?' Anita asked.

The driver paused.

'Never mind. I thought that perhaps you may have researched the street before booking. Just to let you know that it is a bit desolate around where you'll be staying, there's a bus stop down the end of the road which will take you to the centre if you need to...' he eyed them in the mirror, 'you know, in case you need anything.'

The driver came to a stop at a small road with two enormous oak trees placed either side of the entrance.

'This is the furthest I can take you I'm afraid, it's a private road you see and cars aren't allowed down the path, it's only a couple of minutes' walk past those trees.'

The driver was out of the car before them, rushing to get their cases out of the boot before they had the chance to unbuckle their seatbelts. They eyed each other at both the eagerness and the strangeness of the man. Getting out of the car, they walked towards their bags which the driver had left for them on the pavement. They each located their own luggage and started discussing between them who would pay for the ride.

Interrupting their chatter, they heard screeching of tyres and the roar of an engine bellowing from behind. They turned to notice the taxi had driven off at speed. They watched as it zoomed into the distance, disappearing under a tunnel of dust which was flying violently in the air, angry that its previously calm resting position on the undisturbed path had been so suddenly disrupted.

Two

The women stood on the pavement, staring after the man in disbelief. Where they came from, taxis never let you out of the cab without paying first in fear that you would run off. It seemed the people here in Oakdene were far more trusting.

'Hang on, we didn't pay you!' Penny's mother yelled, running after the taxi, arms waving in the air to grab his attention.

'Mum, stop it.' Penny ran after her mother, holding down her arms which were still flapping to get noticed.

'But we didn't pay! We can't not pay, it's dishonest!' Penny's mother looked horrified that she had potentially committed some wrongdoing against the unknown man. 'It seemed like he had been waiting for some time to pick up a fare and then he just drove off without being paid, poor man.'

'He may have thought that we paid him or he may have been confused. He knows where we're staying if he wants to come back and get the money once he's realised.'

'It's just a bit odd that's all, it didn't seem like he wanted to take us here and then he almost pushed us out of the taxi and sped off,' her mother replied, still looking into the distance where the man had raced away from them so quickly.

'Well, we haven't had our walk around yet, maybe the people here are a bit strange,' Anita said, picking up her bag and walking towards the path, not seeming too bothered by the event.

Looking back at where the taxi had disappeared, Penny also found it peculiar but didn't think any more of it; it was his fault if he was careless enough not to do his job properly. She turned to look at the path which the driver told them they were to walk down to find their apartment. The path was barely noticeable, engulfed between two gigantic trees. She spotted a sign which read 'Oak Street'.

'What's the street called again, Mum?' Penny asked.

'Oak Street darling, oh look, it's through there,' she pointed, following Penny's gaze.

One of the oak trees was positioned directly behind the signpost and the other was standing beside it; their branches almost acting as an arrow to show them in which direction to walk. Penny looked closer at the tree which was trying to hide behind the sign and laughed at the way it looked, its skinny bottom trunk supporting the weight of so many thick green leaves at its top. She imagined that was probably how she was looking recently with the extra weight she had put on, her skinny spindly legs supporting her protruding belly.

It was the beginning of spring and Penny thought it unusual for the trees to have so many leaves on them already. She didn't know much about nature but knew that trees of this kind shed their burnt orange leaves in the autumn and began to grow new, youthful, green leaves in the spring. Back at home they hadn't had a particularly warm autumn, and when she had left the city it looked as grey and as miserable as it always did; the small number of trees that survived in the concrete city only just beginning to develop splatters of green on their branches.

Regardless of why they were in bloom, Penny thought they looked wonderful. Just looking at the plentiful trees made her feel as though she was healthier, that somehow she was taking in the freshness by just standing beneath them. She opened her mouth and took a deep breath of the country air but was disappointed when she didn't automatically feel refreshed.

The two trees stood adjacent to each other; almost side by side. Their thick spray of leaves touched each other in the middle of the path, creating a deep archway which made it difficult to see past them. The signpost indicated that Oak Street was down beneath the trees along a tiny cobble path that led the way.

They followed the botanical arrow down the path and as they walked, Penny saw that it was lined with towering trees. Each tree bore skinny, leafless branches which reached out and touched the branch of the tree standing by its side, as though the trees were holding hands through their branches and they didn't want to let go.

Whilst the branches on the oak trees were bursting with life, these trees were the opposite. Although Penny knew the skinny branches had just not regenerated their own green leaves as quickly as the oak trees, Penny couldn't help but think how much they resembled decaying bones rather than leafless twigs. The closer she looked, the more she felt that they were looking back at her, their lankly, intertwined branches seemingly pointing down at the four ladies as they quickly scurried past.

They reached the end of the footpath and saw a grand country estate positioned behind a well maintained, circular garden. Penny looked upwards and gasped as she saw the magnificent building before her. Being raised in a city, Penny had never seen a house as splendid as the one she was looking up at and was instantly drawn by how elaborate and romantic it appeared. She saw that the house was covered with little white windows which surrounded the high, double-breasted wooden door in the centre of the building. To the left-hand side of the main house there was another door, this one much smaller and less maintained, appearing rusty and weathered. The door appeared to belong to a small house that had been added onto the side of the main building, sticking out at an unnatural angle.

There wasn't much more of the small building to see and as Penny was moving her gaze back towards the main house, a movement within the window above the rusty door made her stop and stare up at it. She couldn't be sure, but she thought she had seen something in the corner of the window, looking out at them taking in the view of the house.

She had already looked away but when she registered the movement, she looked back quickly to see what it was, but the flicker had disappeared. She waited a few moments before taking her eyes off the spot, in case the movement made another appearance. When nothing materialised, Penny shrugged and walked towards where her family had stopped and she wondered who was staying in the house alongside them.

As they moved away from the garden towards the house, they saw a young woman hovering near the door of the side house, clutching a clipboard tightly in her hands. She was wearing a smart, grey trouser suit and had her hand placed in front of her eyes in an attempt to get a better view of the group who were walking towards her. When they got closer, Penny saw her tapping one foot on the ground impatiently at their slow walk and lack of urgency.

They reached her and Penny realised she looked uncomfortable standing beside the grand house in her poorly fitted suit. Her bright blonde hair fell loosely in curls around her shoulders which highlighted her youthful and tanned skin. She was standing at the bottom of a step which led into the side door with a smile on her face which did not seem genuine. Rather than being an upward turn, her lips were raised just above a tight line and Penny thought that if she opened her mouth, they would be able to see that behind the smile was a set of firmly gritted teeth.

As she saw the group approaching she started to wave her hands frantically and rushed towards them.

'Mrs Day? Nice to meet you. I am Claire, your representative of Cosy Holiday Rentals,' the woman shook Penny's mothers hand up and down hurriedly. 'Let me show you your apartment, you are on the ground floor of the end house.'

After two shakes, Claire dropped the hand she was holding and turned to face the door, wasting no time introducing herself to the others. She brought a set of keys out from her jacket and said, 'Now this door is very stiff so I don't recommend you lock it.' She fiddled with the door, pushing it backwards and forwards aggressively.

'Well that doesn't really sound all that safe, to just leave a door open,' Penny's mother nervously replied. She was a stickler for safety and Penny knew that this sort of instruction would be making her feel anxious, automatically thinking of the people who could break in as they were sleeping safely in their beds.

'Oh, don't worry about that, you can't open it without a key but just don't double lock it. No one really comes down this street anyway and you're the only ones on this block so you shouldn't have any problems. I wouldn't want you to double lock it and not be able to get in. Our agency is quite far away to be honest and we... we... well it would take us a while to get back.'

'Why aren't we staying in *that* building?' Fiona pointed to the main house, nose upturned when she noticed Claire was opening the door to the side house and not the magnificent one that took their breath away on their approach. 'Why do we get the crappy side block?'

'Oh, I thought you saw the advertisement? Those ones

aren't quite ready yet. You see we don't normally get bookings until the summer and to clean all of those, well they take some time and we… well we thought this one would suit you a bit better.' She smiled at the group, and noticing they were not reciprocating the gesture, turned back to face the door. She pushed it open with her shoulder and took a step down into the apartment.

'Yes, this is the one I chose, dear,' her mother reassured her, trying not to notice that Fiona's nose remained scrunched-up at Claire's response.

They followed Claire into the house and placed their bags by the entrance, looking around at where they would be staying. Once they were all safely inside, Claire returned back to the step next to the opened door and kept her hand firmly on the handle.

'So, this will be your holiday home for the next week, everything you need to know is in there,' she said, pointing to a folder. 'We have put together a welcome pack with some provisions, wine, cheese and chocolate etc. You shouldn't need the heating on as we're due to get nice weather, but if you do, please press the button on the wall by the bedrooms and leave the keys on the table when you leave. You shouldn't need anything else but if you do, please don't hesitate to contact me. Is there anything in particular you want to know?'

'The taxi driver said that we were about a ten-minute drive into town. How do we get there, is there a bus stop nearby?' Anita asked.

'Yes, if you turn right at the end of the path and walk for about five minutes, you can pick up the bus opposite a lovely little pub which will take you into town. Or you can call a taxi; we have left the number of a local firm in the wallet,' Claire answered, reluctantly leaving the step and walking towards where the gift hamper and paper wallet were sitting on a table.

'Here you go, we have also put in some details of the best restaurants so if you fancy eating out...' she stopped midsentence as she looked away from the folder and over the shoulders of the women still standing by the door. She nervously looked around the room, turning around in a circle until she was facing the wall. She stayed there for a few moments before turning back to face the group. Looking straight at Penny, she stared directly into her eyes, not moving them for a few seconds, not even to blink.

'Is there a problem?' Penny asked, suddenly feeling exposed by the way she was looking at her with a disapproving but pitying expression.

Claire thought for a few moments before blinking, shaking her head as she came out of her trance. Turning back to the table, she slammed the folder abruptly shut before striding towards the door.

'Well it was lovely meeting you, please enjoy your stay,' Claire said as she climbed the step out of the opened door, focusing on the floor to avoid contact with the suspicious eyes which were watching her strange behaviour with interest.

'Hang on a second, aren't you meant to show us around?' Anita asked rather rudely. Although Penny's mother was always perfectly mannered, her aunt was not and it wasn't long before her trademark attitude addressed the uninterested woman.

Claire paused, one foot outside the door and turned to face them. 'Well, the thing is,' she said nervously, still clutching onto the handle of the door, looking from one woman to another, 'it is all very self-explanatory, two bedrooms, one bathroom and a kitchen/diner. Feel free to use all appliances, pots and pans and help yourselves to any books you wish to read. I am very sorry but the agency double-booked and I must get off to meet another client,' and with that, she turned again to leave.

'You said we were the only ones on the complex this week?' Fiona queried, trying to regain Claire's attention and get more information out of her.

'Yes, that is correct, we don't tend to get busy really until summer so we don't have any bookings at the moment.'

'Is it only one floor?' their mother asked.

Claire looked at them impatiently and huffed as she said, 'Yes, we rent each floor as a separate apartment. Some floors in the main house are separated into two. The entrance to the apartment on the floor above you is around the side and up the stairs. But as I said, it is completely empty so you don't need to worry about that. You're the first booking of the season. In the summer, we normally...' Claire stopped. Looking again over their shoulders, her eyes were glued to a spot behind them. 'We normally... erm...'

Noticing the abrupt stop in Claire's sentence, everyone turned to look in the direction she was staring. After seeing there was nothing of interest, they returned their puzzled eyes to Claire who, after noticing them looking at her, came round from her trance and said, 'I'm... I'm... I'm sorry I have to leave now; have a good time.'

She turned and rushed out of the door, not waiting to be called back in for more questions she clearly didn't want to answer. They stared at Claire's disappearing figure, in shock at the sudden departure.

Anita walked towards the door and slammed it shut. 'Now we know that the people here really are strange *and* really rude!'

Bewildered by Claire's speedy exit, Penny moved to the window and saw her figure getting smaller and smaller as

18

she literally ran down the path onto the main street. She wondered whether her family had been rude to her somehow, causing her to want to get away from them as quickly as she could. Surely it would have been in her best interest to impress them, Oakdene wasn't exactly the bustling tourist town everyone had heard of, after all. When she could no longer see the strange woman, she shrugged and turned back into the room.

'Let's check this place out then.'

The door they entered led them straight into the kitchen/dining area. In the middle, a large wooden table dominated the room, big enough to fit at least ten people around it, although Penny could only count five chairs scattered around sporadically. Directly opposite the table, attached to the far end of the wall, was an old-fashioned kitchen workstation. Small pine cupboards lined the wall above it from corner to corner, stopping only in the middle to allow room for the gigantic antique oven hood. She walked over to the oven, fingertips trailing the top of the worktops as she moved along and opened the doors. To her surprise they were unexpectedly heavy, and as she pulled them open, a creaking sound vibrated throughout the room.

'Goodness, this looks prehistoric!' Anita said, crouching down beside Penny, coughing as an explosion of dust burst out of the oven door. 'I don't think they cleaned it before we came!'

'Well it's a good job we're not planning on doing any cooking this holiday; we'd burn the place down,' her mother replied, removing Penny's hand from the oven door and closing it firmly shut. She had created a strict rule that apart from breakfast, they would not be doing any cooking or any chores they would normally be doing back at home. She insisted this week was strictly about having fun and relaxing and she pushed the two peering women quickly away.

Penny was grateful there were no plans to cook, none of them having acquired culinary skills that would impress anyone. The dust from the oven was still lingering around the room and as she waved her arms to try and clear it, she noticed an impressive fireplace to the side. The walls surrounding the fireplace were covered in drawings and paintings, each of a different genre and style, which strangely did not seem to match.

'Oo, what is this?' Fiona asked, walking towards the other side of the room.

Penny followed and saw that at the very far side of the room in the corner, a dark black door was positioned between the oven and the fireplace. She wasn't sure how she had managed to miss it when she walked in, the inky black colouring highlighting its presence in the otherwise bright room. It was secured by a big, bulky metal padlock, preventing it being opened. She held the padlock in her hand and turned it over curiously, wondering why a room so visible would be locked. Chips of rusting metal fell onto her hands as she turned it over and saw how old it was. The decay implied that, with a simple tug, it would fall apart easily giving them another room to explore. She tugged on the lock but it rebelled against her efforts, throwing another sea of dust through the gaps of the door as it rattled in her attempt.

'What is with all of this dust?' Anita coughed. 'Why didn't they clean this place before we came? I could've had asthma and this might have put me in hospital!'

Penny rolled her eyes at her aunt and moved away, grateful to distance herself from the thick powdery dust that seemed to be lingering in the spot by the door.

'That is where the bodies are kept,' Anita whispered.

'Oh stop it you,' Fiona walked away from the door and joined her sister on the other side of the room.

'I mean it. Did you not know, this place is haunted? It used to be a hospital for the clinically insane, people used to be killed and their bodies dragged up those stairs…'

'Stop it Anita, or at least wait until later before you start!' her mother interjected, hitting her sister lightly on the shoulder.

Being raised in an Irish family meant that Anita and her mother grew up in a world where telling ghost tales was as common as a bedtime story. They loved them, loved telling them, hearing them, watching them, anything. Penny wasn't sure if they actually believed in the stories they heard and shared, but she couldn't remember a time when Anita had not put a ghostly spin on almost anything they were doing.

Unlike the rest of her family, Penny thought it was all nonsense. Clearly she knew that there was no such thing as ghosts, but she still enjoyed hearing the tales and allowing herself to be scared for a few seconds nonetheless.

'I'm just telling the girls the truth so they don't get scared later when they hear bumps in the night and run into our bedroom scared like they used to when they were little girls!' Anita said, giggling as she watched the despair on the younger women's faces.

'Oh sshh…' Fiona turned back to look at the door, 'I reckon it's just the stairs connecting to the floor above. You can tell that back in the day this whole place used to be one big house, they obviously had to block it off to stop us from wandering where we shouldn't.'

Anita considered this reply before saying, 'I prefer the body idea.'

She turned and walked out of the room and the others followed her into the hallway which they presumed led from the kitchen area into the bedrooms and bathroom. Standing outside the entrance to the kitchen, the hallway was straight and Penny could see an open door at the end of the corridor. She couldn't work it out from where she was standing, but the room appeared to be unnaturally dark, as though there were no windows to light it up. She glanced to her right and noticed two archways which led to the bedrooms and saw that, unlike the room at the end of the hallway, sun from the outside was pouring in.

Penny wanted to head straight to the room she was staring at, but her mother wanted to check the rooms methodically, going into each room as they passed.

They turned into the first room and saw a grand four-poster bed filling the middle of the room, and Penny knew this room was intended for her mother and aunt. Fiona jumped on it as she said, 'Wow this is luxurious, a bed fit for a princess.'

'Gosh I think this is actually an original bed, there's no gap between the bed and the wall,' Penny's mother said, kneeling on the floor and jabbing her finger between the headrest and the wall before sitting beside them. 'Imagine how many people have slept in here since then!'

Penny shivered at the thought and tried to put the image out of her mind. Although not normally one to mind so much about such things, the thought that she would be sleeping in a bed where many had laid before her made her feel queasy. What they had seen in the apartment so far had shown them that the owners hadn't put too much thought into giving the place a thorough clean and she tried not to think about what germs could be lingering in the old bed.

They left the room and continued their exploration of the apartment, travelling down the hallway until they reached an alcove to their right. Penny walked into it and saw an old-fashioned writing bureau propped next to glass patio doors. Running her fingers across the writing desk, her eyebrows lowered and mouth twisted when she realised that, like everything else they had seen so far, it was covered in dust.

Penny placed her head against one of the small glass doors and looked out onto a square patio area, which seemed rather tired and pretty lifeless. She gave the handle a turn but like the black door, it was locked. When they realised there was nothing worth seeing outside the door, they continued their walk onwards until they reached the second archway to their right.

'This must be the other bedroom,' Penny's mother commented as she wandered in. 'This is where you girls will be staying.'

'Jesus it's cold in here!' Fiona exclaimed.

Fiona was right, as soon as they stepped into the room they noticed the sharp, sudden change in the air. Instinctively Penny moved her arms up and wrapped them around her body in an attempt to keep warm. Looking around, Penny noticed there were no windows in the room and the exposed brick walls flowed into the arched ceiling. Penny realised that this was not an ordinary bedroom but a cellar of some kind.

'I don't think I like this room very much,' Fiona said. 'Are you sure we can't have your room? Please?' She looked at her mother, her voice whining the same way it did when she was a child, pleading to get her own way.

'No you cannot. I did tell you before that this room was called the 'cellar' room. You said you were happy with it. You know I can't stay in here because of my claustrophobia.'

Her mother had told them that they would be staying in some sort of 'cellar' room but Penny hadn't thought to ask her what she meant, assuming they would be staying in some quirky feature room. Stood looking into the room, she felt as though the arched walls were becoming more and more circular the longer she looked at them and she found herself desperately wanting to leave.

'Ergh... fine I guess,' Fiona huffed, 'Pen, we can push our two beds together so it is like we have a double, no way I'm sleeping all alone in this creepy room.'

'Well it's a good job I packed an extra jumper; I'll try not to notice the cold!' Penny said, trying to ignore the feeling that the lowered walls were trying to engulf her. She turned quickly and left the room, hoping the others would join her.

The final room they had left to explore was the bathroom which Penny assumed was the door they could see directly from the kitchen. They stood outside and Penny remembered how dark it appeared when she was looking at it from the top of the hallway. As they entered, Penny was amazed by how bright and airy it was. Between the basin and the bath, a large window was located, flooding the room in sunlight.

'Ooo, very nice!' her mother said, head appearing from behind Penny's shoulder. 'Don't just stand there, let us have a look,' she pushed Penny forward.

'It is quite strange though,' Penny said.

'What is love?' her mother asked.

'It's so bright in here.'

'That's a good thing, especially when doing our makeup,' Fiona said, adjusting her hair and pouting in the mirror which was hanging above the sink.

'But, it was so dark when we came in. Well it looked that way anyway. When we stood at the top of the hallway, this door was half open and the room was pitch black inside. I assumed there was no natural light in here but there is. I don't understand why it was so dark?' Penny asked, looking around at the others.

'I didn't notice that, maybe when the door is half closed, it blocks half of the window?' her mother reasoned.

Penny thought this was a logical explanation and decided to let it go. She hadn't really taken too much time to look at it when she was standing in the kitchen and was probably looking at it strangely. Like her bedroom, Penny noticed how cold it was, despite the window being firmly shut and it being unseasonably hot outside. For some unknown reason, Penny suddenly felt lonely, the room slowly sucking all the energy out of her body. The hairs on her neck started to rise and as she took in another gulp of the cold, sharp air, she could feel an overwhelming sense of sadness strangely engulfing her. Penny wanted to leave the room immediately.

She pushed the others out and as soon as she left the room, her spirits instantaneously lifted. They made their way back to the kitchen to collect their bags but Penny couldn't shake the feeling of unease that was beginning to bubble away in her stomach.

Once they had reached the top of the hallway, she glanced back at the open doorway of the bathroom. She could see the doorframe in perfect visibility, but the inside of the bathroom was again the blackest of black.

Three

After disposing of their bags in the rooms where they would be spending the week, the women sat at the table enjoying a glass of wine from the complementary basket.

'Funny, this apartment looks nothing like the advertisement. I know when you book something online sometimes the photos are a bit nicer than the real thing but honestly, it's so different. I even looked at pictures posted by other guests on the review sites to make sure we were staying somewhere nice!' Maggie complained.

'Maybe you were looking at the wrong apartment, like maybe you were looking at the ones next door or something?' Fiona said. '*Those* ones look nice!'

'No, it was definitely this one as I specifically wanted the one at the bottom on the corner of the block in case other guests were loud,' she paused, 'or more likely we were too loud!' She giggled as she raised her glass, taking a sip of the wine.

'It is nice Mum, don't worry! I'm only teasing, I think it's cute,' Fiona reassured her.

Although not the cleanest place she had ever stayed, Penny had to agree with her sister that it certainly was cute. The furnishings and fixtures gave the apartment a certain quaint and homely appeal which made her feel as though they would have a good stay here. She was still confused about the bathroom but as she took another sip of wine, she felt it washing away the uneasiness she experienced when she thought back to the room.

Her mother had said that the actual apartment differed from the advertisement, but Penny didn't think it mattered so much; it was beautifully antiquated and decorated perfectly to fit the style and period of the building. The owners had done a superb job in restoring and keeping as many of the original features as possible. Penny loved history and old, lived-in buildings and for some unknown reason, felt a connection to the house.

'Look, I'm telling you, it's completely different!' her mother said, interrupting Penny's thoughts. As she spoke she brought out a folder from her bag and placed a piece of paper in front of them.

The four women crouched together to look at the pictures she had sprawled across the table and Penny was shocked to see how different it was. The photograph presented an accurate picture of the outside of the house and the basic layout of the floor plan was the same, however the furnishings and decorations inside were dramatically different. The image in the advertisement showed a modernised kitchen and stylishly designed bedrooms. The picture she was staring at radiated so much more warmth then the rooms she had only recently stepped foot in and she wondered how they could ever be regarded as the same.

'Seems as though they falsely advertised. Maybe we can get some pennies back,' Anita said. 'Make sure to take lots of pictures before we leave so we can email them our complaint as soon as we get back.'

Penny could see her mother was disappointed by the way she looked downwards at the glossy pictures in front of her. She was focused on the advertisement and Penny thought she saw her hands tremble slightly when she picked up the remainder of the papers and put them back neatly in the folder and into her bag. She had put so much effort into organising the trip, Penny knew she wanted it to be perfect for the four of them and how much this would have mattered to her, even though it didn't matter to them.

'I think it is really nice, Mum,' she said as she walked around the table and put her arms around her. 'It doesn't matter what it looks like as long as we're together.' Her mother patted Penny's arm and smiled, grateful for the gesture of reassurance.

'So, what is the plan for the rest of the day then?' Fiona asked, trying to distract her. Penny looked at her watch and realised that it was now 3pm. Their mother had planned the train times meticulously to ensure they had the maximum amount of time in Oakdene and Penny knew she would have organised exactly what they would be doing for the rest of the evening.

'Well as it is quite late I was thinking that maybe we could go for a little walk around the area, get our bearings a bit and have dinner somewhere local. I have a full day's activities planned for tomorrow, which really requires us to leave by 9am, so I think an early night will do us good!' she responded, suddenly more enthused with the chance to discuss her plans.

'Okay, I need to get freshened up first. Does anyone mind if I take a quick shower?' Fiona asked. 'I absolutely cannot go out in this.'

Fiona moved her arms up and down her body as though there was something wrong with her appearance. Penny rolled her eyes in response to her gesture; she looked perfect as always, the sticky air seemingly not having any effect on her perfectly applied makeup.

'Hurry up then,' her mother shooed her away. 'Is anyone else getting changed?' she asked the others who both responded with a shake of the head while Fiona ran hurriedly out of the room.

Stiff from sitting at the table on the uncomfortable wooden chairs, Penny stood and started walking around the kitchen table, trying to take note of some of the items she had missed when they looked around earlier. She walked towards the fireplace and stood in front of the art which was hanging at various heights across the wall.

'These pictures are weird!' she commented after she had walked around once.

She moved back towards the pictures and took a closer look at them. Most of them seemed ordinary enough, one was a portrait of a woman, another was of a horse in the countryside, one of a vase and so on. She walked forward to get a better look and ended up in front of the black door. She stopped and eyed it curiously.

The more she looked, the more she considered it odd that the agency had locked the door. If her sister was correct in her assumption that the door was a passageway connecting their apartment to the one upstairs, why did they not just seal off the staircase, or more simply, replace this tattered looking door with one that had a lock and key?

Penny could hear her mother and aunt discussing how best to phrase their letter of complaint, noticing how high-pitched their voices had become with the more wine they consumed. Zoning the chatter out, she focused her attention on looking at the picture that had been hung between the door and the fireplace. Unlike the others which seemed to be randomly placed, this one looked as though exactly that spot had been chosen for it. Penny couldn't explain why it appeared this way, apart from the fact that everything around it seemed to be out of place whereas this one was sitting perfectly square in the centre of the wall.

This particular item was a sketch in a simple wooden frame. Inside the top right of the picture, a tall, thin man was standing in a black suit, hand on a walking stick. Although she squinted and moved her head closer, she was unable to see the man's face due to him being far down what appeared to be, a road. She noticed that the drawing was incomplete and had been started but never finished by the way the lines of an intricately drawn road led into a blank space of white nothingness. There was only one house that had been drawn at the far right of the image, which had also not been completed. On the opposite side of the drawing, a woman stood looking away from the man, appearing to be the only image in the picture that had been completed.

The woman was dressed in a simple, but wide, skirt which came down to her ankles and a tight bodice that showed the slenderness of her frame. Her head was looking away from the man and out of the frame, but Penny could not see her face. She moved her head away from the picture and looked at the outline of the house and its surroundings. For some reason, the scenery in the drawing seemed strangely familiar, but she couldn't figure out why.

'Look at this one,' she pointed, 'it doesn't seem to have been finished.'

'It says 1801 something or other,' Anita said, coming up behind Penny, glasses perched on her nose as she reviewed the bottom of image. 'I can't read the signature. Hey, maybe it is a famous artist and this is one of his unfinished drawings; it may be worth something. Look it up!'

Penny picked up her phone and clicked the Internet App. 'Ah damn it, there's no Wi-Fi connection'

'No there isn't. There's no phone signal either; I tried to call Paul and the kids before my shower but I couldn't get through. We'll have to call them when we head out.' Fiona appeared in the doorway looking even more incredible than she had before, dressed in tight denim jeans and a loose black blouse.

'Oh, it said it came with Wi-Fi?' their mother said, once

again looking disappointed.

'I've searched around the place and there's no landline here either so we are completely cut off!' Fiona added, looking frustrated.

'Come on girls, you don't need all that technology rubbish. How do you think me and your mother survived when we were youngsters? We had no mobiles and had to walk twenty minutes to the nearest phone box. A few evenings without your phone won't kill you,' Anita added.

Penny knew that Anita was right; she was far too dependent on her phone these days. Already she had found herself pulling it out of her jeans pocket at least a dozen times to see if anyone had contacted her. Maybe they should go back to basics for a bit, it might even be nice to spend some family time together without any distractions.

'Although… It probably isn't very good to be completely out of touch with the outside world. What if we need to call someone, an ambulance maybe?' her mother once again looked anxious.

'Don't worry, Mum; I'll only try to kill you when we get somewhere near a payphone,' Penny mocked.

'I'm serious, there should always be a phone around in case we need someone.'

'She's right you know. I don't think it's good that we have no chance to call for help if we needed to. It's how all good horror films start. What happens if someone tries to break in and kill us in our beds…?' Anita was trying to scare them once again.

'Well it's a good job your bedroom is nearest the door. They'll get to you first and we'll hear you scream and be able to make our escape,' Penny laughed.

'I can see this is what it is going to be like the whole trip.

Honestly you lot…' her mother added, shaking her head. 'Ready to go?' She looked around the room and the others nodded, still smiling at Penny's teasing.

'Shall we take a selfie then, to mark the first night of our trip? I want to send it to Paul when we get outside?' Fiona asked.

Although not a fan of having her picture taken and especially not keen on taking 'selfies', Penny agreed to get into the picture with her family. Trips like these created memories and Penny knew that there would come a time when memories begin to fade and the only thing that will reconnect you back to a particular time and place is a moment frozen forever within a photograph. They all huddled to where Penny was standing, in front of the unfinished drawing, and posed for the picture. Despite the accommodation not being quite what they had expected, they were all filled with happiness that they were together and away from their normal lives. Penny put her arm around her mother and Anita and pulled them tightly towards her. Her sister crouched down at the front and they heard the shutter of the camera flick once, capturing their excitement of the first day.

'Right, let's go then, who has the keys?' her mother queried, ushering everyone out of the door. 'Shall we leave a light on do you think? I'd imagine that road gets quite dark at night.'

They all agreed that that was a sensible idea and decided to leave the light on in the kitchen; that way they would see where they were going as they returned. Anita grabbed the keys and closed the door behind them, turning the light switch on as she left.

They made their way down the path towards the oak trees, excitingly discussing the night's adventures, their animated chatter following them as they headed towards the night.

As soon as their voices could no longer be heard in the apartment past the oak trees, the light in the kitchen slowly flickered off.

Four

'Can you see the door, Fiona?' Anita was asking her niece as they stumbled down the path towards the house, slightly worse for wear after drinking five bottles of wine between them over the course of the evening.

'Here it is I think. Didn't we leave the light on?' Fiona asked, her words coming out slow and raspy due to the number of drinks she had consumed.

'This is it, pass me the keys Fi,' Penny said, pushing her sister out of the way, getting irritated that she was taking so long to put the keys into the lock.

The door opened after Penny pushed it with her shoulder a few times and when it finally did, a blast of cold air burst through the doors, taking the women by surprise. Her hands fumbled across the wall to find the light switch, annoyed at her aunt for failing to leave the light on as they had planned.

When the room was finally filled with light, the others stumbled in eagerly, almost pushing Penny over in their attempt to get past.

'We told you to leave the light on!' Penny glared at Anita.

'I did!' she replied, looking offended. Penny raised her eyebrow at her aunt; doubtful that she was telling the truth. 'Honestly I did. Where are all the chairs?' She looked around the room.

Thinking this was another one of Anita's games, Penny

turned to tell her to stop and take something seriously for a change. Her head felt slightly giddy and she was more giggly than usual, but she didn't think she was as tipsy as the others, who had seemed incapable of walking in a straight line on their way home. Penny was annoyed that Anita couldn't follow a straightforward instruction properly.

As she turned to open her mouth, she stopped when she saw the five chairs had been placed at the top of the table, right in front of the fireplace. She could have sworn they had left them where they were sitting, which she was certain was around different sides of the table.

'Were we sitting that side of the table? I thought we were near the door?' Penny asked the others.

'I thought so too,' her mother replied, looking curious. She shrugged her shoulders and added, 'Maybe we were just tired from travelling and the wine! I doubt any of us really paid attention.'

Penny considered this and thought that her mother was probably right; it was possible that she had been mistaken, certainly it wasn't something that she would have thought to check before she left the house. She tried to convince herself this was the case but the more she thought about it, she wondered how likely it was that both of them would get it wrong. She shrugged it off but couldn't help but feel apprehensive when she looked back at the chairs sitting neatly in a row, sitting as though they had been specifically placed there, enthusiastically waiting to be occupied.

Although the table was large in length, it was rather small in depth and the chairs were squashed together, the backrests bumping against each other. What a strange apartment, Penny thought. Unexpectedly she felt her stomach pulsate, but quickly she pushed the feeling away. There was nothing to dread within the apartment, just a few

---

things she hadn't worked out yet. Her mother was right, they were overtired.

'I think we need a cup of tea. It's freezing in here!'

Her mother interrupted her thoughts which Penny was grateful for. She didn't want her mind to be distracted by things she couldn't explain and so she went over to help her mother. She picked up the ancient kettle and placed it on the hob, laughing when she heard it whistle as it began to boil. She hadn't seen a kettle this old and didn't think they existed any more.

'How cute are these?' her mother said, placing a tray and a collection of cups and saucers in front of them. 'I have washed them don't worry,' she said, noticing Fiona's repulsed glance as she placed the tray of old porcelain cups that she found in front of her.

They held their steaming cups of tea close to their faces, soaking up the warmth radiating off them. Their walk outside the apartment had certainly cooled them down but as they were heading back to the apartment, they had noticed that they didn't need additional layers to keep warm. Strangely, it seemed as though the apartment was cooler than it was outside, the strong cold blast that had hit them hard as they walked through the door not having disappeared as yet.

'I've found these,' Anita said entering the room with an armful of blankets. 'They were at the bottom of the cupboard in our room; there are loads in there. The agency must know how cold it gets here!' She threw one to each of them who hurriedly wrapped them around their shoulders.

'It's like we're camping, only we are inside,' Penny laughed, enjoying the sight of the four of them wrapped up as though they were sitting around a campfire and not a holiday apartment.

'That agency woman said the dial for the heating was on the wall somewhere, but I haven't seen any radiators so far!' her mother said taking a sip from her drink and looking around the room.

'They're most likely enclosed somewhere, they've done such a good job in keeping the place old-fashioned, they probably didn't want anything too modern to intrude.' Penny reasoned.

'Let's look in the morning. Let's get this down us and go to bed,' Anita said, hands wrapped around the mug, steam still rising into her face, making her almost invisible to the others. 'What do we have planned for tomorrow?' she asked her sister.

Maggie smiled, 'Well, tomorrow morning there is an antiques market at…'

Suddenly, a loud thud echoed around the room, causing her mother to stop short her sentence. The room was silent; they were all shocked to hear the unexpected noise which had interrupted them without warning. They looked around, trying to work out where the noise had come from. Noticing nothing amiss, they all stayed still and Penny noticed her sister pull her blanket tighter across her shoulders.

Anita opened her mouth to speak when all of a sudden, another noise exploded around the room. The noise had come from above them, from the supposed vacant floor. This time the sound didn't stop, and the ceiling rattled loudly once again. Listening carefully, Penny was able to work out that the sound was that of footsteps walking from one side of the room to the other, stopping directly above where the table was situated.

'I didn't think anyone was staying upstairs,' Penny said, looking up in the direction of the ceiling.

Five

The footsteps stopped abruptly once they reached the centre of the room, directly above where the women had congregated at the table. Each pair of eyes had moved upwards and they sat there in silence for what seemed to be an age, waiting for the sound to reoccur. Whatever had moved above them had stayed silent since their eyes had darted towards the ceiling, as though it knew it was being listened to and wanted to avoid revealing any more details of its location.

'Maybe it's rats?' Penny's mother questioned, shrugging her shoulders.

'Pretty big rats!' Anita replied, eyeing each of them in turn.

'Funny, I did think that I saw someone in the window upstairs when we walked down the path earlier. I only saw it once, but maybe someone *is* staying upstairs?' Penny added.

Anita looked around the group and noticed no one else was speaking, but were still looking at the ceiling. She saw this as another opportunity to scare the group and lowered her voice as she whispered, 'Or, maybe it is that body that was locked behind the door; whoever is upstairs heard us discuss it and thought it was best to drag the body up the stairs across the floor, into the…'

'Stop!' Fiona said, abruptly interrupting her aunt mid-sentence. 'Normally I like your scaremongering but maybe we could wait until after our first night here. Something about this apartment gives me the creeps a bit.'

'Why are you scared? You know she's just teasing!' Penny laughed at her sister's reaction.

'I don't know, it's just this place is so old, I just don't feel like scary stories right now.'

'Don't be silly Fi, it's probably the old pipes making a noise. That or someone has moved in above and that weird letting agent forgot to tell us about it,' Penny said, reaching out to hold her hand. 'She did run off very fast.'

'You're probably right, it did sound like there was more than one person up there,' Fiona said, looking back up towards the ceiling. 'Maybe we can knock and see who has moved in tomorrow?'

Anita let out a sigh, 'Okay, I'll keep my stories about the bodies at bay until tomorrow but be warned, stopping me telling the story now means it will be ten times scarier tomorrow.' She dipped her fingers into her tea and flicked them at Fiona, sending little speckles into the air, landing on her nose.

'Wow, I can't believe it is so late,' her mother stated, looking at her watch. 'It's 11pm! Time flies and all that...'

Anita stood and let out a yawn, 'I'm tired, let's call it a night.' She started packing the cups back onto the tray and moved towards the sink.

'Are you double sure you don't want to change rooms with us?' Fiona pleaded with her mother, using the same whiny voice she had earlier.

'No, you two will be fine. Push the beds together and it'll be like you are little again.' Her mother turned Fiona around by her shoulders when she saw that she was trying to enter her room. 'Go on, bed now.'

Fiona sulked as she and Penny made their way towards the cave-like room. When they entered, Penny was annoyed to feel the room hadn't warmed up. She reached for her bag and pulled out her comfortable, but unflattering, nightdress. She hated to leave things unorganised, but her drooping eyelids were telling her that she was far too tired to unpack. She hadn't realised it until they stepped into the room, but she was exhausted.

Penny looked at her sister's bed, surprised at the speed in which she had managed to take everything out and lay it perfectly in front of her.

'Is that all you have?' Penny questioned her. She looked around at the small collection of items on the sheet, a folded-up silk nightdress, a toiletries bag and a few cashmere tank tops.

'Silly, of course it's not,' Fiona laughed at the suggestion. 'I found an empty cupboard when I had a shower earlier and decided we would use that considering there is no other furniture apart from the beds in this room.'

Penny followed her sister out of the room and watched her open a door which had been built into a wall adjacent to the room they would be sleeping in. As the door was pulled open, Penny wasn't surprised to see a row of beautifully coloured dresses and trousers hung up neatly, arranged systematically in colour.

'I thought you were travelling light?' she nudged her sister, looking at the fully packed row of clothes. 'I can't be bothered to do mine now, will do it in the morning.'

As she was standing looking into the cupboard, her thoughts became distracted she turned to face the open bathroom door next to her. She wasn't sure what it was that made her look in that direction but now her head was turned, she couldn't pull her eyes away from the darkness that seemed to suffocate the room.

She could hear her sister speaking beside her but she wasn't listening to what she was saying, instead keeping her gaze on the opened door. Although not quite as dark as it had been when she was looking at it from a further distance earlier in the day, she still couldn't see clearly through it. Her stomach rose as she viewed the door, but she pushed it back down. She wasn't keen to acknowledge the sense of dread that had overcome her unexpectedly. Although she tried as much as she could to ignore the feeling, the bathroom was magnetically pulling Penny towards it in a way it was hard for her to ignore.

'Penny!!' Fiona's voice broke through her daze and she turned to face her sister who was standing with her hand on her hip, obviously annoyed that Penny wasn't listening. 'You never listen to me!'

'Sorry, I got distracted. Do you not see the darkness in that room?' She nodded her head in the direction of the opened door.

Fiona screwed up her face as she eyed her sister suspiciously, 'No, I see a bathroom with tiled flooring.'

'Oh, must just be me then.'

Noticing Penny's disappointment, Fiona added, 'It is a little dark I guess. Go and get washed up, then we can push our beds together and have a gossip before we go to sleep.'

She closed the cupboard door and went into the bedroom, Penny following closely behind her, not wanting to be left standing by the bathroom door on her own. She collected her nightdress from the bed, but before reaching the hallway, she hesitated, 'Fi, would you mind coming in there with me, just for tonight? It kind of freaks me out a little bit!'

Fiona looked at her for a second, puzzled by her uncharacteristically apprehensive behaviour, 'Of course silly! Big sisters are supposed to protect their little sisters, which clearly you need, scaredy cat,' she mocked pushing Penny out of the room.

Penny tried not to make it too obvious, but she walked slowly towards the bathroom so that her sister would enter first. When she saw that she entered the room with no problem, Penny followed. Fiona shut the bathroom door behind them and wasted no time in getting changed. She dumped a heavy toiletries bag onto a shelf and began emptying the contents, covering the whole ledge, without thinking where everyone else's cosmetics would go.

Looking at her sister slowly pulling out each item made Penny instantly regret having asked her to accompany her into the bathroom. For her, getting ready for bed normally meant a quick splash of water before she hurriedly brushed her teeth in a rapid rush to get tucked under her duvet. In contrast for Fiona, it meant staying in the bathroom for at least twenty minutes, using an array of products all designed to combat the different signs of aging. When Fiona had eventually finished her drawn-out beauty regime, she walked out of the room without telling Penny to follow. Penny rolled her eyes and ran after her.

'I'm glad our beds are able to be put together. I have just realised how much I would hate to sleep alone, I haven't done it for so long,' Fiona said after they had pushed their beds next to each other as soon as they entered the room.

As she tried to get comfortable in an unfamiliar bed, she imagined what she would be doing if she wasn't away. She knew that she would most likely have been getting into bed quietly beside Jason, her boyfriend of five years, having turned her laptop off after prepping for the back to back meetings she had the following day. Penny hadn't thought about Jason since she left the apartment earlier that morning and the memory of him lying silently in their own bed at home caused a twinge in her stomach.

Although she was excited to spend time with her family, she knew that missing Jason this early on wasn't a good sign. She had been tempted to invite him along for the trip, but knew that her sister wouldn't want her husband to come along. Fiona radiated the perfect life on the outside, but Penny knew that her sister struggled juggling all her duties and that she was very much looking forward to some much needed alone-time.

Realising there was no point in dwelling on what she was missing as it would only make her feel worse, she plumped her pillows and lay down, noticing the uncomfortableness of the firm, starchy sheets underneath her. She moved her body further down the bed, desperately trying to find a comfortable position and placed her phone under her pillow, once again checking for reception.

Optimistic in effort but pessimistic in thought, she glanced at the phone before letting out a sigh. She didn't think she'd be able to get reception in a room with sinking ceilings if she wasn't able to get it in a room next to an open door and the lack of little bars on her phone confirmed she was right. Although she was aware the message would not send, she sent Jason a goodnight message nevertheless.

'We haven't shared a bed together since we were kids.' Penny turned at her sister's voice, jumping as she realised she had moved herself so far forward that their faces were almost touching, 'Do you have any gossip to share? How's things with you and Jason?'

Penny turned on her back and smiled, not only at the thought of Jason but also in gratitude for the opportunity to spend time with her sister. Fiona was right, they hadn't shared a room for a very long time and she suddenly felt strangely homesick when she remembered all the nights they shared when they were teenagers.

'Really good,' Penny smiled, rolling back to face her

sister, 'work has been very busy recently though so we haven't had much time…' she was interrupted by the sound of snoring. Her sister was still facing her, hand behind her head, her mouth wide open, and Penny realised that she too must have been exhausted. She thought her sister deserved some relaxation and she straightened the bed sheet around her as she let out soft, gentle snores.

She could hear giggles from the top of the hallway which were gradually getting louder and louder. She sat upright, confused about where the noise was coming from until she recognised Anita's familiar cackle. She waited until she saw her mother and aunt's heads pop around the archway, looking into the room. Her mother was smaller than Anita and the way they were peering into the room, heads in, bodies out, made Penny laugh out loud. Looking at their floating heads, Penny had to cover her mouth to stop her own giggles escaping and waking her sister.

'I was too scared to come to the toilet on my own, it's so far away from our room,' her mother giggled. Penny suspected that she'd had an extra glass of wine on her way to bed which had made her unusually giggly. 'Fiona's right, it is a bit creepy.'

'Sshh,' Penny whispered, finger raised to her lip, still holding down her own laughter, pointing at Fiona. 'Turn the light off in the hallway when you come out.' She ushered them out of the room from her bed, shooing them away with her hands. She blew a kiss to both of them before lying down, face turned towards her sister.

She smiled remembering the sight of the two older women as she closed her eyes. Feeling her body relaxing, muscle by muscle, a deep tranquil sensation flowed through her veins. Her breathing was slow and deep and she drifted towards the welcome destination of sleep.

Six

Penny opened her eyes and gazed around the room, surprised by how light it was. She pulled herself upwards so she was sitting at a perfect right angle and rubbed her dozy eyes as she tried to remember where she was. She was surprised at first when she turned over and felt the unfamiliar stiffness of the mattress underneath her and it took her a few moments before she remembered she was not in her own bed. Although she had been sleeping for what seemed to her hours, she let out a long yawn and felt her eyes trying to force their way back shut. Penny snuggled back down into the scratchy bed; she'd had a deep sleep but she did not feel rested. Remembering her mother had meticulously planned a full day which she needed to be up for, she begrudgingly forced her eyes to reopen and shook her head in an effort to wake up.

She turned to look where her sister had been lying the night before and saw she was no longer asleep beside her. She reached for her phone underneath her pillow and noted the time, ten in the morning. Hearing plates clattering in the distance, she decided it was time to leave her not so comfortable resting place. Knowing her mother would most likely be annoyed that she had slept through their precisely planned early departure time, she mentally braced herself for the nagging that was in store.

'Are you up yet?' Fiona's head peered around the doorway. Noticing that her sister was awake, Fiona leapt into the room with such enthusiasm it almost gave Penny a headache. It annoyed her that her sister had so much energy when she had so little. 'You were dead to the world this morning, I tried to wake you but you didn't budge, you must have really needed the sleep!'

Penny yawned and outstretched her arms, 'Do you know what, I don't actually feel too amazing, I'm still so tired.'

'Sometimes that happens when you deprive yourself of sleep, as soon as you get more than you've had for a long time, your body clings onto it, desperate for more. You know I do a great relaxation massage at my salon you should try. Free for you of course.' Fiona was always trying to get Penny to try one of her treatments.

'Yeah okay, after this trip yeah?' Penny pushed her sister off the bed with her feet and made a move to get out of the bed. 'Last night when we...' She stopped her sentence and felt a hiccup rise up her throat. Covering her mouth with her hand she looked at her sister, both shocked at the noise that had come out of her, 'Sorry, I'm not too sure what that...' Another hiccup passed through her lips.

Penny took a deep breath and noticed a tight knot in her stomach that seemed to be suddenly soaring towards her throat. She dashed out of the room and made her way into the bathroom before being violently sick in the basin. Her sister chased after her, holding her hair back as she curled over the sink. Penny tried to move away but decided against it, grateful for the comfort. After she stopped retching, she wiped her mouth and immediately began brushing her teeth, desperate for the acidic taste to leave her mouth. She pushed her sister away and told her firmly that it was okay, the comfort she sought only moments before now becoming highly irritating. She felt herself become hot and sweaty and couldn't deal with the hands which were trying to touch her to make sure she was okay. Looking hurt, Fiona left the bathroom and Penny was able to compose herself.

She splashed herself with cold water and looked at her

face in the mirror, watching the water fall off her nose in droplets as she tried to catch her breath. Penny noticed that she was looking paler than usual and her eyes had become bloodshot from the violent heaving. She figured the random sickness must have had something to do with what she had eaten, but remembered she only had a simple salad the night before and so doubted it would have been that. Trying to be rational, Penny reasoned that the change in routine must have been unsettling her body, it wasn't used to such rest and maybe it was confused with what was going on. If this were a normal working day for her, she would have had already been on a long run and drunk four cups of coffee by this time in the morning. Penny thought that she was desperately craving caffeine, the sharp throbbing in her head telling her she needed her fix urgently.

She took off her clothes and stepped underneath the steaming hot shower, breathing in as she felt the hot water splatter across her body. Steam was rising already and she tipped her head backwards and felt the water hit her scalp, almost burning her as it connected to her skin. Her body was grateful for the scorching and powerful force of the water, the tiredness she'd felt as she rose from her slumber quickly evaporating as she scrubbed her skin.

Once she had washed herself awake, she stepped out of the shower feeling revived. She tried to forget the taste of the sickness and tried to focus on the nice day she had spent with her family the day before and look forward to the day to come. Pulling on the same pair of black jeans which she paired with a baggy white jumper, Penny made her way to the kitchen, pulling a comb through her tangled wet hair as she went.

'Mmm, smells lovely,' Penny commented as she pulled up a chair next to her mother. Her stomach immediately started rumbling as she hungrily looked at the spread in front of her.

The table was lined with hot croissants and English muffins, the aroma of the pastries hanging lightly in the air, teasing her stomach for the deliciousness that was in store as soon as she took a bite. Anita and Fiona were already seated at the table tucking into their food, not stopping to acknowledge Penny's arrival into the room. Penny grabbed a chair and stuffed one of the muffins into her mouth. She started to eat before she had fully sat down, stopping only to sip her freshly made coffee which immediately stopped the shaking that hadn't eased up since before she showered.

'Are you okay love?' her mother said, moving across the table to pat her forehead to check her temperature. 'Fiona said you were a bit unwell?'

'I'm fine, I was a bit sick but I think that is just because my daily routine has changed. I felt exhausted last night,' she replied, mouth full of the muffin. She shot her sister an evil glare. She was always the one who went running to their mother to tell on her, even if she knew it would make her worry.

'I always tell you you're working yourself into the ground, you need a rest,' her mother commented, sounding concerned.

'Don't be silly; I'm fine,' Penny said, roughly swotting away her mother's hand. She was still clammy from either the shower or the sickness and the fussy touching was aggravating her. 'I'm sorry I slept past the time we were meant to be up and out, you should have woken me.'

'We only got up about an hour before you love,' Anita said, words barely recognisable as she spoke with her mouth full. 'We fell asleep almost immediately.'

'What's the plan for today then, Mum?' Fiona asked, trying to take the attention away from Penny and back onto herself.

Her mother's face lit up as she got her chance to once again bring out the itinerary which she had placed neatly on the counter behind them. 'Well we are a bit late to do what I had planned, no one's fault of course,' she nodded to Penny. 'I thought that maybe we could spend the day in Charterville, looking through some of the shops, have a nice lunch and then come back here before dinner tonight. I have made reservations at one of the top restaurants in the city to celebrate being together.'

'Sounds fabulous,' said Fiona, returning her gaze to the compact mirror she held firmly in her hands, applying her makeup perfectly. 'I'm looking forward to shopping, I really need a new top!'

'Eat your breakfast dear, we're going to be pottering around for a good few hours today,' her mother said, pushing another English muffin under Penny's nose.

Although she had eaten one already, Penny heard her stomach grumble loudly in gratitude at her mother's offer. Instinctively she reached out and began eating it, enjoying the buttery taste as she took a bite, the little rolls around her belly laughing at her lack of will power.

She looked around again at the kitchen as she enjoyed her cup of coffee. She had noticed its quaintness when they arrived, but she hadn't had time to really see the details of the room. She looked past the fireplace and the pictures hanging on the wall and saw that behind them, the paint had cracked. On first sight, she had thought the wall had been painted a pale yellow but the more she stared at the walls, the more she realised that time had aged a once bright, white wall into this dull and lifeless colour.

'I don't think they've actually done anything to this apartment since they bought it!' she told her family, pointing to the colour of the wall. She stood, cradling her coffee and walked towards the fireplace, moving her hand along the wall, noticing its roughness. 'I don't think this wall has been repainted.'

'Funny you should say that, we mentioned that last night didn't we Anita?' her mother replied, nodding in Anita's direction.

'Another thing to add to our complaint list! Really the advertisement is totally misleading,' Anita complained. She reached inside her bag which was lying on the floor beside her and brought the advertisement of the apartment to the table. 'Look again will you!' She pushed it into Penny's hand.

Penny picked up the paper and glanced over it. She really didn't need to see it again but thought she would humour her aunt and agree with her regardless. She stopped and looked up at the kitchen she was standing in and then back to the advertisement. As much as she didn't like to encourage her mother and aunt with their conspiracies and constant complaining, she couldn't help but notice how different the two images were. Reluctantly she felt compelled to agree with them.

'The thing is, it's so beautiful and quaint, I'm sure a lot of people would want to stay in a period house decorated to the time in which it was built. I don't understand why they didn't just put that on the internet and put the correct pictures up?' her mother pointed out, looking disappointed once again.

'Maybe they just put the wrong photos up?' Fiona shrugged.

Penny thought about this but doubted its validity. The images of the building were exactly the same but the insides had been decorated very differently. It was almost as though they were looking at an advert of what it would look like after an expensive refurbishment and they were standing in it before the makeover had taken place.

'Let's check out the advert again when we get on the bus. I'm sure there'll be an explanation,' Penny reasoned.

'There'd better be. Maybe we should call that woman…'

Penny zoned out again, knowing where this conversation would lead, and decided instead to head towards her room to collect her bag. As she was walking, she stopped by the bureau and peered out of the glass doors. She was doubting her outfit choice and wanted to go outside to see what the weather was like to ensure she was appropriately dressed. Head pressed against the window, she saw the sunshine gleaming through the doors but also noticed that the small amount of plants which had been placed around the terrace were swaying in the wind. She attempted to open the door but the brass handles which secured them did not budge. She tried once again to push them open, but without any luck, she turned and made her way into the bedroom thinking that she would put on a jacket just in case.

When she returned to the kitchen the women were all on different sides of the room, each doing their own thing. Her mother was at the sink washing up the plates, Anita was packing her bag with various pointless items Penny knew she wouldn't need and her sister was standing at the door, frantically waving her phone in the air in an attempt to get a signal.

'I thought you were ready! You're always fussing about something!' Penny moaned.

'Sorry love, I just want to make sure the place is clean for when we get home. You know you could always help with the washing up which will make it quicker?' her mother said, not turning to look at her from the sink.

'Still no bloody reception,' Fiona moaned from the doorway, 'I really wanted to check on the boys.'

She pushed the door open and stepped outside. Penny thought of her own phone's lack of reception and her mother's suggestion that she help her with the dishes. She decided to follow her sister outside, not so keen on the idea of doing chores she thought were meant to be excluded from the trip. Whilst Fiona paced backwards and forwards, arms waving in the air, Penny began walking towards the centre of the garden to get a better view of the apartments.

Looking up at the house, she was almost overwhelmed by how magnificent it looked, sitting on its own behind the neatly cut lawn and guarded securely by the oak trees behind her. She focused on the apartment they were staying in first and laughed at how little and cute it looked tucked in at the corner, engulfed by the grand building to its left. She looked up at the windows of the main house directly above where they were staying to see if she could detect any activity from them, remembering the bangs they heard the night before. All that was visible from where she was standing was the outline of curtains which seemed to be closed, blocking light from entering. Surely if people were staying in the apartments, they would be drawn.

Penny looked back at the door and wondered how someone would gain access to the various apartments, especially those that were on the top floor. Thinking about the noises, she returned her gaze to their small apartment to the side. She thought she remembered the letting agent telling them that the apartment above them was accessible around the side of the building. If this was the case, it would mean that their building was totally separate from the main house, although it looked connected from where she was standing. Penny turned to look at her sister who was still pacing around in a circle with her hands in the air and she thought she may as well go and take a further look.

She passed their apartment with the door ajar and heard her mother and aunt giggling at something as she walked past. When she turned the corner past the front of their apartment, she looked up and confirmed what the agent had told them; there was a small staircase which led up to the second floor. It almost looked like a fire escape, with the banister and steps a rusty black metal. At the top of the staircase she saw a door which she assumed led into the floor on top of theirs.

From where she was standing she was unable to see any movement in the room and so decided to go up to the front door, knock and introduce herself to the people staying there. It was a good idea, she thought, especially if they were to be loud, which was possible considering the amount of alcohol they had brought with them. Penny raised her foot to stand on the first step and instantly regretted it. As she brought her full weight onto the metal step, she felt the staircase rattle angrily beneath her. Unsure it would be able to hold her, she hesitated before seeing that it was securely attached to the wall. When she was certain it was able to bear her weight, she started to climb, swallowing her fear and refusing to notice that the rattling had not subsided with each step she took.

The higher she climbed, the more she wondered whether it was normal for a staircase to sway as much as this one was, being rocked sideways by the wind. As she travelled upwards she began feeling lightheaded. The harshness of the wind began ringing loudly in her ears, as if it was warning her not to go any further.

When she reached the top, she had to catch her breath and steady her feet before knocking on the door, grateful that she had made it up safely in one piece. After a few moments when no one answered, she knocked again and called out to see if anyone was there. She thought she could hear shuffling behind the door but still no one came to answer it. She reached out to turn the handle to push it open, but it refused to budge. Stepping away from the door, she saw that there were two windows to the side and she slowly walked towards them. Her hands were firmly holding onto the railings behind her and she tried not to notice that the wind was pushing heavily on her back and the staircase was swaying even more now she was at the top.

The curtains had been pulled together, however there was a tiny gap in the middle which allowed Penny to get a closer look if she crouched down. Letting go of the staircase, she put one hand above her eyes to block out the sun and she strained to see what was inside. The windows were dirty, thick from grime and dust and looked like they hadn't been washed in some time. The room behind the curtain was dark and she was only able to make out shapes of what was in the room. From what she could see, it appeared as though she was looking into the window of someone's bedroom. She was certain that she could see a large bed and a bedside table opposite but couldn't make out the finer details.

She pushed her head further against the window to try and see more, even though she knew it a pointless task. She squashed her face so tightly up against the window that she could barely breathe through her nose and the more she tried to focus, the more the items in the room became distorted. Frustrated that she couldn't see, she decided to put her efforts into concentrating on one object, hoping that if she looked at it long enough, it would begin to be clearer. Pushing herself further forward, she tried to focus on a point at the back of the room.

It was no use; all she could see was darkness and shadows. Deciding she'd spent enough time on the creaky staircase, she was about to leave until suddenly, something dashed past the window before disappearing back into the darkness.

Without thinking, Penny's body jerked backwards in fright as her heart tried to catapult out of her body. Penny realised the staircase wasn't the only thing that was shaking; she could feel her legs trembling as she tried to compose herself from the sudden shock. When she was able to stop the shaking, she moved back towards the window, scrunching her nose back onto the glass but this time with more care. She didn't want to miss anything and took in the sight of the room more carefully, looking through the window for what could have been the shape she had seen, wondering whether someone was in there trying to hide from her curious eyes.

'THERE YOU ARE,' Fiona's voice pulled Penny away from the window, 'What on earth are you doing up there? Get down, it doesn't look safe!'

'I was checking if there was anyone in there!'

'And?'

'No one, I don't think, although…'

'Come down, the wretched thing is shaking. Quick before Mum sees you, she'll have a heart attack!'

Penny made her way down the staircase much more quickly than she had travelled up and re-joined her sister on the safety of the ground. She paused for a moment as she tried to steady her dizzy head, realising that the staircase had been swaying more than she realised.

'There is still no reception! I literally cannot believe it, what sort of place are we staying in where we can't even get a phone signal?' Fiona despaired, hands waving in the air.

Penny was vaguely aware of her sister talking to her but her mind was elsewhere. As they turned the corner back towards their open door, she looked back up at the window, thinking about the shadow that flashed past her so suddenly but had refused to show itself to her again. When they reached the kitchen, her mother and aunt were sitting at the table with their bags on their laps and their coats tucked warmly around them waiting for Penny and Fiona.

'Are you ready to go?' Anita asked.

'Yeah, let me just grab my bag,' Penny turned around to pick up her bag that she had left on the table earlier. 'By the way, I don't think there is anyone upstairs, I went around by the side of the house and up those stairs. To be honest, it doesn't actually look like a rented apartment!'

'What do you mean?' Anita asked her suspiciously.

'Well it doesn't look like a proper front door to start with and the curtains were drawn. When I looked inside, the windows were really dirty and the room looked a bit of a mess. I think it was someone's bedroom. I can't imagine the agency would rent it out in the condition it was in,' she replied, pulling the strap of the bag around her body.

'That can't be right. We have literally just heard a noise up there when you were gone,' her mother answered.

'When was this?' Penny queried, surprised at the response.

'About five minutes ago, that's about right isn't it Anita?' her mother asked Anita who responded with a nod of the head. Penny thought back to five minutes previous and wondered if that was the same time she nearly toppled over the banister in shock when she saw a movement in the window. She tried to remember what she saw, thinking the noise her family had heard was most likely the movement of the thing dashing past.

'Actually, I think I saw…'

'Come on, I want to get out and call the boys,' Fiona impatiently called from outside of the door, stopping Penny mid-sentence.

They walked out of the front door, Penny being the last one through. She picked up the keys that were resting on the table and realised that the task of turning everything off had been left to her. She turned around to face the room and looked up to the ceiling as if daring it to make another noise. When no noise was forthcoming, she turned to make her way outside, stopping to glance back quickly at the black door. She wasn't sure why, but something inside had urged her to stop and look back. She was glued to the spot momentarily, all thoughts going out of her head as she slowly felt a chill travel up through her spine, making her shiver as it navigated its way upwards. Feeling uneasy, she turned quickly and stepped outside the door, closing it firmly behind her.

Seven

They arrived back at the apartment just after nine which was much later than they had anticipated, happy and content with the pleasant day they had shared together. They pushed their way through the open door and collapsed onto the chairs placed around the table. Penny counted them as she walked in and was pleased to see that they were all standing in the same spot they had been left; she had made a mental note of their positions prior to leaving to ensure they didn't do a rearranging act again.

Anita pointed out to the group that they had a bottle of wine which had been cooling in the fridge and almost as soon her bottom touched the wooden chair, she rose straight back up again heading towards it, collecting glasses on her way.

'What an amazing day,' Penny's mother commented, kicking off her shoes and leaning back into the chair, face grimacing as she moved backwards. All the walking had taken its toll on her it seemed.

Anita returned to the table, full glasses carefully held in her hands and handed one to each of the others. 'Let's hope the rest of the week is as much fun!' She held her glass out in the air, inviting the others to copy the gesture until they all clinked their glasses to toast the trip.

*

That morning, after they left the apartment, they hopped onto a bus which took them into the city centre of

Charterville and they headed into the first bar they saw to celebrate their first official day in the city, giggling like school girls as they drunk expensive champagne which Fiona had insisted on purchasing. Sitting in the bar, they gossiped until the bottle was empty, as though they were a group of friends meeting up after a long time as opposed to a family consisting of two generations.

Although Fiona had pleaded that they stayed and share another bottle, her mother could not be swayed, not wanting to deviate too far away from her plans and instead insisted that they complete at least some of the excursions she had planned. They made their way to the designated bus stop where they caught an open-air bus which took them on a tour around the city, getting off when they saw something of interest and then jumping back on when they had seen enough.

The more they pottered around the more Penny fell in love with Charterville. Similar to Oakdene in its old-fashioned appearance, each street they walked down was lined with cracked cobbles and the roads were narrow, allowing only a limited number of vehicles to drive up and down. Her mother's research was accurate; the little town they were staying in was very small and quiet, but this city was bustling with people going about their business and wasn't short on things to do. The paved roads were lined with trendy bars, small bookstores, and cafes where the seating areas were arranged out front which gave it an almost Parisian feel. Walking through the city centre, Penny failed to spot a high-street brand, seeing instead lots of smaller, local, independent businesses. Looking at the people who strolled past, Penny realised that they all seemed to be walking at a snail's pace, in no real rush to get anywhere fast but seemingly peacefully happy with this lack of urgency.

Within three hours, they had walked nearly the whole

city and had visited all the main tourist destinations. Their feet were sore from the walking and as the day slowly became night, they noticed the air becoming chillier, providing relief from the warm heat which had made them somewhat uncomfortable during the day. They decided to abandon their fancy dinner reservation and opted instead for a relaxed dinner in one of the eateries they had passed, feasting on a three-course menu, washed down by a delicious mix of fruity cocktails.

*

Back in the kitchen, Anita raised her glass, 'Cheers to our trip and to making new memories.' They all stood and chinked before giving each other a hug. 'Now let's put some music on while we drink this!'

They huddled around the table like they had the night before and started discussing the day's adventure, music playing gently in the background from the tablet that Anita had brought with her.

'There is so much history in this area, I love it!' Penny said.

'Me too,' her mother smiled, 'although I didn't like the way that woman completely ignored us when we were in the shop buying our groceries.'

Her mother was talking about Claire, the letting agent who had shown them around the apartment. After they had decided that they were not going to go out for their dinner as planned, they agreed that they would stop by a local store on their way home to pick up some drinks and chocolates to continue their night in the apartment. As they were doing so, they noticed Claire ahead of them in the shop.

Anita had spotted her almost as soon as they entered and mentioned that they should march straight up to her and say something about the coldness of the apartment and query why the advertisement was so different to the reality. As the people in the queue filtered into the various checkouts, the women hurried forward and realised that they were standing at the till adjacent to Claire. Penny's mother said a casual hello and the letting agent made an enthusiastic spin, turning around to face the ladies with a wide smile. It took her less than a second to place them and when she did, her smile dropped as quickly as she had turned around.

She faced the women, looking from one to another, keeping her mouth gripped in a firm line, the smile that was spread across her face only moments ago now a distant memory. Noticing the rapid change in facial expression, Fiona asked her if she had had a good day and her question was met with silence, Claire's eyes still quickly moving across them. A minute passed as they all stood staring at each other, and then Claire turned on her heels and walked straight towards the door, failing to look back or pick up the bottles of beer she had brought with her to the checkout, leaving the group, and the cashier, startled and confused.

'I think that most certainly deserves a complaint. She point blank ignored us and ran away!' her mother exclaimed.

'Well she was off duty, Mum, she probably didn't want to get involved with work stuff tonight,' Fiona reasoned.

'I understand, but all you said was hello and she looked at you as though we had hurled obscenities in her direction! I don't think that is a good representation of the company or the town!' Maggie replied, shaking her head.

'Like I said yesterday, people here are rude and don't enjoy us Londoners invading their space,' Anita commented, looking completely unbothered by the incident, concentrating more on not spilling her drink as she took another sip of wine. 'You must have seen the people today walking around with smiles on their faces. I tell you, there is something wrong with people who are that happy all of the time!'

'What's wrong with being happy, you miserable old bat?' Penny teased.

'Nothing, I just don't trust them, that is all.'

'Well let's add it to the list of things to mention when we check out!' her mother said, shrugging her shoulders once again.

Fiona stood up from the table and stretched out her arms, 'I'm going to get into my pyjamas I think.'

'No, you're not allowed to go to bed yet; we have all evening!' Anita told her off, raising the bottle which was now half empty, clearly indicating that she had no desire to retire to bed early and had every intention of finishing the bottle and perhaps starting another.

Fiona laughed, 'Don't worry, I'm just going to get into something more comfortable so I can enjoy the evening better and tuck into those chocolates without feeling my jeans press into my stomach!'

She turned to leave the room but stopped suddenly as a large bang sounded loudly from above their heads. Fiona slowly turned to face her family who were sitting very still, eyes pointed up towards the ceiling.

Penny opened her mouth to speak but before she could say anything, Anita said, 'The body doesn't want you to get changed… yet…' She made a deliberate point to pronounce each word very slowly, hoping that the pause would cause suspense and ultimately, fear.

Fiona looked at her for a moment, unsure how to react and then let out a laugh, 'Is anyone else scared by that noise?' she asked the others. As she did, another noise was heard from above. This time the noise wasn't a loud bang like before but more a light tap on the ceiling which was repeated three times.

'We hear you!' Anita said, standing up and looking at the ceiling. 'Do you want us to drink another bottle of wine? One tap for yes, two taps for no!'

Penny's mother pushed her hard on the shoulder, 'Stop it, and don't mess with whatever it is!'

'It's just the pipes, Mum,' Penny said, trying to convince herself more than anyone else.

'One tap for yes, two taps for no,' Anita continued, ignoring her sister. Penny looked around the room and saw they were all anxiously holding their breath waiting for a response. She was certain that no noise would respond to the request but she could feel her heart flutter nevertheless. She didn't really believe in such things, but what she had seen in the upstairs apartment scared her more than she would like to admit and she wasn't sure that inviting something to converse with them was a good idea, even if it wasn't real.

Anita shrugged and returned to her seat, 'It's a boring thing whatever it is! Look at your faces you silly lot, I was joking! Penny's probably right about the pipes, stop being so daft! God if I knew that it would be this easy to scare you I would have rattled on the ceiling myself.'

Fiona walked towards her sister and took her hand firmly in her grasp, pulling Penny out of her seat. 'You're coming with me to get changed, be it a pipe or not!'

Penny was pulled along by her sister down the corridor and couldn't help but laugh as she was dragged forwards. The amount of wine she had consumed during the day and evening was beginning to catch up with her, making her more cheery than normal. She barely felt her feet as she travelled down the hallway, giddy and light-headed. 'I can't

---

63

believe you are so scared! You know what she is like, that's two nights in a row!' Penny teased.

'I wasn't scared actually, I just wanted some company!' Fiona said defiantly. As soon as she entered the room she immediately began taking her clothes off and pulled on her pyjamas.

'Aren't we going to spend like an hour in the bathroom tonight then?' Penny baited her, reaching for her own nightdress to quickly put on.

'I'm... having a... night off!' Fiona exclaimed, Penny noticed the slight slur in her voice and the drawn-out sentence and realised that she wasn't the only one who had been affected by the wine.

They hurried back into the kitchen, hands firmly held together as they did when they were children, eager to get back to the others. They saw that another bottle of wine had been opened and the music had been turned up. The pair of sisters snuggled into their respective chairs and wrapped the blankets Anita gave them around their shoulders.

'What have we missed?' Fiona said, moving her seat closer to her mother.

'We're talking about the history of the house,' Anita replied.

'How would you know what the history of the house is?' Penny questioned.

'We are thinking about theories!' Anita clarified. 'Did you get a look at the outside of the house? This apartment sits on its own at the end.'

'And?' Fiona queried, topping up her glass.

'Well, as this is on one floor, we reckon this was the servant's chamber and that door over there,' Anita pointed to the black door, 'was the passageway to the upstairs quarters. It acted as a go-between for the servants and those upstairs. The cooks made the food right where we are sitting now and brought it up to those upstairs for one of their fancy fine dinners.'

As her aunt was speaking, Penny pictured the scene she was describing. She turned to face the cooker and imagined a short stocky woman with her hair pulled back tightly in a bun standing in front of it, hands moving frantically as she stirred whatever it was she was cooking on the stove in front of her, steam flooding the kitchen. She thought of the room she had spotted earlier upstairs and tried to imagine someone Anita was describing living there. She looked back towards the black door and she imagined what it would be like on the other side.

As if reading her thoughts Anita interrupted, 'I know, tonight let's open the lock on the door and see what's inside!'

'We can't do that, it's vandalism' her mother interjected.

'At the stroke of midnight, we'll…'

'Why midnight?' Fiona interrupted.

'Because that is when the spirits come out, my dear!' Anita moved her head forwards towards the table. 'We'll open the lock…'

'How will we open the lock?' Fiona did it again.

'Well, if you'd let me finish!' Anita shot Fiona a sharp look and then moved her head back towards the centre of the table and spoke again, this time her voice lowered, 'At the stroke of midnight, the lock will mysteriously open and the door will be ajar. Curious, we will all gather at the door and ponder whether or not to go in. Of course, it is not the most sensible idea we have had, however curiosity gets the better of us and we make our way through the open door. We'll push Fiona in first of course…' they all laughed,

Fiona rolling her eyes. 'What we first notice as we make our way through the doorway is the smell, hitting us like something we've never smelled before. Once we have managed to catch our breaths we…'

'Where did the smell come from?' Penny asked.

'The bodies,' Anita huffed, annoyed at the interruptions, 'but of course, we do not know that until we make our way further up the staircase. Getting back to what I was saying… We've pushed the unlocked door open and the smell hits us as we hear the creak of the doorway echo throughout the abandoned corridor. The light is terribly bad and all we can see from the darkness is our hands stretched out in front of us, holding on to each other as we make our way through. Once we are all inside, we find a lamp on the floor that we pick up and use to navigate our way through, seeing stairs facing us…'

'Why would there be a lamp left on the floor if the door hadn't been opened for some time?' Fiona jeered.

'Some things you can't explain!' She threw Fiona a frustrated look, warning her not to interrupt her again.

'We're huddled together now at this point because the room is colder than we have ever experienced. We raise the lamp over the staircase and notice the cobwebs lining the steep steps. We start to feel scared and decide not to continue our exploration and then BANG!!'

Anita shouted and banged on the table, forcing her listeners to jump suddenly, Penny's wine spilling over the edge of her glass from the force of her jolt.

'We turn around and notice that the door has suddenly slammed shut behind us in the wind. Well, there is no choice but to go up the stairs with the hope that there will be an exit. Still holding onto each other, one by one we slowly climb until we reach the last step and reach a door. We start pushing the door and…'

Suddenly, a sharp ear-piercing noise echoed throughout the room, silencing Anita and causing the rest of them to jump for the second time.

Penny rose as if by instinct and started walking towards the black door, her bare feet feeling the cold as they connected with the tiled floor beneath them. Eyes firmly on the locked door, Penny was unaware of what had caused the noise, or what had made her move towards the door, she wasn't even aware what she was doing. It was as though a magnet was pulling her forwards, the compulsion too strong to resist.

As she crossed the room, her foot closed down on what felt like a million little spikes of glass piercing sharply through her skin. Her eyes remained on the door as she continued walking, her mind failing to register the pain that was slowly rising through her body from her feet. When she reached the door, she stopped and looked downwards, still in a comatose state. She couldn't focus on anything other than the line of blood which was leaking from her foot which was effortlessly navigating its way around the shattered shards of glass. The red lake slid towards the door like a snake, staining the floor a deep shade of red as it slithered forwards. She looked back up at the door and listened to the silence of the room. The only noise to be heard was the tinkling sound of the final shards of glass finishing their spin and collapsing in defeat onto the floor.

Eight

She felt a strong pull on her arm and her body move sideways into the force that was pulling her. Her head felt giddy as she swayed into the arm holding her, her gaze being forced away from the door. The air around the room seemed sparse and Penny now focused on the floor, looking at the sparkling pieces of glass spread out across the bright red surface. Somehow, she had been disconnected from the room, the air around her making her confused about where she was. As she fell sideways, she began to regain her awareness and to keep it, she tried to focus on the floor, although it seemed to be spinning in circles underneath her. Penny was aware of the sharp throbbing pain that stabbed at her foot, slowly making its way up her body, getting stronger and stronger as it moved upwards.

'Penny, you're bleeding,' her mother said, letting go of her arm. With a forceful push, Penny was placed into the closest chair, 'Let me see if I brought any plasters with me.' She hurried out of the room.

Penny sat back into the chair which she hadn't realised she had left and felt an aching in her foot that was becoming more and more intense with each second that passed. What had started off as a sharp tickling sensation had developed into a violent stabbing pain shooting up her leg, causing tears to roll down her cheeks.

Now fully aware of what was going on, Penny pulled the throbbing foot onto her lap and moved it as close to her face as she could. As she held onto her foot tightly, she saw a perfectly straight, sharp, glass point protruding out.

Without giving it a second thought, she placed her fingertips on the tip of the splinter and yanked it out with one fast, determined pull. She winced as she felt it leave her pierced skin in one fluid motion. As quickly as the piece of glass was removed, the blood that had been slowly trickling out now gushed forcibly through the hole in her skin, no longer being held in place by its barrier.

'What happened?' she asked the others, who were now standing around her in a circle, concerned looks on their faces.

'A glass fell off the side there!' Anita pointed to the side of the kitchen cabinet. Penny's eyes moved from the counter back to the floor and imagined the glass tipping off the edge in slow motion and the explosion of glass as it hit the tiled floor. Her mother came back in, arms filled with first-aid items, and crouched on the floor to examine the wound.

'It's not that bad, a plaster will do,' she said, attempting to stop the blood flow as she pressed firmly on the skin before tightly attaching the plaster.

Penny's attention had turned back towards the door. A moment ago she was transfixed, unable to tear her eyes away from it. She wasn't aware until she was pushed back into the chair, that she had gone to the door. 'How did it fall?' she questioned.

'Anita unnerved something upstairs; it fell right at the same time she was talking about that door,' Fiona said, fear splashed across her face. Penny noticed that she was looking very pale and the fear seemed to have removed some of her makeup, showing her slight imperfections that were normally hidden. As she said the words she began edging away from her aunt and closer towards her mother.

'I was making it up, I didn't know a blooming glass would fall!' Anita replied looking offended. She paused for a moment and then said, 'However, it was great timing; couldn't have planned it better if I had tried,' she laughed, expecting the others to find humour in the situation. When the rest looked at her with blank faces, she realised they had not.

Penny saw her mother and Fiona exchange concerned looks, her mother nudging Anita with her elbow at the tactlessness of her comment. Penny raised her hands towards her face and noticed that they were shaking. Annoyed with herself, she placed them beneath her legs so she couldn't see the sign of weakness and the trembling ceased momentarily, although she was sure she could still feel them vibrating. She tried to think back to the moment when she rose from her chair and tried to figure out what had come over her to walk so determinedly towards the black door. She remembered being sucked into the tension of Anita's story, hanging onto her every word in anticipation of what was on the other side of the door, even though she knew it was just another one of her stories. The next thing she remembered was the sharp throbbing pain in her feet as she was standing in a puddle of her own blood.

'I thought you were going to clean up the glass at first but then you continued to walk over it, as if you hadn't even heard it smash,' Fiona said, still standing close to her mother's side.

'I honestly can't tell you why I got up. I don't remember it at all,' Penny replied. The others looked at her as though they thought she was keeping something from them; like she wasn't telling them the whole truth. Not appreciating their suspicious glances, she thought back again to the story to try and figure out what it was that possessed her to leave her chair. It was no use, she couldn't remember getting up, let alone remember why she chose to.

'Maybe I did go to clean up the glass but then got distracted?' Penny tried to rationalise the situation. 'Weird huh?' she added as a final thought, wanting to draw a line under the conversation.

Her mother searched for something to clear the shattered glass away from the floor as Anita returned to her seat. Noticing the tension had lifted slightly, she saw this as a perfect time to say, 'Actually, I didn't want to tell you this in case you got afraid, but when the door opened, it unleashed a…'

'Okay,' Penny interrupted, holding her hand up in Anita's direction to silence her. 'We won't continue the story tonight, just in case.' She realised that there must be a logical explanation for her strange activity, and she didn't want to even contemplate the idea that there wasn't.

'I think it's time to go to bed,' her mother said once the last stray shards of glass were cleared up.

They didn't disagree, the events of the last five minutes had put a dampener on their night.

Penny collected her phone and followed them down the hallway where they walked in silence to their rooms. As she left, she realised they had left the kitchen lights on and turned to switch them off. She stretched her hand around the corner to reach the light switch but before flicking them off, stepped back into the room and looked towards the black door. Inquisitively she stood for a few moments, head to one side, trying once again to understand why she was so drawn to it.

Realising it was useless, she flicked the switch and made her way towards her bedroom, hobbling from the pain in her foot as she went. She let out a long yawn; the tiredness that had been slowly trying to break through had finally succeeded and all she cared about now was getting to sleep.

'How's the foot?' Fiona asked as Penny entered the room. She was already tucked under the covers which were wrapped tightly around her body, with only her head to be seen, poking out of the end. 'It's still so cold in here!' she added, noticing Penny laugh out loud as she saw her.

'Not too bad now, I didn't even realise what had happened until Mum yanked me away,' she responded, looking around for her jumper to sleep in. She had hoped the coldness in the room might have improved, but if anything it seemed colder today than it had been the night before. Penny still couldn't figure out why; it had been so warm outside and she couldn't see anything in the room which could be causing the chill. The kitchen hadn't been particularly warm, but it was distinctly warmer than it was in here.

'It was slightly creepy though, don't you think? The way Anita got to that part of the story and the glass just suddenly fell off the top like that.' Fiona still had a scared look as she said the words and the way she looked at her younger sister for reassurance made Penny forget that her sister was a mother herself.

'Oh stop it; you know all of the stuff she makes up is hocus pocus. She must have thought she had hit the jackpot when she set foot in this place and saw how old it is. She probably spent all of last night planning the different ghost stories she could tell us to get exactly the reaction you're giving off right now,' Penny laughed as she got into the bed beside her sister. 'Anyway, you're meant to be the tough one.'

Fiona looked away from Penny and didn't seem convinced, 'Don't tease me! I don't know, there is something about this apartment I don't like. I mean it is beautiful and everything but it gives me a weird feeling.'

'Don't be silly. We just need some sleep,' Penny

dismissed her sister. She thought it typical that she was being so dramatic; there was no reason to be so fearful about something that did not exist.

As Penny tried to get comfortable, she felt the throbbing in her foot become more intense. Penny kissed her sister on the head and turned her back to her, hoping she would be able to sleep through the pain which now seemed to have removed all the tiredness she was feeling only moments ago. Penny tossed and turned in the uncomfortable bed and became more and more frustrated when she heard her sister's breathing become slow and heavy. She tried to clear her mind from the pain and the strange black door, but her attempt to relax was interrupted by a noise coming from beyond the room.

Penny tried to discard the noise as being a figment of her imagination but the more she tried to push it out of her mind, the louder the sound became. Now fully awake, Penny opened her eyes and pushed herself upwards on the bed. She strained her ears to determine what it was she was hearing and as she did, thought it sounded as though someone was giggling in one of the other rooms. The noise sounded muffled, but she thought the sound was coming from the room behind them; the bathroom. She looked towards the opened archway and saw a bright beam of light shining through, stopping at the end of her bed. She hadn't noticed the light before; perhaps that was what was stopping her from getting to sleep. Annoyed, she reluctantly pulled the sheet from around her and jumped out of bed, ready to turn it off.

As her feet touched the floor the giggling sounds became louder, making her jump, the noise disrupting the otherwise silent room. She listened and thought it sounded familiar and she remembered her mother and Anita's bobbling heads peering around the doorway the previous night when saying goodnight. The giggling continued to get louder and what she thought was heart-warming and amusing when she saw them last night, was now making her tired and restless self highly irritated. She was pleased that they were having a good time and although she was normally not one to ruin anybody's fun, there was a time and a place for such a thing and when she was trying to get to sleep was not the one.

Penny rose from the bed and started moving towards the light. She moved through the archway of the room and turned towards the bathroom. The giggling had stopped and had been replaced with loud muttering. Funny, she didn't think it sounded like the two older women and wondered if the walls were thicker than she had originally thought. The closer she got to the door, the louder the muttering became and the more unfamiliar it sounded. She shrugged away the thought, cursing her aunt even more for putting ridiculous ideas into her head. She put her hand on the doorknob and placed her ear against the door, attempting to listen to what was being said. All she could make out were loud distorted moans and so she began to turn the handle which she moved slowly towards the right. As soon as it had made a full turn, the muttering came to an abrupt stop. Penny paused, hand frozen on the knob, surprised by the sudden silence. She didn't want to acknowledge that her heart was now beating faster than ever. Composing herself, she rationalised that the two had heard her approach and were startled by her attempt to open the door, causing them to keep quiet.

She pushed the door open, 'How long have you two been up for? You're keeping me awake.'

She barged into the room but stopped when she reached the centre. She turned around to face the toilet and then back around to face the basin. She repeated this motion again and turned around in a circle once more. Her eyes darted over the walls, covering every inch of the room. Penny made another turn of the room to ensure she hadn't missed anything. The room was empty.

Confused by the emptiness and the silence, Penny wondered if she had been asleep the whole time and had dreamt the laughter, although she was certain she was awake. She wondered if this was another one of Anita's tricks to scare her. She could tell by the look in Anita's eyes earlier that she enjoyed seeing the girls get spooked by the broken glass and the strange noises coming from above. Penny knew that as soon as she saw these things happening, she would have been planning all the stories that she could tell and the pranks she could play on them to ensure they were thoroughly scared senseless by the time they left. Now certain that this was exactly what had happened, Penny turned and marched towards their bedroom.

She stormed forwards and as she was walking, noticed the beam of light which was creeping through her room was coming from the overhead hanging lampshade. She hadn't looked at the ceiling of the hallway since they had arrived but as her head moved towards the light, she realised that she was standing directly underneath the spotlight, the bulb almost touching her head. Although she had thought earlier that the hallway seemed be reducing in height as it descended, it was only at this point that she really understood how low the ceiling actually hung. She moved her gaze towards the rest of the hallway at the far end towards the kitchen, and spotted three identical lampshades omitting light into the corridor from staggered points along the hall.

Penny glanced back upwards and stared directly into the light, trying to get a better view of the lampshade. This one appeared old and rusty and from the small size of it, it seemed impossible that it would be able to generate as much light as it was. She turned to look at the other three lamps and noticed that they were also the same, swinging slightly back and forth as a breeze moved them from their normal, restful position. Seeing them sway made Penny notice the iciness in the air and she wished she had stopped to pick up her dressing gown before leaving her room. Distracted by the lights, Penny had almost forgotten why she was standing in front of the bathroom door and then heard the sound of laughter once again coming from the other end of the passageway.

She huffed as she heard the noise, the chill in the arctic air was making Penny even more awake which sparked a rage inside her. As she moved forwards, Penny realised that it would have been impossible for the two women to make their way from the bathroom to the bedroom so quickly. Penny had got out of bed as soon as she heard the noise and she didn't think that she heard the footsteps as they left the bathroom, but perhaps she had been mistaken. She was almost certain that the noise had come from the bathroom initially, but she supposed she couldn't be sure.

The noise grew as Penny walked closer to the bedroom and the closer she got to her destination, the more it began to sound less like laughter and more like raised voices, as though the voices were in some sort of argument. Worried about what could be going on between her mother and aunt behind the door, she turned to run towards the room.

Before she was able to move forward, her body froze, one leg still lifted in front of the other.

The noises had stopped.

The only sound she could hear was that of her own heart beating rapidly in her chest so loudly she thought that everyone else in the apartment would be able to hear it too, the blood vibrating hard in her ears as though it were close to pouring out.

Frozen, she moved her eyes slowly to the left and the right.

The lights had flickered out, sinking her into deep darkness.

*

Penny stayed frozen for what, to her, seemed ages. The pulsing of her heart was beginning to increase rapidly as she tried to calm herself down. Adrenalin was soaring around her body and if she'd had any doubt that she was asleep before, she certainly didn't any more. The grogginess that had been consuming her only moments before was now replaced with a sudden alertness, her eyes open and wide, trying to adjust to the darkness that engulfed her. Penny stood motionless, trying desperately to see better in the shadows. She had done a good job in trying to push away the fear that was slowly building under the surface of her emotions over the past day, but it was no use trying to ignore it now. Being rapidly plummeted into blackness had taken her by surprise and she was startled by it.

Her first instinct was to run back into her bedroom, jump under the covers and force herself to sleep. She turned on the spot ready to retreat, when reason began to override fear and a voice inside her told her that she shouldn't give up on her attempt to check on her mother and aunt in the bedroom. It had seemed as though they were arguing before and she didn't think the darkness would have changed that.

After she had recovered from the initial shock and was able to slow her breathing into a more manageable rate, she marched towards their bedroom. Trying to overcome her fear, she reasoned that, like the pipes, the electrics in the house were old and therefore it was not surprising that they would trip, causing the lights to flicker on and off. Taking deep breaths in, she swallowed the fear and told this to herself repeatedly as she made her way towards the bedroom.

Unable to walk as fast as earlier due to the lack of light, she had to take small steps to get to the room even though she desperately wanted to run with all her might to get there faster. She wrapped her arms around her body, feeling tiny little bumps that had formed in reaction to the chill in the air which seemed to be getting colder the longer she walked. She let out a sigh and noticed that despite the blackness that swamped the room, she could still see the mark her breath had left when it hit the air.

As there was no longer a pathway of light for her to follow, Penny attempted to look around as she hobbled down the hallway, trying to feel some of the fixtures she had seen earlier on in the day, eyes searching for something she recognised. Eventually she reached a doorway to her left just before the entrance to the kitchen. She stopped to listen to see if there was any noise coming from the room as there had been earlier, but complete silence filled the apartment. Her hands searched for the doorway and on locating it, she pushed it open so forcefully that it bounced against the wall behind it.

She reached her hands out to the wall and fumbled until her hand met a light switch that she turned, causing a dim light to leak into the room from a poorly lit lamp beside her mother's side of the bed. She stepped forwards and looked down at the two women and saw that they were both peacefully tucked under the duvet, facing in opposite directions. She waited a few moments, expecting them to spring upwards to scare her even more but when no movement was forthcoming, she moved her head closer and heard soft gentle snores indicating that they had clearly been asleep for some time. Penny straightened her back and remained at the side of the bed, head tilted to one side, looking at her mother and aunt with interest. If it hadn't been them making the noises, then who was it?

Although standing beside the two women who had protected her all her life, Penny suddenly felt vulnerable in the semi-lit room, scared of who might be watching her. Thoughts started whirling around her mind when she tried to piece together what had happened until she forcibly stopped them, telling herself off mentally for being so ridiculous. Of course there would be a reasonable explanation for everything, she just needed to get some sleep and think about it again in the morning. Relieved that the pair hadn't been arguing, she pulled a blanket which had been discarded onto the floor over their duvet, not wanting them to be affected by the chill which was showing no signs of improving.

She turned to leave the room and let out a little laugh as she thought about how scared she had been, now coming around to the idea that there would be a logical explanation once she thought about it during the day, when her tired thoughts were not clouding her judgement. It had been a while since she had stayed overnight in anywhere other than a hotel on work trips and therefore her body and mind just needed to become adjusted to her new surroundings. Her strides back to her own bedroom were quicker and more assertive and she was looking forward to getting tucked back into bed and putting this madness behind her.

She marched onwards with such a speed that she hadn't realised the pain in her foot was asking her to slow down. She reached the bedroom and started to enter the room. Once again something forced her to stop. Without knowing why, she sensed something in the air had changed. Something about the chill seemed icier, the silence even more empty. Slowly, she turned away from the bedroom and into the hallway.

Penny looked towards the kitchen, the outline of the entrance still visible from where she was standing. She heard a buzzing noise and saw light sparks zapping out from the lampshade nearest the kitchen. Suddenly, a bright light was gleaming out, illuminating the area vividly; shining brighter than it had done before it had cut out.

She stood, mouth open, looking at the light, the goosebumps on her arm standing out even more. Not knowing what to do, she stepped forwards towards the light, when suddenly she heard the buzzing sound once again.

All at once the next light in front of it catapulted into life, shining just as brightly as the one before it. This time there had been no flickering and light suddenly flashed from beneath the shade. Almost as soon as the second lampshade had lit, the third one was brought to life and then the forth, as though the lights were switching on in a domino effect. The final light to illuminate was the one that she hadn't realised she was standing directly beneath, spotlighting her presence in the otherwise empty hall.

Without thinking, Penny turned and ran into her room.

Nine

Opening her eyes, Penny expected to see darkness, but was shocked to see light filling the room, telling her she had slept through the night. She remembered diving into bed, pulling the covers over her head so she wouldn't be worried by the noises or lights anymore; desperately willing sleep to come. She was doubtful, after being scared more than once, that she would be able to sleep and had resigned herself to a disturbed night. However, as she pushed herself up on the bed, she realised she hadn't had any trouble drifting off at all. She rubbed her eyes as she took in the brightness of the room, the darkness from the night before seeming a lifetime ago.

Penny took a deep breath in and unlike the previous morning, felt surprisingly rested which was strange considering everything that had happened the night before. Her mind couldn't help but relive those moments again causing her to doubt their validity, wondering if she had dreamt it all. She remembered the strong sense of annoyance she had felt when she first heard the noise, the curiosity that developed when she couldn't identify the source of the sound and then the spine-chilling fear when she was pushed into darkness. There was no doubt about it that those feelings were real, meaning she had to have been wide awake.

Fear was not a common emotion for Penny. Always thinking logically, she never allowed herself to be fearful unless there was a real risk to her life, which was next to never. In the darkness of the night before, all rationality had disappeared. She curled up under her duvet, her mind racing back to all the stories Anita had told them in the past and at that moment, had no doubt that they could actually be real. Now she had woken up in a new day, she wasn't altogether sure what she believed. She was not as frightened as she had been and she didn't believe there was anything 'haunting' about the apartment like her sister had said, but she was finding it difficult to rationalise all the strange events that were happening.

As she left her bed she had a quick glance at her phone to check the time and was pleased to see that it was approaching 8.30am. Her mother would be glad that she was up in time to complete a full day's activities. She was aware from the empty spot in the bed next to her that her sister had also risen early and could hear voices coming from the kitchen. This time there was no mistaking that they were real, no one could fake her sister's high-pitched tone echoing around the apartment. She stood, but had to reach out her hands to support herself as the room began to spin in swooping circles as she got to her feet. Hands holding onto the wall, she feared she would collapse into a heap on the floor until the room finally began to balance itself out and she felt steady enough to be able to walk unaided.

She showered with speed and entered the kitchen. Once again her mother had put on a massive spread of pastries and the other three women were helping themselves. Penny had pulled on another pair of jeans and was ashamed that the second pair she had bought with her were tightly pressing against her stomach. As she struggled to do them up, she remembered that she had vowed not to eat any more bad food on this trip, but when she arrived in the kitchen and looked down at the spread laid in front of her, her stomach grumbled loudly as the smell entered her nostrils, telling her to take no notice of her mind. Reluctantly she leant forward and put one of the sweet treats into her mouth, instantly grateful she hadn't listened to the voices telling her to resist.

'Morning, love. How's the foot?' her mother asked as she too tucked into one of the croissants, the copious amount of butter she had spread on it falling like droplets onto the plate in her hand.

'It's okay, a bit sore to walk on but not too bad,' she replied. 'It took me ages to go to sleep though.'

'Oh yeah?' Anita asked not meeting her eye, seemingly not bothered by Penny's evening.

'You two were keeping me up late and I came to tell you off,' she answered.

'What do you mean keeping you up late? We were asleep as soon as we got into bed,' her mother replied, looking concerned.

'I heard a noise and I went to go and tell you off as I thought it was you two mucking around,' she shot the pair a disapproving look, 'but when I came in to look at you, you were both asleep.'

'What type of noise?' Anita asked.

'Laughing I think, but then when I came to look you were fast asleep!!'

'Maybe you're hearing things love. An old place like this, maybe it's easy to hear funny noises,' her mother reasoned.

'So, it wasn't you?'

'No love, we went to bed as soon as we got in our room.'

'And it wasn't you, Anita?' Penny stared at her aunt, waiting for her to cave in and admit that she had pushed the joke too far.

'Your mother's right, out like a light we were.'

'Hmmm, I don't believe you but it doesn't matter, I got to sleep in the end.' Penny took another bite of her pastry and added, 'Oh and by the way, I think there's something wrong with the lights, they turned on and off a few times.'

'What do you mean?' Anita asked, urgency in her voice.

'Just that they turned off and on. It's no big deal,' Penny was confused by the worried tone in Anita's voice. She knew that what had happened was strange, but now that she was up and about it seemed less important; the apartment was just old and tired.

Anita continued to look at Penny, watching her face, eyebrows arched together obviously confused by what she had said. Not wanting to dwell on the matter any further, Penny walked over to the sideboard where her mother had kept the itinerary and glanced over what they had planned for the day. She was pleased that her mother had factored in some culture for the trip and had planned a visit to the local museums. Although the trip had technically been arranged for Fiona, she was grateful it also included a few things that she would like to do too.

'What type of museums are they, Mum?' she asked, pointing to the piece of paper she had in her hand.

Noticing her daughter's interest, Maggie's eyes lit up and a wide smile crossed her face as she said, 'Some local ones that tell us about the history of this place. Thought we could try and get a bit of everything in.'

'Oh no, today is the boring day then,' Fiona huffed as she snatched the paper out of her sister's hands. 'Are there any shops nearby I can look at while you lot do that?' Her voice was miserable as she sulked about the choice of activity. It didn't come as a surprise to Penny that her sister was not looking forward to the outing. Ever since they were little she absolutely hated anything that involved walking around and looking at things, much preferring a more energetic activity that could hold her captive imagination.

'The trip is not just about you, you know!' Anita said, pulling her up on her stroppiness. 'I wanted to go; you'll just have to put up with it.'

Fiona glanced around at all of them, looking for an ally but saw there would be no way of changing their minds. She let out another long sigh and walked towards the door, 'Fine, I'll meet you out here,' she said.

'Best we go and join Miss Stroppy Pants!' Anita huffed as she pushed herself up from the table and headed towards the door.

*

It had seemed a longer day than the one before and they spent most the time pottering around Charterville and visiting the tourist attractions they had missed the previous day. Penny's mother was very keen for them to get everything of 'importance' completed on the first two days so they could have the final days catching up on anything they missed off her list without feeling rushed. Penny felt exhausted as she considered how much ground they had covered so far and could feel the throbbing of her feet pulsing through her trainers as they expanded with each step she took. She hadn't noticed the pain in her foot when they left the apartment but as the day got on and her feet smacked against yet more cobbled stones, its pounding became more intense as a reminder of the strange events of the night before.

'Please tell me we will not be doing any more walking tomorrow. I came here to relax!' Fiona said, head falling onto her opened arms which were laid on the table in front of her. Penny noticed Fiona's dishevelled look, loose strands of hair falling beneath her neat and tidy headband that should have been keeping them in place. Penny wasn't used to seeing her sister like this and couldn't help but let out a little laugh at the sight of her, her pained expression almost making Penny forget about her own discomfort.

'Well it's a good thing we have the spa tomorrow then isn't it?' Maggie snapped at Fiona, giving her an exasperated look. Fiona hadn't stopped whinging about the boring day since they left the apartment and it was beginning to take its toll on their normally patient mother. 'I did plan it this way for a reason you know; think about someone else for a change!'

Fiona was taken aback by the shortness of her mother's reply and threw her an equally irritated look. 'I think about plenty of people, thanks very much!'

At this short exchange, Penny realised the whole group were completely shattered from their long day which was making their irritation levels rise. In an attempt to lighten the mood, she said, 'It was interesting though wasn't it? The museums I mean.'

Fiona rolled her eyes. 'If you think walking around looking at stupid dirty things that existed years ago interesting then... yeah!' She made a point of sarcastically pronouncing the last word to emphasise her boredom.

'Just because not everything revolves around looks and beauty parlours doesn't mean it isn't interesting!' Penny snapped back, annoyed at her sister's reaction.

'Two nights you've been back together and you're at each other's throats like you are teenagers again. Pack it in!' Anita eyed them both sternly, 'Yes Penny, it was interesting, especially what we found out about this street.'

*

They had already been into two small museums by the time they turned a corner and reached the final one, tucked away in a small corner of a residential street. Although she hated to agree with her sister, by this point Penny had to admit that she was bored. The museums they had visited were distinctly average with nothing of interest catching their attention. Being unaware of the city, she had no previous knowledge of its history and therefore couldn't seem to rustle up any particular interest when she was passing various old artefacts in the museum. At one point, she was tempted to tell her mother to abandon their cultured day and head towards the nearest bar when, without meaning to, they stumbled upon the last museum.

Not expecting much, they entered the small house-like building and were greeted by a friendly old lady who was so excited that she had paying customers for a change that she made a point of showing them around personally. The woman almost jumped off her chair when she saw the four unfamiliar faces walk through the door and her normally wrinkled face looked line-free as she broke into a gigantic smile at the sight of them.

Simply named 'The History of Charterville', the woman explained to them that she had on display various objects which demonstrated how the city's history and culture had been formed. Not wishing to be rude, they allowed the woman to walk them around and show them various pieces on display. They listened to her tell them how Charterville was one of the greatest cities in one of the medieval wars. Penny hadn't heard of the war she mentioned and was sceptical of its existence, however she continued to feign interest to please the woman. Like the previous places they had visited, they had little interest in what they were being shown, but the little old woman was so enthusiastic that they were unable to leave. They continued to follow her painfully slow footsteps around the building, umming and aahing at the facts they were being told.

The group's attention was immediately grabbed when the woman walked them past a tall glass cabinet littered with photographs. The lady paused as she reached the stand

and spoke about some of the photographers who had captured some of the town's memories. Penny's gaze stopped on one photograph which she found familiar. Tucked away in the corner of the cabinet was a black and white photo of a grand house standing proudly behind two gigantic trees.

'Oh look, that looks exactly like where we are staying!' Her mother reached out her finger towards the stand, speaking Penny's thoughts out loud.

The woman, whose age had impaired her eyesight somewhat, pushed her face up against the glass and said, 'Oh yes, I had heard they started renting that out. It is down in Oakdene you know, lovely little town a few miles from here.'

'Yes, we are staying there.'

'Oh, how nice!' The woman smiled, 'That was the house of Lord and Lady Peel. They called it Oak Tree House, presumably because of those trees. They always seemed to be in bloom, if I remember correctly.'

'Who were they?' Penny asked, intrigued to find out a bit more about where they were staying.

'I'm not too sure what they actually did to be honest but I do recall my grandfather telling me stories that were passed on from his grandfather. Very wealthy family I believe. I think they had one child but I don't think she was all there really.' She made a looping gesture with her finger pointing towards her head, 'I think she married a doctor of some sort when her parents passed away but I don't think it ended too well for her.'

'What do you mean?' Anita too was captivated by the story.

'Huh?' The woman looked confused.

'To the girl?'

'The girl… let me think. Well I think there was an incident of some sort; I am not too sure what but I don't think it was good. Quite ugly by all accounts, for all those involved. I don't think she could have the child that they wanted. I think she died in strange circumstances. They found her body under… under…' Her eyes glazed over as she struggled to remember the rest of her story and she looked away in the distance, as if something had suddenly caught her eye.

Not seeming to remember their earlier conversation, the old lady said, 'Anyway, I heard they have started renting it out. Maybe you could catch a bus down there and see it for yourselves, although I wouldn't recommend going there what with everything that went on and all.'

Ten

'Maybe the noise we heard upstairs was the crazy child! Maybe that's why the door is locked, to keep her out!' Anita leant forwards on the table. Her eyes lit up as she said, 'Told you there was a body behind that door, what did I say?'

'Damn it, I keep forgetting there is no bloody reception in here.' Fiona threw her phone onto the table, ignoring her aunt, 'I was going to look it up on the internet. What incident do you think the batty old bird was talking about?'

'Don't!' Penny cut Anita off, noticing her mouth opening to create yet another ridiculous story that would no doubt end up scaring her sister for another night. Anita looked annoyed at this interruption and shot Penny an offended look, sad that she was ruining her fun.

'I don't think we will know until we can look online,' Fiona replied. 'Maybe we could do it tomorrow?'

'But the body…' Anita said.

'The woman was clearly confused,' her mother interjected. 'You could see that she had lost some of her marbles, poor lady. Old place like this, there are bound to be some old folktales flying around.'

Penny thought about what the woman had been able to tell them and felt strangely comforted that she knew a little bit more about where she was staying, although it was not much. Oak Tree House had a nice ring to it and it was no surprise to her that it was once the home of a Lord and Lady, the grandness of the main house being too elaborate for anyone else.

As she was thinking, she remembered peering into the window upstairs which had a strange resemblance to a bedroom and thought about what the woman had implied about there being a 'crazy' child within the family of the household. Could this bedroom have been the child's room? Penny shook her head as she considered this; obviously a bedroom would not be left untouched for hundreds of years. As she had made the loose connection she realised that Anita probably had too. She looked across at her and saw a wide smile stretched across her face. She was obviously ecstatic to hear the word 'body' and 'crazy' regarding their residence and she had no doubt that she was probably concocting wild stories in her head at this very moment.

Her mother let out a long yawn, stretching out her arms as she moved backwards in her chair. It wasn't particularly late but the day's activities had worn the foursome out once again.

'I'm really sorry but I think I'm going to have to go to bed,' she said. 'Why don't you all stay up and share a bottle of wine? I'm afraid I'm knackered.'

'Actually, I'm shattered too and my foot is killing me,' Penny replied. The throbbing in her foot had reached a new level now that she had discarded her shoe.

'Boring,' Anita huffed. 'We haven't even spoken about the body yet!'

'And we don't need to!' Fiona said.

'What if the body is behind the door and escapes at night? Surely we should consider our options…'

'Goodnight Anita.' Fiona got up and kissed her aunt on the top of her forehead.

'But now we know about it, it has awoken the deadly

spirits upstairs.'

'Night night.' Penny also kissed her goodnight.

'It's how all good horror stories start you know, people hear about the story but choose to ignore it and then are surprised when things start to go horribly wrong.'

Penny and Fiona smiled as they followed their mother out of the room, leaving Anita sitting at the table, mouth open at being rejected. Penny figured she'd stay up and have a glass of wine, contemplating what stories to tell them tomorrow. The walk to the bedroom seemed longer this evening as Penny had to hobble along on her swollen foot. Exhausted, she began to take off her jumper as she limped, with the aim of getting into bed as soon as she entered the room. Instantly she regretted this decision as the coldness made her gasp; the difference in the temperature of the room enough to take her breath away. She pulled on her nightdress and then put the jumper back on in the hope that it would provide some warmth through the night.

'Are you not going to have a wash?' Her sister looked at her, eyebrow raised, disgusted with her lack of self-care. Penny knew that Fiona didn't approve of such a lack of self-preservation but she didn't care. She would have to confront the dark shadows under her eyes when she greeted herself in the mirror the following morning, but for now, sleep was calling out to her too much to worry.

'Not tonight, I just want to sleep,' Penny moved towards the bed.

Fiona didn't bother saying goodnight to Penny and turned around to face the wall. Penny noted, but did not comment, that her sister had done the same as her and scurried into bed without following her precise beauty routine. She made a mental note to ridicule her over this in the morning when she would no doubt tease her on her slovenly appearance.

Penny tried to go to sleep. Unlike yesterday she was sure that she would be able to fall asleep quickly, exhaustion flowing through her body, the ache of each muscle throbbing from the day's activities. She tried to relax and forget about what happened the night before, trying to push it away from her thoughts, telling herself it wouldn't happen again. As she took deep breaths, she began to feel more relaxed, the pain in her foot subsiding as she kept it still and she felt herself dozing off.

Interrupting her descent into sleep, she heard a noise coming from the hallway. The noise was getting gradually louder, forcing her out of her attempt to sleep and into full consciousness. She sat up from the bed and once again saw a single beam of light entering the bedroom as she strained her ears to listen out for the noise. The noise was definitely real but it sounded distant and far away. Confused, Penny wrestled with the idea of getting out of bed or forcing herself to go back to sleep. She finally convinced herself that it was all in her imagination and she threw herself back onto the bed, this time bringing her spare pillow around to cover her ears.

She tried to fall asleep, forcing her eyes to remain shut, but the drowsiness that recently filled her body had disappeared and despite not wanting to, Penny found herself listening out for another noise. The sounds were still there in the background but she couldn't figure out what they were. At first they sounded like hushed voices but with the pillow covering her ears she couldn't be sure. Slowly and reluctantly, she moved the pillow away from her head so she could hear better. She opened her eyes to see if her sister had also been woken. If she hadn't, Penny would most certainly wake her to confirm that she was not alone in hearing these things and wasn't going mad as she was starting to believe.

She moved her hand towards where her sister was lying

—

but felt an empty bed beside her. She sat bolt upright and looked around the room. Fiona was nowhere to be seen and the sheets she had been in moments before lay perfectly straight and un-creased as though she had never been there at all.

Convinced her mind was playing tricks with her, she moved her hands frantically back over the bed. She thought that perhaps her sister had got up to go to the toilet without being heard and maybe Penny had actually drifted into sleep without realising. As her hands moved across the bed, she realised she couldn't feel the dent where the two single beds had been pushed together the night before. She jumped up and moved towards the light, hand searching the wall for the switch to give her better vision. The light illuminated the space around her and Penny let out a gasp as she saw she had been lying on a small wooden bed, completely different to the one she thought she had been sleeping in.

Penny slowly walked towards it and around to the spot she had just quickly jumped out of. A basic wooden headboard protected the thin mattress which was secured against the wall. Penny convinced herself that she must be dreaming, wanting to believe it more than ever, willing it to be true. To be sure, she began pinching herself repeatedly on her arm, the same way her mother had taught her when she was younger and having a bad dream, hoping the pain would jolt her back to the real world in an instant.

She closed her eyes tight as she felt the pain of the pinch rush through her body and the blood from her arm zoom to her head. Cautiously, Penny opened one of her eyes, keeping the other firmly shut; expecting herself to be looking down upon her sleeping sister in their two pushed together beds.

Penny thought her heart had stopped when she looked down, before it quickly picked up its pace and started hammering aggressively in her chest. Fiona was not in the bed and the one she had been lying in a few moments ago had been replaced with a small, wooden one.

She couldn't deny it this time around, no matter how hard she tried to push the fear away. She was scared. It was hard to see the rationality in the situation as she stared down at an alien bed and the spot where her sister had vanished. Apprehension began to grow in her stomach. Her body began to feel tingly as she tried to accept the fear inside her and the room started to spin in circles around her. She was disorientated and confused and frantically trying to figure out what to do next in this bizarre situation in which she found herself.

The noises in the background continued, pulling Penny away from looking at the bed. Although not wanting to, she couldn't help but listen to them getting louder and louder. She heard sobbing break through the chaotic sound. Heart-breaking, desperate sobs. Instinctively she thought of her sister and began running towards the sound, shouting her name as she rushed forwards. Penny barely looked where she was running as she travelled down the hallway, focusing only on moving towards the noise in the shortest amount of time possible. She hadn't heard her sister cry in some time but, not knowing who else it could possibly be, automatically assumed it was her and barely a thought had entered her mind before she started running, the fear replaced with the urgent need to protect her only sibling.

She stopped suddenly when she reached the kitchen, almost tumbling over when she came to an abrupt halt. She saw a figure standing in front of the main door which led out of the apartment. The running had made her mind clearer and although she was taken aback when she saw the figure, she felt strangely reassured, assuming it was Fiona and that she was okay. As the initial panic began to subside and she was able to catch her breath, she felt irritated that another member of her family had made her get out of bed for no reason. Why on earth had Fiona been sobbing so loudly?

Her heartbeat did not remain steady for long. She opened her mouth to call out at her sister but then looked at the silhouette in closer detail, not recognising the broad shoulders and wide legs. She quickly remembered what had happened in the bedroom and the transforming bed and the sobbing she'd heard that brought her here. Her stomach tightened as the dread she had been trying to ignore intensified, as though it was a spider spinning its web at such speed, desperate for a catch of its prey. She couldn't attempt to ignore it anymore; the dread spider was slowly creeping up her spine, getting closer and closer to her heart. Something was not right.

She stood at the doorway looking in. The lights were still out and the kitchen was filled with an unnerving darkness which made Penny want to hold her breath, in case just breathing might unleash something she wouldn't want to see. A single light was entering through the tiny glass window at the top of door, trickling through as though it urgently wished to light up the room and rid it of the darkness which was consuming it. It was surprising how such little light could illuminate the figure standing before her in perfect visibility. The figure appeared to be at least six feet tall, although Penny was not sure if the way the light was reflecting down upon it was giving the illusion that it seemed larger than it was. Like the rest of the room, the silhouette was black and she realised that had there been no light entering the doorway, she would not be able to see it, the colour of its profile blending in perfectly with the other shadows in the room.

Penny looked at it again and realised by the stature that it was a man, dressed all in black. Her head turned sharply left as she heard the sobbing once more. She noticed that there was a second figure on the floor in front of the black door, curled up in a tight ball. The painful sobbing continued, causing Penny's stomach to knot in reaction to the tragic sound. Straight away she knew these people were not her family, although she had no idea who they were and what they were doing inside the home they had rented. Although disconcerting, Penny felt an overriding urge to comfort the person on the floor who clearly needed some sort of assistance, not even stopping between sobs to catch a breath. Penny didn't know why she didn't question why they were there, all Penny wanted to do was comfort the person on the floor whose sobbing interrupted any other thoughts she had. She could make out that the ball of a person was a woman, her long hair falling below her shoulders and the obvious curves of her womanly bodily outlined in the dark. She was shaking as she let out the desperate cries and Penny felt anger towards the man at the door who clearly didn't intend to help this person.

Penny attempted to move forward but when she tried to lift her leg, no movement came. She tried again but all she felt was a heavy weight pulling her leg downwards. She looked around the room, at the woman on the floor, and then back to the man at the door. Rage started building inside her and she was furious at herself for being so stupid and naive. Of course it wasn't okay for there to be unexplained people in their apartment; why hadn't she sensed the danger in the situation and fled when she had the chance? She opened her mouth to scream but no sound came out. She kept trying to push the words out of her constricted throat but as she tried, she felt her chest become tighter and tighter as though someone was slowly closing their hand around it, blocking her from getting the air she so desperately needed. She felt the room slowly closing in on her as the air around her became sparse. Losing her ability to move had paralysed her mind with it and she was unable to think clearly, her mind full of a red fuzzy haze. Desperately, she attempted to move her legs and speak once more but found she was still gripped to the spot. The redness in her head was becoming brighter and brighter the more panicked she became.

She glanced back at the silhouette who was now beginning to turn back to face the woman who had rolled over to address him. Penny was unable to see her face, the darkness in the room only allowing her profile to be outlined. From the way she was sitting, Penny thought she was crouched forwards, head bowed into her arms as though she was carrying something, although Penny couldn't see what. It was depressingly dark in the room, but she could see one colour perfectly.

Surrounding the woman was a rich, vibrant puddle of red which was lighting the darkness of the room as though there was a ferocious fire burning on the floor. When Penny realised the red puddle was blood, the dread spider came back and continued to spin its web, now with even more speed. The woman was bleeding. Penny tried to move her legs once more but the more she fought to move, the more stuck she became, the floor refusing to let her go.

The man turned and started slowly walking towards the woman, mouth open as if he was talking. Penny tried but it was no use, she couldn't hear what he was saying, the bubble that was keeping Penny in one place was acting as a sound barrier too. As he was walking, he picked up pace and pushed his arms in front of him, outstretched towards the woman.

Suddenly the sound barrier had been broken and Penny heard a spine chilling scream, 'Nooooooooooooooo…'

Eleven

'Penny, Penny!' She could feel her head being shaken backwards and forwards, flopping in whichever direction it was being thrown as though the bones in her neck were no longer functioning. She raised her arms and tried to push away whatever was holding her, remembering the man zooming towards the defenceless woman on the floor, worried that he was coming for her.

'Calm down, calm down.'

Tears were streaming down her face and she felt a gentle touch on her knee and heard a recognisable voice trying to get her out of whatever state she was currently in. She opened her eyes and tried to stop crying so that she could focus on where she was. Fiona had a firm grip on Penny's shoulders and was trying to hold her still as Penny attempted to release herself out of her hold.

Seeing Fiona in front of her, she realised that she was safe and that it wasn't her who had been crying. All at once the tightness that had held her chest loosened and she was able to take deep breaths into her lungs, clearing the red haze that had been clouding her mind. Fiona's hold was tight and once Penny was certain she was out of danger, she felt her arms go numb with the forcefulness of her grip.

Penny wiggled free from underneath her sister's hold and darted off the bed. Although the disappearing redness had allowed her to think more clearly, all her thoughts were still in a muddle. She blinked a few times as she tried to understand where she was.

She saw that the old, wooden bed had been reverted back to the two single metal beds that she and Fiona had pushed together the night before. The side of the bed Penny had jumped from was crumpled and it was clear that Penny had been lying there only moments before. She turned away from Fiona and placed her hands on her head as she tried to make sense of the situation. Penny could feel the beads of sweat that had been forming along her brow slowly travel down her face, stinging her eyes as they rolled downwards.

Penny felt tired, severely exhausted, and when she turned back to look at the bed and the concern in her sister's eyes, she realised that she must have been sleeping and that she had dreamt it all. She let out a sigh of relief and would have laughed at her reaction had she not been so terrified. She lowered her hands and realised that they were trembling, still trying to catch up with the logic of what she had just experienced.

'What happened?' Her mother rushed into the room, almost tripping on her trailing nightdress as she burst forwards. 'I heard shouting!'

'She just started screaming NO, really loudly. Over and over,' Fiona replied. She had let go of her sister's arm and was talking about her as though she was not in the room. Although she was tired, Penny was certain that she saw her sister shoot her a disgusted look as though whatever it was that she had just dreamed would be contagious.

'Did you have a nightmare love?' Anita hurried into the room as her mother quickly ran from it.

'I... I... I'm not sure.' Penny shook her head, trying to remember what had just happened. 'I heard noises again. At first I tried to ignore them as I didn't want to have another night like last night but they started getting louder and...'

'Another...?' Anita interrupted.

'Yesterday. I heard noises. I thought it was you two mucking around, I told you this earlier,' she nodded at Anita, her speech quick as she tried to regain a normal breathing pattern. 'But it wasn't you. Then tonight I heard the same noise only this time it was different…'

'Different how?' Fiona asked her, moving Penny's hair away from her face.

Penny glanced between her aunt and sister who were both perched on opposite sides of the bed, their eyes squinting at Penny as she told them what happened, as if they were having difficulty in understanding what she was saying. Penny didn't want them to worry about her, she was worried enough about herself as it was. She couldn't face dealing with the burden of having their anxiety piled on her as well, at least not for tonight. She shook her head a few more times and sat back down on the bed, looking into her lap where her hands were folded in front of her, knuckles white from clenching them.

'I've got you some water, love.' Her mother had returned into the room and pushed a glass of water into her hands. She was out of breath as though she had run some distance and her expression made Penny realise that she was just as concerned about her as the other two.

'What noises did you hear, Pen?' Anita moved forward and grabbed Penny's hand. The movement startled her and the drink spilt a little as she jumped backwards from the touch.

'Not tonight Anita, she's obviously had a bad dream,' her mother scolded her sister.

'I just wanted to know. After what we were told today maybe…'

'Not tonight!' she interrupted her forcefully. 'Take these as well, they will help you to get back to sleep. You're all clammy, you must have had a fright.'

She pushed two little blue tablets into her daughter's hand and raised them towards her mouth. Penny didn't like taking medication unless it was absolutely necessary and pushed her mother's hand away. It was only a bad dream, she thought, that wasn't unusual, she'd be able to get to sleep if she pushed it out of her mind.

'Well I'll leave them here for you anyway. Just in case.' She placed the tablets on the bottom of the bed.

'What time is it?' Penny asked.

'Just gone half two,' Fiona answered, picking her phone up off the floor to check.

Penny was embarrassed that she had caused all three of them to get out of bed so early in the morning, disrupting what should have been a peaceful sleep. She especially felt bad for her sister who, on a normal day, had to get up frequently throughout the night with the children. Fiona was especially looking forward to getting a few nights uninterrupted sleep and Penny was pained that she had ruined this for her.

'God, I'm sorry. Go to sleep, I'll be fine, it was just a bad dream,' she said.

'I don't mind staying up if you want me to?' Anita still had that look on her face and Penny couldn't stand it; she didn't understand why she seemed so bothered.

'No honestly, I'm tired and I just want to go to bed so we can have a fun day tomorrow,' Penny replied, forcing a cheery tone to echo through her words, although it didn't sound convincing.

'Do you want to swap beds with Anita and get in with me if you're not very well?' Penny's mother asked, making Penny smile.

'No honestly, I'm not ill, just a bit tired. It was only a dream! Honestly, go to bed now.' She pulled the covers higher up to cover her body, indicating to her mother and aunt that they should leave the room. To make her point even clearer, she placed the glass on the floor and put her head back onto the pillow. 'Thank you for checking on me and thank you for the water, it's made me feel better.'

'Well if you're sure,' her mother said, still looking concerned. 'Promise you'll wake me if you start feeling unwell or have another bad dream?'

'Promise,' Penny replied, kissing her on the cheek.

As her mother and Anita left the room, Penny pulled the covers closer to her body. Although she was hot to the touch and now sticky from the sweat, she was still freezing. The scare had made the chill in the room even more noticeable and even with the duvet pulled up to just under her neck, she was still cold.

'Are you sure you don't want to talk about it?' Fiona asked, facing her sister on the bed.

'Honestly, it was just a dream; I don't even remember properly what happened. Let's just get some sleep,' Penny leaned over and gave her a kiss on the cheek too.

Fiona smiled and turned her back away from her sister as Penny edged forwards towards her. She was eager to be close to her in case the bed mysteriously transformed the way it had done just moments before. She had been lying to her family when she said she wanted to go back to sleep; adrenaline was shooting urgently throughout her body meaning any drowsiness had completely evaporated. Penny didn't want to close her eyes as she didn't want to be reminded of what had happened. She had never allowed herself to think outside of the world in which they live and was petrified that her mind had taken her to a place it would never dare to go when she was conscious.

103

She had always been able to control her emotions, think clearly and see the bigger picture. The fact that she was unable to figure out what had just happened sparked an anger inside her, making her stomach gurgle in an aggressive protest as it tried to register the strange feelings. She thought back to the dream and tried to piece together what happened and what it could have possibly meant. Every thought in her head was muddled and unclear, making it hard for her to tell what was real and what wasn't.

Although clearly a dream, there was part of Penny that simply could not accept that was true. It had seemed so real, unlike any other dream she had before; she could still feel the sharp panic in her chest and the way her feet had been cemented to the floor, restricting her movements.

She heard the faint sounds of her sister breathing and realised that it hadn't taken long for her to drift back to sleep. She contemplated going back into the kitchen to see if she could stir up whatever it was that she had seen, to try and make sense of what had happened. But although the heart-gripping fear was slowly subsiding, the thought of leaving her bed made it rattle inside her again and she realised that she wasn't brave enough to face that right now. Instead, she snuggled back into the bed and edged closer to her sister.

Penny closed her eyes but reopened them a second later. The total darkness she saw when they were closed was enough for her to want the light, afraid of what the darkness would bring. She considered her options for a few moments and reached forward, patting the bed in hope that the pills her mother had left her had not been lost in her attempt to get comfortable.

She found one lying by her feet and popped it into her mouth, desperately hoping it had the desired effect of putting her into a deep sleep.

Twelve

'What do you think she was dreaming of?'

'I don't know.'

'Didn't she say anything to you when we left?'

'No, it was 2.30 in the morning, I was knackered. We went to sleep.'

'What was she like?'

'I don't know.'

'Was she okay?'

'God, why are you asking me all these questions? It was only a dream.'

'My ears are burning,' Penny interrupted Anita and Fiona, who were gossiping about her in the bathroom. 'It was just a dream Anita, don't go on about it.'

Like the previous mornings, Penny had not woken in a good mood. Even before she had a chance to think about the evening before, she knew as soon as she opened her eyes that she didn't feel right. She felt like she had not slept at all, although she knew this was not the case. The last thing she remembered was popping the pill into her mouth, fretting that she would never be able to sleep again and then suddenly waking to a new day. The next moment she was standing in the bathroom listening to herself being spoken about, as though only a few seconds had passed rather than half the night.

Her head had felt heavy as she lifted it from the pillow,

tight and painful to move as though a million needles were pressing against her forehead in sharp forceful motions, pain splintering within her head with any movement she made.

'Did anyone bring any painkillers?' She pushed past them to look inside her sister's toiletry bag.

'In that bag,' Fiona nodded to where Penny was already searching. 'Someone's happy this morning.'

Penny decided to ignore her sister, who got the hint and sulkily left the room. The needles were beginning to stab her with more force now. She couldn't bear to listen to her sister's whingey voice for longer than she had to; the shrill sound when she spoke was doing pushing the needles in even further. Anita had stayed and was lingering around. Having lost all her patience, Penny ushered her out of the room too. She almost felt bad as she slammed the door on Anita's concerned face when she opened her mouth to speak but she didn't care, she needed to be alone.

She scurried through her sister's bag and downed the painkillers, cupping water from the basin with her hands. Waiting for the tablets to offer some sort of release from the pain, she splashed her face with the bitterly cold water, hoping it would wake her up.

Crouched over the basin, she watched the water drip from her face as she tried to convince herself she was feeling better. The refreshing tang of the cold water forced her to wake from her comatose state briefly, although the pain remained; the tablets not being as fast acting as the one she took to get to sleep.

She lifted her head to look at herself in the mirror and scrunched her face when she saw the reflection staring back at her, seeing how rough she looked. Her hair was tangled and the little grey circles that were normally beneath her eyes had morphed into big black sacks. She cursed herself for going to bed without taking her makeup off; her mascara had smudged in the night and was running in a stream from her eyes down to her chin. She looked as though she'd had a heavy night on the town, not one that was forced into sleep with drug-induced help. Penny let out a groan as she regarded herself once more in the mirror and then got into the shower, wishing that she had more energy to look after herself better.

Although she was in no real rush to finish her shower and get ready for the day in front of her, she also had no desire to stay there for longer than needed, getting bored the moment she felt the water connect to her skin. As she was lathering her body with soapy water, she realised that she felt the lowest she had ever felt. A dark cloud lingered heavily over her head, quashing any attempt to feel remotely happy, forcing her to feel overwhelmingly miserable and depressed. Despite this mood, she continued to scrub, hoping that as she did, she would create a new skin which would bring with it a better mood. Once she saw her skin was red raw from all the scrubbing, she decided she'd had enough and reached over for the towel she had left on the floor.

As she stepped out of the bath and wrapped the towel around her, she felt acid rising up her throat. Her head began to feel woozy and the room started to spin as soon as her wet feet touched the cold tiles. Knowing what to expect, she reached out her arms and grabbed the basin to steady herself. She could almost taste the bile before it came up and she tried her hardest to swallow it down. Unable to make it to the toilet in time, she crunched over the basin as she threw up, retching from the bottom of her stomach.

What was wrong with her, she thought, once there was nothing left in her stomach. She'd had a fright the night before, but she didn't think it had scared her enough to make her vomit so violently. She never really got unwell, never allowing herself the time to mope around and instead she just pushed through whatever illness she had caught. Although she felt that she had just thrown up everything they had eaten since arriving, she didn't really feel unwell. Feeling sluggish and lethargic, she was unable to summon enough energy to move, remaining in a curled-up ball beside the basin, pitying herself for her lack of strength. The sickness hadn't done her any favours in trying to lift her mood.

When she realised she couldn't stay lying on the comfort of the cold tiles any longer, she pulled herself up from the floor, realising as she did that her illness must have been something to do with the tablets her mother had given her the night before. Penny made a mental note to never take those tablets again; insomnia would have been better than the feeling she was experiencing now.

She splashed her face again and stared at herself in the mirror. Even accepting that she wasn't looking her best, she was startled by how much the reflection staring back at her didn't look much like her at all. If the reflection hadn't copied the gesture she made as she raised her hand, she would have been doubtful that it was even her. She looked more closely at her likeness and resolved that maybe it was time for her to give in and take a trip to her sister's salon. She couldn't carry on looking like this, haggard and tired as though she had completely given up on life despite not yet reaching thirty.

Trying to make the mess she was staring at better, she picked up a brush to pull through her wet hair. She huffed as she realised it looked duller, recalling she only recently had it dyed, annoyed at the apparent waste of money. She moved her head closer to the mirror, trying to convince herself that it was the light and gasped when she saw her eyes were no longer round and large, but were now small and squinty, appearing almost cat-like. She shook her head as she took in this new image of herself; the tablets obviously messing with her eyes as well as her body.

Still looking in the mirror, she moved her head even closer to look more carefully; so close that her nose was almost touching the glass. She raised her hand to touch her face but pulled it away immediately as though the glass was too hot to touch.

Jumping back in astonishment, she realised that the reflection hadn't copied the gesture. She was looking back at herself standing completely still, but she could feel herself physically shaking, staring at the stranger in the mirror.

Slowly, she moved forwards again. Not being able to pull herself away from the reflection, she stared directly into its eyes, noticing they were not her own. Breaking the stare, the eyes she was staring so intently into turned away from Penny and gazed into the distance.

Startled by seeing her reflection come to life and moving without Penny doing so, she flew backwards and almost toppled onto the floor as her foot slipped on the wetness of the tiles. Her heart was racing and although she was certain she wasn't ill, she could feel her stomach churning as though she was going to throw up again. She took a step closer to the mirror to check the reflection was actually hers.

Her dishevelled reflection had returned, her big, round eyes beaming back at her and the shine of her hair glinting in the mirror as it reflected the sun which bounced around the room. Taking a deep breath to calm her nerves, she felt better seeing that her own image was back. To make sure her mind wasn't playing tricks on her once again, she reached out and touched her reflection to make sure it was really her. She turned slowly to face the room. She knew there would be no one else there but her hands began shaking in anticipation that someone would jump out, now realising she didn't know what to expect within the apartment any more. Of course, there was no one else standing with her in the room but the goose bumps that popped up all over her arms as she turned in a circle were enough for her to run out in a hurry.

She slammed the door firmly behind her causing a loud echo to vibrate along the hallway. She dived into her bedroom to get changed and then darted towards the kitchen where she knew the others had congregated. Suddenly she had no desire to stay within the apartment a second longer than she needed to. She couldn't explain what she had seen in the mirror but she most definitely didn't want to hang around figuring out what it was. When she reached the table, she saw all three women were dressed and sitting discussing something meaningless that Penny didn't have the patience to try and feign interest.

'All ready to go out then?' she prompted them, trying to hide the panic in her voice. She decided not to tell anyone about what had happened in the bathroom, partly because she didn't know if the sleeping tablet had made her imagine it but also because she didn't want to be reminded of what had happened.

'How was your sleep, darling?' her mother asked, handing her a cup of coffee.

'I don't want any thanks,' she pushed the cup away from her mother. 'The sleep was good, made such a difference. I want to get out and about to be honest.' She spoke very fast, and looked around at the women sitting at the table, annoyed with their lack of urgency. 'Are we ready to go?'

'What has got into you, eager beaver?' Fiona looked at her sister with a puzzled glare. 'It's not like you to turn down a cup of coffee?'

'What? I just want to get out; it's spa day today right? I am so ready for some relaxation.' She tried to convince her sister, laughing as she said the sentence to emphasise her point, but she saw Fiona's eyebrows arch in suspicion.

Penny wasn't technically lying, she was indeed very much looking forward to going to the spa for the day, having never been to one before. As soon as her mother had told her about the planned trip, the excitement for a day of pampering started building immediately. For the past two months, all she could think about as she was working herself into the ground, was that soon she would be soaking her feet in a bubbly foot spa, closely followed by a luxurious massage. Penny tried to focus on this point, she needed this today and she needed to get somewhere which would take her back to reality. She would be able to check her phone, speak to Jason and stop thinking about what was and was not happening in the strange apartment.

'Are you sure you're okay? You look pale. Is there something you're not telling us?' Anita walked towards her, a quizzical look on her face.

'I'm fine,' Penny laughed, not meeting her aunt's direct glare. 'I just want to go!' Her voice came out louder than she had planned and not wanting to be probed any further, she turned and marched towards the door.

'As long as you are sure you're okay? We're all ready to go, we were waiting for you to get up,' her mother said, moving their used plates to the side by the sink and picking up the itinerary for the day. 'Give us five minutes.'

Her mother went into the bedroom and her sister went out of the opened door. Anita stood up slowly from the table and eyed Penny apprehensively, as if trying to compel her into telling her what was really on her mind. Penny turned and looked her in the eye before quickly turning to follow Fiona, feeling uncomfortable with the weight of Anita's suspicious stare.

Once her mother had finished collecting her things from

the bedroom, she and Anita joined the two sisters outside and they headed out for their day of relaxation. Penny strode forwards, leading them all out beyond the oak trees. Despite feeling a strong urge to turn back and look at the house, she resisted and tried her hardest to stop her mind wandering back to what had happened that morning. She concentrated on the path beyond the trees and hopefully, her refuge away from her troubled thoughts.

Thirteen

Despite her mood, Penny managed to enjoy the ultimate girly day full of pampering and relaxation, which lifted her spirits and put a smile back on her face. They had spent their time mainly lounging by the pool, dipping in and out of the sauna, followed by getting two expensive treatments each. Penny opted for a manicure and a deep tissue massage and she certainly wasn't disappointed with her choice. She had never needed relaxation more than she did at that moment and was trying to convince herself that if she got away from the house and focused on herself for a change, she would realise that her tired mind had been playing tricks on her, imagining things that weren't real.

As she stepped into the velvet-lined massage room, she tried to forget about the apartment and jumped on the bed, hoping that she would be transported to a place of pure self-indulgence. She told herself before she entered the room that she would put the unsettling series of events out of her mind as, despite her best efforts, they were still tumbling through her memory, begging to make sense.

As she was staring at the therapist's feet through the hole in the massage table, she found her eyelids become heavier and as she allowed them to shut, her mind flashed back to the reflection she had seen in the mirror that morning, the movement she saw in the window upstairs and the figures she saw in the kitchen the night before. As quickly as they entered her thoughts she pushed them back out.

Penny decided to keep her eyes open for the remainder

of the treatment so she wouldn't have to deal with the flutters in her stomach more than she needed to. It wasn't as relaxing as being completely in the 'zone' but it would have to do. It was more relaxation than she had experienced in months and she was damn sure she was going to make the most of it, even if it did mean focusing most her energy trying to steer her mind away from the disturbing thoughts that were trying to pollute it.

They didn't do much talking throughout the day as they were too preoccupied with spending the time enjoying their own company and absorbing the pampering they were receiving, taking only the time to speak to each other as they moved between the various different rooms within the spa. Penny was aware that Anita was cautiously watching her and Penny made a point not to end up alone with her for fear that she would make her tell her what was wrong. She hadn't made sense of it herself yet and she certainly didn't want to drag Anita into it, dreading that she would make more out of it than it already was.

Overall, they spent more than four hours in the health resort. Although they had spent the majority of those long, drawn-out hours lying down, the quietness and nothingness that had filled their day had made it seem as though they had been in there forever. Their eyes had to adjust when they left the building, as they came out of the dark tranquillity into the bright light of day and they decided to opt for a relaxed, chilled out dinner to complement their lounging day. After they had spent a pleasant hour or so enjoying the local cuisine, they decided to get a taxi back to the apartment, too tired to want to worry about getting a bus home.

*

'I feel incredibly relaxed; should think we'll get a good night's sleep tonight!' Penny's mother said as she kicked off her shoes and leant backwards into the chair she'd flopped herself into once they entered the apartment.

'My skin is going to be perfect tomorrow, it feels so smooth,' Fiona glowed as she looked at herself in her compact mirror which she pulled from her handbag resting on her knee.

'Your skin is always perfect!' Penny said, taking the mirror off her sister to look at herself.

For the first time in years, Penny actually liked the image she saw. She looked radiant and fresh, no longer tired or ill looking like she'd appeared earlier that morning when she was throwing up. The horrifying dark circles which had been bordering her eyes were now hardly visible and her greying skin was glowing. 'I actually don't look too bad myself! Maybe we should do this spa malarkey more often!'

Fiona jumped in her chair and clapped her hands in excitement, 'I said you needed to start looking after your skin more. If you put a bit more time and effort in, your skin will look like that more often!'

'Yes well, some of us don't have any more time or effort that we can put in. Some of us work long days you know!' She threw the mirror back at her sister, Fiona catching it in her hands to avoid it hitting her in the eye. Penny laughed and considered taking her sister's advice; it had been a while since she had looked after herself and maybe she should use this trip as a step in that direction, much preferring how she looked now compared to earlier on.

'Did you manage to get a phone signal when you two wandered off?' Penny's mother asked the pair.

*

Earlier as they were approaching the spa, Fiona and Penny decided to hang around outside to use their phones, Fiona to call the boys and Penny to try and connect with Jason. As soon as they reached the path beyond the oak trees, their phones instantly began to buzz, picking up the telephone signals flying in the air which somehow their apartment seemed to block. She saw she had a few messages from Jason which brought a smile to her face, telling her he missed her and that he was looking forward to her coming home. She hadn't missed home that much since their first evening and reading the messages made her heart swell with an ache for normality. She had to take several deep breaths to push down the solid lump that was forming in her throat at the thought of not being with him, the separation affecting her more than she had anticipated.

Even though Penny and Jason lived together and saw each other every day, during the times they spent apart they were always in touch with each other and were forever sending text messages back and forth. Although she had expected to be sad not seeing his face every day, she had clung onto the thought that they would still be able to talk to each other regularly. Every time she noticed the little bars build indicating that reception was in the air, she desperately sent him a message asking if he was okay. Penny had tried to call him before she went into the spa but annoyingly there was no answer. As soon as she had hung up she received a message from Jason telling her he was busy but he promised to call her as soon as he was free. Penny let out a sigh as she texted back, telling him there was no point in him calling as she would be unreachable for the next couple of hours (knowing the spa had a no phone rule) but that she would contact him as soon as she left.

*

Penny slouched on her chair, her hand propping up her tired head as she remembered the afternoon and her promised call back to him. She jumped up quickly when she realised that she hadn't called him back as promised, too preoccupied by her thoughts on the luxurious day she had just had. Annoyed that she had missed yet another opportunity to speak to him and aware that he would have been waiting for her call, she jolted from the chair and headed towards the door. She knew that she only had a few more days left before they returned and she got to see his face but suddenly she felt anxious about being separated from him and felt the need to speak to him immediately.

'I forgot to ring him back! He'll be waiting for my call!' she said as she pushed open the door.

'Where are you going? It's getting dark!' her mother called after her.

'I've tried; you won't get any reception out there either.' Fiona brushed her off, noticing Penny had her phone in her hand. Ignoring her, Penny rushed out.

She hopped off the step that led out of the kitchen and began walking towards the middle of the garden, the crisp spring air making her hair blow in the wind as she made purposeful strides in a desperate attempt to find some sort of connection. She pulled out her phone and moaned when she saw the tiny reception bars had not materialised but she pressed the dial button nevertheless. Disheartened when the phone failed to ring, she was determined not to give up and began to frantically wave her hands in the air the same way Fiona had the other day in an agitated attempt to obtain even the slightest bit of reception.

After a few attempts, she knew Fiona was right; it was useless. She wouldn't get any reception and this would be another night where she would be unable to speak to him. Feeling defeated, she fell to the floor. She looked towards the opened doorway of the kitchen knowing she ought to spend time with the others, but at the same time she didn't really want to go in yet either. She was enjoying the time away with her family, but she was beginning to feel claustrophobic being so cut off from the outside world the moment they walked down the path towards the apartment.

The gentle heat that had been warming the town as they headed back from the spa had disappeared and had been replaced with a sharp, bitter breeze. Enjoying the feel of it gently blowing across her face, she laid down on the grass, placing one of her hands beneath her head. She hadn't wanted to acknowledge it as they travelled home, but coming back to the apartment meant she had to confront what she had been feeling over the past few days and try and figure out what the hell was going on. As much as she tried to push the feelings out of her mind, trying to explain them with a level of rationality, she couldn't help but dread walking down past the oak trees. Butterflies instantly came alive in her stomach the moment she approached Oak Tree House, nervous apprehension rapidly growing with each step she took.

She felt safer lying on the grass away from those four walls and tried to piece together some of the events that led to her fears before trying to summon the courage to move from the spot she was lying on and face the night in front of her.

There was the person she saw in the window as she first walked down the path. She thought nothing of it at the time, obviously assuming it was a tenant in another apartment. Then there were the noises coming from above which confirmed her earlier thoughts. She remembered the shadow that darted across the window upstairs when she went to investigate, which made her jump with such force that she almost toppled over the banister in shock. And then there was the broken glass, the people she saw last night and the changing reflection in the mirror. Her mind was still desperately trying to figure out a reasonable explanation to connect all of these events but the more she tried to focus on one, the more it was unclear, as though she was trying to focus on an image which was being moved away quickly from her eyes.

The butterflies were zooming around her stomach now urgently as she remembered all the weird things that had gone on and, feeling defeated, she realised she had to admit that something weird and unexplainable was happening.

Penny figured that she would have to tell someone, knowing that she couldn't keep it bottled in for much longer. She couldn't tell Fiona, on the off-chance that she was wrong. Telling her would cause a frantic panic and although Penny wasn't well versed on how to handle such situations, she assumed that this would not help their predicament. She didn't think her mother would believe her and knew that she would be disappointed that the trip, which was supposed to give the ladies some well-deserved R&R, had instead caused her normally sensible and calm daughter to be fearful and frantic. Penny knew the only choice she had was to tell Anita, although she wasn't entirely sure how she would take it; wondering whether she would think she had turned her own games against her or offer her help.

She looked up towards the sky and noticed the sun was slowly going in, descending beneath the trees, desperately trying to rest its head for the night. That made two of them she thought as she let out a yawn. She placed her other hand underneath her head as she continued to gaze upwards, the carefree feeling she enjoyed earlier in the day now all but gone.

Penny closed her eyes as she continued to lie under the sky, allowing her body to be pulled towards the earth. She felt bad for not contacting Jason again and hoped he understood that she wasn't neglecting him. Now more than ever she desperately wanted to hear his voice. She picked the phone up once again, wishing it had somehow picked up her sense of urgency and made a connection. Knowing it hadn't, she held it in front of her face as she tapped away on the screen, sending him a further message apologising and reassuring him that she'd call him as soon as she could.

Outstretching her arms in front of her, the phone positioned above head, she noticed little bumps rising slowly from her wrist all the way up to her shoulder. A shiver ran over her as the wind suddenly became forceful. She placed the phone onto her chest and saw the tops of the trees swaying violently in the wind from side to side. She sat up slowly and looked around, seeing that like the trees, all the other plants and grass were swaying just as aggressively. Penny shivered as she realised the bumps on her arms had quickly turned into a cool coat of coldness.

The abrupt change in temperature meant that she could no longer enjoy the calm evening she was appreciating as she was lying on the ground. She stood to her feet and dusted off the loose fragments of grass which had attached themselves to her, preparing herself to reluctantly head back into the apartment. Standing in the wind, facing the house, she took in a deep breath, trying to summon the courage to face whatever it was that was lurking within the apartment. Once she had readied herself for the challenge, she secured her phone inside the back pocket of her jeans and walked forwards. She made her way across the garden in front of the grand house but stopped suddenly before she reached the doorway.

Something had flickered in her peripheral vision, causing her eye to dart upwards to see what it was. She wasn't sure what had caught her attention, it had moved so quickly. She looked around but couldn't see anything of interest.

The wind had picked up pace now and she felt the full force of it pushing against her back, trying to push her over, its angry roar shouting from behind as it bellowed through the trees. Trying not to let her imagination run away with her, she told herself that the wind must have blown something past her quickly and as quickly as it passed her by, it was blown elsewhere. There was nothing to be afraid of.

Shaking her head to rid her of suspicious thoughts, she picked up her walk towards the house, now freezing from the wind which had turned into a violent gust, throwing loose leaves angrily in its rage. She marched forward but didn't get very far and stopped once again. She had seen the flicker once more.

This time she knew exactly where it had come from.

There had been a movement in one of the windows directly on top of where they were staying.

She froze when she saw it but then it was gone again. She daren't move, hoping her stillness would cause the movement to happen again. She stood still, staring silently into the empty black window. Penny blinked and when she opened her eyes, the window was bare no more.

A white face flashed into sight, face pressed tight against the glass. It was there for no longer than a second before it disappeared again.

She was certain she knew who it was.

The face that had been standing in the window watching her was the man who was standing in their kitchen the night before.

He had seen her too, seen her watching him, watching her.

Fourteen

Penny continued to stare up at the window, willing the figure to come back into sight so she could get a better view of him. She now knew that there must be people living in the upstairs apartment and for some reason, they were watching Penny and her family.

Although still scared, adrenaline was pulsing through her body, replacing fear of the unknown with fear of the present. She had thought there were people staying in the apartment above them and seeing the man's fleeting image had confirmed that. Feeling slightly relieved that she had seen a real-life person and was able to attach some sort of explanation to what had been going on meant it wasn't all in her head after all. Her hands begin to tremble as she considered why he had been staring down at her so intently. Why had he been in their apartment late last night, and who was the young girl with him?

She turned and saw the door of the kitchen had been left open and knew that she had to go in there and tell her family what she had seen and get them out of the house immediately. They would get a bus straight into town and call the letting agency, or stay in a motel, or catch a train home. Whatever they decided, they were getting out.

The wind continued to blow, picking up speed as it swirled in angry circles around her. She turned back and looked towards the trees, surprised by how dark it had suddenly become. The trees were now swaying with such force they appeared close to tipping over. She looked down to see the blouse she was wearing blow frantically in the wind, gripping to her skin as it tried to desperately avoid flying off into the sky. She had one last look up at the window and when no face reappeared, decided to head back into the apartment before she herself was picked up and carried along by the storm which was building around her.

She entered the kitchen and fought to pull the door behind her. The wind protested against her advances as though it too was desperate to escape the outside and seek refuge in the warmth of the apartment. Finally, she was able to slam the door shut with a colossal bang which bounced off the brick walls of the kitchen, the echo lasting longer than Penny thought was natural. She turned to face her family where she assumed they would still be at the table. 'God, it has really picked up a wind out there. We need to leave, I've just seen…'

She looked at the table but saw that it was bare, the family she had left sitting there having disappeared. She listened out for any sound of them but noticed that the apartment was unusually silent, the only noise audible being the sound of the wind roaring in the background and its rattling against the window pane, still making its plea to get inside.

Remembering the man in the window, Penny knew she had to get them out, or at least come up with a plan on how to tackle the people upstairs. She had a flashback to the night before and shivered as she thought how easily he had been able to access the apartment without them realising. If he had gotten into the apartment then, he certainly would be able to do it again. She recalled the way he was watching her from the window, his body motionless, his stare cold. She knew he had no intention of being a friendly neighbour.

She looked around the room and saw that all the chairs had been pulled out, meaning the only pathway out of the room and into the hall was around the back of the table past the black door. Having not walked past it since she was drawn to it the other night, she paused as she approached and noticed the heavy padlock which had secured it before was no longer attached to the handle.

Puzzled, Penny wondered if Anita had succeeded and persuaded the others to open the door after all. Knowing that her mother wouldn't let them go against the rules so brazenly, she backed away. Penny had an overwhelming desire to stay away from the door, but she couldn't help but wonder where the padlock had gone. Perhaps this was the way the man had granted entry into the apartment, although that still didn't explain how the lock had been removed. It had to be removed from the side where she was standing, meaning whoever had opened it had been standing on her side of the door.

Realising it must be a sign, she stepped closer to examine further when, without warning, shuffling noises made her spring away. She looked around, curious as to where the noise had come from but realised she was still alone in the room. Loud bumps and scrapes were coming from further down the hallway, as if heavy furniture were being pushed from one side of the room to the other. She thought of her family and remembered that they were in one of the rooms. Knowing they wouldn't be interested in rearranging furniture, she felt beads of sweat forming on her brow as she tried to think of what else could be going on.

For a moment, Penny wondered if she should go towards the noises or turn and run out of the door she had battled so hard to close and get help. Knowing there were no neighbours nearby, she knew she had more chance of being swept away by the wind than of locating someone who could help them.

Reluctantly, she walked down the hallway towards the noise. As she was making her way towards the sound, she saw the door to the bathroom had been left half open. She had forgotten how dark it appeared from this angle, the gap between the door and the wall showing a deep sea of blackness, but she certainly remembered the feeling that overcame her when looking from the outside in. An icy hand gripped her heart and her body turned cold as she stared into the room, the temperature in the hallway seeming to have fallen several degrees while she was standing there.

Pulling herself away, she remembered why she had started to walk down the hallway in the first place and picked up pace as she walked towards her bedroom in the direction of the sounds. She stopped outside the entrance to the room and, not wanting to go in, peered around the open doorway and called out for her sister. When no one responded, she went right into the room and looked around, gasping as she did.

Not believing her eyes, she stepped in further so she could get a better view. The two single beds had once again been replaced by one single, small, wooden bed. The scattered sheets had been discarded onto the floor as though someone had recently left in a hurry. She stepped a bit closer and noticed there was a puddle of red on the sheets, causing them to sink inwards in the middle. Going forward, she moved her shaking hands over the sheets, recoiling in horror when she realised they were wet and there was an overpowering smell of iron. Penny knew she was touching blood.

She stood there in the middle of the room, her whole body quivering as she tried to wipe the blood off her fingers. Whose blood was it? Something made her think it wasn't from one of her group and that she wasn't standing in the same apartment she had been only moments before. Another noise came from the hallway, focusing Penny's thoughts away from her confused state. This time it sounded as though something was opening and closing with such force it made the floor shake with every movement. Penny held her breath as she contemplated what to do next. There was a pounding in her head which told her she wasn't dreaming, although she didn't feel completely awake either; what she was seeing was too strange to be real. Regardless of what was going on, she knew she couldn't stay in the room with her hands covered in blood, and so the only choice she had was to find out where the noise was truly coming from and who was making it.

Taking a deep breath in and pulling her shoulders back to give herself enough confidence to move forward, she strode out of the bedroom and back into the hallway. Still not wanting to fully accept the horror that was trying to take over her whole body, she told herself that when she made it to the kitchen, her family would be sitting around the table, hysterical that their practical joke had spooked her so much. The more she walked, the more she knew this wasn't going to happen and as much as she tried, her mind couldn't help but wander back to the man and question who he was and what he wanted.

Too scared to look around, Penny kept her eyes firmly on the ground as she made her way back into the kitchen. Not brave enough to raise them in case she didn't like what she saw, she kept them focused on her feet as she walked instead. Her ears were sharp, listening out for any sound of movement, her hands stretched out beside her, ready to protect herself from anything that took her off guard. She stopped as she reached the centre of the hall. In the eerie silence, she could hear something rattling slightly to her left. Penny stayed in the centre of the hallway and held her breath as she listened to the noise. Although she had built up the confidence to leave the bedroom, she wasn't sure she was brave enough to face what may be next to her and wanted to ensure the noise was real before looking up.

The noise continued, getting louder and louder by the

second. At first it sounded like it was far in the distance, barely audible, as though it was coming from a radio and the volume had been turned down. As she stood there, trying to take deep breaths to slow down her heartbeat, which was now thumping so much it was vibrating all the way up to her throat, the noise became more refined as though it had been tuned just for her to listen. She counted to ten before gradually opening her eyes. She turned her head to face the noise, her chest moving quickly up and down as it tried to match the pace of her pounding heart.

Penny saw a woman sitting at the oak writing bureau, the largest wooden panel now fully down, exposing a writing pad and smaller drawers inside. Penny opened both eyes and turned her body towards the woman so she could get a better look. The woman was sitting on a stool in front of the writing desk, her hand moving angrily across a sheet of paper. Penny recognised her and realised it was the woman she had seen in a heap on the kitchen floor the previous night. She was only able to observe her from a side profile, not daring to take a step nearer to get a better view. She could see that the woman was young, her skin radiating a glowing youth. The woman was chewing on her full, ruby-red lips as she scribbled on the page in front of her, her wavy brown hair falling effortlessly around her shoulders and her cat-like eyes screwed up as she looked down at what she was writing.

Penny was certain that if she got closer to the woman she would see she was beautiful despite her troubled expression, eyebrows arched in a frown as she stared down at the page in front of her. Penny gathered that whatever she was scribbling was causing her a large amount of discomfort and pain, her shoulders rigid, causing her back to bend over as she wrote, her long dress covering the stool she was sitting on. As Penny was standing watching the woman, she saw a single tear splash onto the white sheet of paper, followed by a stream rapidly rolling down the woman's peachy cheeks.

Noticing the paper getting wet, the woman quickly wiped them away with the back of one hand, the other hand moved to protectively rub a large bump in her stomach comfortingly.

Once again Penny felt conflicted and wondered if she should go over to comfort the woman. Quickly she pushed away the thought; the reality of an unknown woman sitting in the hallway of their rented apartment told her this was not the time to offer solidarity. She wasn't as scared as she had been when she saw the man; somehow the woman's presence didn't seem as intimidating, something about her level of vulnerability made Penny feel calmer. When she first saw the man, she had believed that he had come from the apartment upstairs, but seeing the woman sitting before her in her old-fashioned dress, Penny realised the explanation couldn't be as simple as that.

Looking at the woman's protruding stomach and the way she was cradling it, Penny presumed that she was pregnant, and by the size of her, very nearly due. As she was rubbing her unborn child, Penny saw the expression on her face rapidly change. Her tears had dried and within an instant, her peachy cheeks had transformed to a sickening white, her eyes wide. She dropped the pen and moved both hands to her stomach, doubling over so her head was nearly touching the bulging swelling. She opened her mouth and let out an agonising scream.

Instinctively Penny rushed forward. She didn't know what she was planning on doing but she knew she couldn't leave the woman screaming and in pain. Although only a few moments ago Penny had been wondering who she was, in that split second all Penny saw was a young, pregnant woman in need of some help. She neared the woman and moved her hand to touch her shoulder to offer some sort of comfort but as soon as Penny's hand got close, she disappeared, causing Penny to topple over against the stool the woman had been perching on.

'I've changed my mind – you can't…' A scream came from the kitchen.

The impulse she felt when she heard the scream was strong and Penny turned to rush towards the kitchen but just before she did, something made her stop still. A warm breath blew against her neck and Penny knew there was someone standing uncomfortably close behind her. Assuming it was the man, she didn't want to turn around to face him, still scared from the way he looked at her the night before. An eerie silence filled the space around her and the feeling that someone was standing close by intensified. Realising that she couldn't stand still in the hallway in silence forever, she turned quickly on the spot, hoping that the speed at which she turned would take the man off guard or shock him into disappearing once more.

It wasn't the man who was staring back at her. Instead, a different woman was standing in the archway of the doorway to her bedroom, head poking out of the door. It wasn't the same woman as the one by the bureau, this one was much older and tired looking, her hair sticking out in sharp, messy points erratically from her head. Penny could see from her wide-eyed expression that she had been startled and was scared. Penny opened her mouth to speak but as soon as she began to move forwards, the woman vanished.

Another scream came from behind her, once again tearing Penny away from her confused thoughts and she turned to follow the noise. When she reached the kitchen, she could see the crying woman standing beside the table and screaming towards the front door. Penny looked in the direction she was staring and once again saw the silhouette of a man standing by the doorway. Although his back was turned, shivers quickly crept down her arms, proving that this was the man that she had seen at the window; the same one from the night before.

She turned back to look at the woman, who looked as though she was frantically screaming at him, still clutching her stomach. Although the screaming had brought Penny to the kitchen, now she was there she could not hear any sound. She tried to take a step forward but her legs wouldn't move. She opened her mouth to call out to the woman, but no noise was forthcoming. Penny realised that she was inside her bubble once again, able to see everything but unable to move.

The woman rushed forwards and as she did, the man turned slowly to face her. Looking at his face, Penny gasped in terror. It was cold and emotionless, his dark black hair emphasising the whiteness of his face, his eyes dark and empty. He screwed his face up in a look of pure distaste, hatred filling every inch of his gaze. He shook his head and then made long strides towards the woman. The calmness in his walk yet the cruelty in his eyes momentarily paralysed Penny, as though he had sucked all her thoughts and feelings out of her body and she was left staring at him from a lifeless shell. She could tell by his determined tread that he was going to have full control of the woman and no matter how much she screamed, she would never win.

His strides were long and powerful, although the distance between the door and where the woman was standing was not far. As his foot reached the ground on his second step, he stopped and stood there for a moment, legs astride. Slowly, his head moved from the spot where the woman was standing and turned slowly to face Penny in her bubble, although Penny didn't feel as though she was protected in her bubble any more. The man was staring directly at her. He cocked his head to one side as he took in the sight of her. Penny held her breath and remained still, as though by not making a movement it would somehow make her invisible. It didn't work and he continued to look, starting with her feet until he reached her face. The corners of his mouth turned upwards in an attempt to smile, however this was no ordinary smile, it was a menacing, evil grin full of wickedness. He changed his route so he was walking directly towards Penny, seemingly forgetting about the other woman who was still screaming for his attention.

The air in the room was suddenly constricted. Penny tried to open her mouth to allow air into her lungs but she was unable force it open. She tried to raise her feet, but they were too heavy to be lifted. The man continued his walk towards her, now raising his hand to point his thin, long finger in her direction. The air in the room was getting sparser. Her heart was beating so fast she thought it was close to exploding in her chest.

Keeping her eyes on him moving towards her, his image was beginning to blur, distorted with a million black spots which now dominated Penny's sight. Although the air was tight, she didn't have the strength inside her to try and open her mouth another time to get the air she desperately needed to flow through into her lungs. The room began to spin, her head becoming dizzy.

Darkness was quickly replacing the black spots, restricting her sight and although she desperately did not want to give in, she felt her heavy eyelids close and she fell heavily to the floor.

Fifteen

As she regained consciousness, she was vaguely aware of people touching her, pulling her head away from the cold slab it was currently resting on. A sharp pain was pounding through her forehead, pulsing through her body as it navigated its way around her brain. Realising she was lying down, she tried to push herself up but the pain in her head was too much that when she levitated it upwards, she had little choice but to lower it back into its resting position.

'God, are you okay? Get a wet towel Anita!'

Someone was shouting in the background. The voice sounded familiar. She tried to place it but every time her brain tried to claw its way around her memory, the thud in her head became louder. Instead she tried to focus on the blurry images in front of her and was comforted when she saw that the voice belonged to her mother, her round figure coming slowly into focus.

She was shouting, the noise piercing Penny's ears, as the shrill voice reached her pounding head. She opened her eyes and found herself back in the kitchen of the present, her family gathered around her, once again looking down at her with concern. She saw Anita come into her vision, carrying something in her hand and gently, she lifted Penny's head onto her knee and placed a wet cloth underneath.

'This is far too much now, Pen. You're obviously not well, we need to take you to a hospital. Your head is bleeding!' Her mother crouched down at eye level with her.

'I'm okay, don't worry!' Penny pushed herself up onto her knees, grimacing at the pain in her head that thumped with every movement she made. 'How did I end up on the floor?' she asked, confused as to how she could have been in one place seeing unexplainable things one moment and be on the floor the next.

'You came back in from outside and stood in the doorway. You stood still as though you were in some sort of trance, staring into space. We tried to call out to you but you wouldn't listen, you just kept staring. Then suddenly you just dropped to the floor; it seems as though you fainted,' her sister said.

Penny had never fainted before and the unexpectedness of it had taken her by surprise. She remembered how tight her chest had felt and her rapidly beating heart, which was still pounding so fast that her body was vibrating up and down to match its pace. Penny knew that she hadn't fainted due to illness, she had fainted due to heart-stopping fear.

'I don't like this, first the sickness and now the fainting. Is there something you're not telling us?' her mother asked forcefully, no longer having the gentle tone her voice normally had.

'Like what?' She had to admit that this behaviour was out of character for her and she wondered how much they knew.

'I don't know, anything?' Fiona asked sheepishly.

Penny knew what was happening, it was the apartment. Something strange was happening and for some reason, something was trying to get her attention. It certainly was working.

'I think I must have a bug or something. Ever since we came here I've been feeling funny but I haven't wanted to ruin anyone's trip.'

Her mother hugged her as she helped her to her feet and carried her towards the table, 'I said you'd been pushing yourself too hard. It not healthy for someone as young as you to be working so many hours. This is your body's way of telling you need to slow down.'

Penny suddenly felt claustrophobic in the room with the other women, heads pushed in close to hers, their hands moving across her body, trying to get her into the seating position. She understood their concern, but she wanted to be left alone to think about what had happened. Looking her mother in the eye, she knew she couldn't share her secret with her; there was no way she would believe her.

'I'm sorry, I didn't want to ruin your trip. Maybe I'll have an early night and then just rest tomorrow.'

'Well you can't go to sleep yet, you've had a bang on the head. But yes, maybe a day in will be good for you. How about we all have a day in tomorrow, play some card games and order food in?' she said, trying to make Penny feel better.

Penny noticed the disappointment in her sister's face and suddenly felt terrible. This trip was meant to be a relaxing week away for her, away from motherhood and her adult responsibilities. The look on Fiona's face in reaction to her mother's suggestion made Penny feel guilty she was ruining it for her.

'Don't be silly, I will be okay on my own, I don't want to you to waste a day because of me.'

'Do you know what? All this walking has really made my legs ache,' Anita said. 'Maybe I'll have a day in with Pen and catch up on some sleep, you two can go off go to those shops you wanted to see that, in all honesty, Penny and I aren't really that interested in?' She nodded to Penny.

'No it's okay, I don't want to ruin your day out either,'

Penny replied.

'Honestly, I could do with a day in. I am knackered.'

'No, I'd rather be on my own.' Penny was curious as to why she was so eager to stay in with her.

'Well you don't have a choice, I'm afraid. I'm looking after you. Stop complaining or I'll give you a bump on the other side of your head.'

Penny considered Anita's offer. It hadn't gone unnoticed that she had been looking at her curiously over the past couple of days, every time she had felt something strange go on within the apartment. She remembered sitting on the grass outside, which now seemed forever ago, when she had resolved to tell Anita everything. Penny realised that now things had somewhat escalated, she most certainly needed to speak to someone. Suddenly she was overwhelmed with gratitude that her aunt was prepared to ruin one of her days out to help her, sensing that she had an idea that something was going on.

'Well if you're both sure?' her mother asked. 'I should really stay in with you too?'

'Well what about me? I can't go out on my own, I'll get lost!' Fiona whined.

Maggie eyed each one in turn, obviously conflicted about which daughter to support. Penny made it easier for her and said, 'Mum, Anita will be with me. There is no point us all being stuck in, we'd be bored of each other's company in no time. I will most likely sleep all day anyway. As you said, I have a lot of catching up to do. You go out with Fiona and we'll meet you later.'

Reluctantly her mother nodded.

'Now shall we go to sleep?' Penny rose from her chair, trying to not show the dizziness that was causing her vision to swivel in circles as she extended her legs to support the weight of her body.

'But your head?' her mother sounded concerned.

'I'm okay.'

'But they say you shouldn't go to bed if you have hit your head…'

'MUM!!' Without meaning to, Penny angrily snapped at her mother. She wasn't in the mood to entertain her fussiness on top of everything else that had happened. 'I'm fine, trust me. I just need to sleep.'

'Well fine, but if you die in your sleep it's not my fault. Let's help you to the bedroom.'

The three women helped Penny towards her room, Penny not having the strength to walk on her own unaided. As they were walking, Penny turned her head to look at the bureau and imagined the woman sitting there crying, cradling her stomach.

'Are you sure you're going to be okay love?' Her mother was still fussing as they put Penny in the bed.

'Mum, she said she was fine. Honestly, I don't fuss this much over the boys,' Fiona said and Penny felt a silent gratitude towards her sister for sticking up for her, obviously sensing her need to be on her own.

'Well maybe you should. I really don't feel comfortable in letting you go to sleep…'

'She's okay, Fiona will look after her.' Anita placed a hand on her sister's arm, 'You forget that they are adults sometimes you know! She only had a slight bump, she'll be okay.'

Penny could tell her mother was reluctant to leave, but Penny couldn't stand being fussed over for a minute longer.

She leant forward out of bed, not revealing that the dizziness hadn't worn off, and gave her mother a kiss on the head to tell her that she was okay.

When they left the room, Fiona said, 'I would really make the boys stay up you know. Maybe she's right. Are you sure you're okay?'

Penny smiled at her sister's concerned face. 'I'm fine honestly, I just need to sleep.'

'That was well weird. It was like you were possessed. This place still creeps me out. Good job you don't believe in all that stuff, eh, otherwise I think you'd be screwed!'

Penny let out a muffled laugh, trying to ignore the irony behind her sister's words. A few nights ago she would have laughed at herself, sitting in bed fearful of the unknown, when now it was all that was consuming her thoughts. It was as though everything she had ever believed in was slowly slipping out of sight, everything that she had ever been certain of was becoming more and more unclear with each day that passed.

'Shall I stay up with you? Card games don't sound like a bad idea. Although I can't remember the last time we played one.' Fiona queried.

'Thanks, but no thanks. You've got a full day ahead of you tomorrow, you should sleep.'

'We're going to go shopping,' Fiona squealed and sunk into the bed. At that moment, Penny was happy for her sister's excitement and forgot momentarily about what had happened, Fiona's excitement becoming infectious.

'Night night. Buy me something nice.' Penny snuggled next to her sister. She put her arm around her once more, trying to ensure she didn't do a disappearing act again.

Penny decided it would be best to go to sleep, force

herself if need be; she would be no good to anyone if she was tired. As soon as she closed her eyes she realised it would be pointless, her mind was too preoccupied by her scattered thoughts. She lay in the bed, tossing and turning, the sheets becoming a tangled mess underneath her with each turn. Every time she found herself drifting towards sleep, her mind would suddenly bring her back to consciousness, reminding her of what happened last time she drifted off. She saw the darkness of the room gradually get lighter as night turned into day and she began to hear birdsong trickle through the apartment walls telling her she had missed her opportunity to reach a peaceful slumber.

Looking at her phone, she saw it was now 4.30am and she thought that enough time had passed for her to give up on her attempt to fall asleep. Bored of being restless in the uncomfortable bed, she decided to get up and head to the kitchen, not knowing what she would do when she got there. She figured that at this time in the morning she would be up before the others and despite what she had said earlier, she decided that she would go out for the day. She had been thinking about what she and Anita would do as she tossed and turned. She knew that if she chose to stay in there would be nothing to do. She reached for her dressing gown which had been discarded on the floor and made her way into the kitchen, wrapping it around her as she walked.

As she was waiting for the kettle to boil she wandered around the room, stopping when she reached the black door. The padlock was back and she held the lock in her hand as she examined it, turning it over as she stared at it curiously. She heard the kettle begin to whistle and she rushed over to remove it from the stove before it began to sing too loudly, mindful that the two women sleeping in the room directly behind it might hear and be woken. After she had made a drink and had it firmly in her hands, she started walking around the room. She realised that she was bored and needed to look for something to do. Having no technology in the apartment meant she couldn't pass the time watching whatever would normally be on television at that hour, nor had she packed any books to keep her entertained.

After she had taken the last sip of her drink, she placed the cup back onto the table and let out a sigh. Although the caffeine was meant to wake her, it had done the opposite and Penny felt tiredness rear its head, trying to persuade her to rest. Not wanting to go back to the bedroom, Penny slumped onto the table, head resting on the outstretched arm in front of her. She nestled her head into the crook of her arm and as she began to drop off, she spotted Anita's tablet which they had been using for the duration of the trip. Suddenly, forgetting her plan to sleep, Penny reached towards the device, hopeful that she would be able to connect to the internet and find something to preoccupy her time.

Penny pressed the on button and a gallery of pictures appeared instantaneously. She remembered Anita snapping away on their adventures outside the apartment and began to scroll through them. They had purchased the gadget for Anita the previous Christmas and Penny remembered the delight on her face when she opened such an 'extravagant' present. Looking through some of the poorly lit and wonky photographs, it was obvious that she was still getting used to working the camera on the device, many being blurry or out of focus. Penny laughed as she scrolled through, remembering all the giggles they had on their explorations of the city, before the thoughts of the apartment began to overwhelm her. There were pictures of them sitting in the bar, on the open-aired bus and even of them sitting around this table, glasses of wine in their hands in a toast.

Penny stopped when she reached the final picture, which would have been the first one which was taken. The four women were standing by the black door taking their own picture, the joy of being on the trip clearly evident from their joyful faces. She moved her fingers across the screen to enlarge the image to get a closer look at their expressions. As she was doing so, she stopped as she saw what was in the background, recognition arousing her curiosity.

She continued to zoom into the image and as she did, saw the unfinished picture of the man and the woman, the man being at the back and the woman at the front. She widened her index finger and thumb until the full screen displayed only the people. Her heart began the recognisable thumping she had encountered so many times since she stepped foot in the apartment and realised that the two people in the image were the people who had been visiting her in her dreams.

Penny jumped from her chair and rushed back over to the door, looking for the picture, her tiredness now having evaporated completely. She gasped as she moved her eyes closer to the frame, stopping to rub them in case she was seeing things unclearly. She was now standing with her nose almost touching the frame as she examined the drawing closely. Rushing back to the table, she picked up the tablet and looked back at the image and then back to the picture. The device showed the image in the drawing exactly how she had seen it on her very first day, the woman standing in the front of the frame with the man at the back. In this image and the one in her memory, the faces had not been drawn in and nor had any of the surroundings apart from the outline of the road.

She placed the tablet back on the table and stared at the updated version that was hanging in front of her. In the drawing, the houses were still yet to be drawn however the cobbles had been filled in fine detail. The man was no longer standing at the back of the frame but was now halfway down the road, arms raised as if pointing towards the woman. Penny once again scrunched her eyes to see if she could work out the faces but that amount of detail had

140

not been added. In the first image the woman was standing with her face looking out of the frame but now it was turned back towards the man, shoulders hunched over as she cowered under his stare.

Penny was transfixed to the spot as the reality started crushing down upon her, making it hard for her to stand. She knew then what she had been trying to ignore the whole time.

Something was happening within the apartment, something that made the people in pictures move.

Something much more sinister than she would ever have imagined.

Sixteen

Anita appeared in the kitchen looking tired and restless about two hours after Penny. She hadn't moved from the spot by the painting and was still standing there glued to the same position when Anita walked in.

'Everything okay, love?' Anita asked quietly, causing Penny to jump. She was so engrossed with what she was looking at that she was taken by surprise by the sound of her aunt's voice, breaking the trance with the painting.

Penny reluctantly pulled her gaze away from the image. 'Sorry, did I wake you?'

'Not at all, I'm an early riser, especially when I'm somewhere new. Fancy a cuppa?' she said as she made her way to the stove. 'For a moment there I thought you were sleep-walking, especially after what happened last night. You were standing there ever so still, facing the wall; I could barely see that you were breathing. Scared me a little bit.'

'Sorry, I couldn't get back to sleep after I fainted so I've been up all night. When I came in here I started looking at these pictures again.' She moved back to the table to sit opposite her aunt.

'Is everything okay? I know you had a bad night's sleep but every time we come back to the apartment, you just don't seem yourself?' she asked.

Penny realised that now was the opportunity to confide in Anita and reveal all that had been going on over the past couple of days. She thought carefully about her words before she spoke, not believing she was about to try to explain something so unexplainable.

She gulped and said, 'Please don't think there is anything wrong with me, but… I think there is something weird going on here. I can't explain it. I know it sounds crazy and I'm probably overtired but…'

'I don't think you're crazy, love,' Anita interjected, filling her cup with the boiling water that had just brewed.

'You don't?' Penny said. She didn't think it would be possible to feel such an immediate relief at these words, finally being able to breathe a little easier, as though someone had relaxed the tight grip that had been holding onto her throat over the past few days.

Anita took a deep breath inwards and looked directly at her. 'I don't think you are crazy and I agree that something weird is hanging in the air around here. I feel it, each night it's getting stronger.'

Penny eyed her aunt cautiously, 'Are you trying to wind me up again or get me scared, because I don't think I can be mocked at the moment, I'm too tired.'

'Penelope, I'm going to tell you something but you mustn't tell your mother I told you. I enjoy the ghost stories and making people scared, that much is true, it's in my nature. I'm only like that however, because I believe in ghosts and I believe in spirits. Of course, I make stories up when I know them not to be true, but I also know my fair share of real-life ghost stories, trust me.'

'Like what?' Penny probed.

'It doesn't matter, you don't need to know, but I'm telling you that ghosts are real and live amongst us. I believe that two worlds can live within the same time and place, interlinking. I enjoy my fair share of joking around, but I would never mess with anything I truly thought would harm anybody.'

'But you tried to conjure a response from a 'spirit' when you heard those noises on the first night?'

'Yes, because I believed the same as you, that there was someone staying upstairs. I saw how spooked your sister was getting and I even noticed a tiny hint of fear in your eyes. I didn't think anything else of it.'

'But the black door, you said…'

'I thought it was a just a black door, love. You know I like winding you up.'

'When you say you feel something, what do you feel?'

'Well there was obviously a sharp chill the first night but I just thought that was due to the age of the building. But when that old woman in the museum started telling us stories and you started taking funny turns, I started putting some of the pieces together.'

'Like what?' Penny felt as though she could cry with relief, she wasn't alone after all.

'Well, the way the letting agency woman ran away from us in the shop, the advert being so different, you saying you saw something upstairs, the noises, your dreams, the way you were staring at the door the other night. It's all too odd to be a coincidence, especially as you're normally sensible and stuffy.'

'No I'm not!' Penny took offence to this comment, even though she knew Anita meant this teasingly.

'There is nothing bad in that, love. We each have our own little quirks. Your sister is the fantasist, you've always been the realist, which is why it has made it so weird.'

'And what do you think about here? Do you think there

are ghosts? Have you seen any?' Penny moved her head in closer, finally being able to accept what was going on.

Anita eyed her niece and took in a deep breath, 'No love, I haven't seen any. I haven't quite worked this place out yet but I most certainly think there is something here. Since I have started putting it together, I have noticed the chill in the air and the bad energy that consumes the place. There is an overwhelming feeling of sadness about the place, don't you think? As though if you sat still for long enough it would consume you.'

Penny hadn't thought about it that way before. She had been too busy thinking about her own feelings and the unsettling way they were making her question everything she thought was real.

'No, I've just been scared mainly.'

'Well that's not a bad thing I guess. You're not too far in it if you haven't noticed that. But you are starting to worry me, these dreams you're having, that glass being knocked over and you standing in front of the pictures like that when I walked in, I do not like. If something is trying to pull you in, resist it!'

'Why?' Penny asked.

'You don't mess with spirits. You don't know if what is trying to connect with you is good or evil and you can never be sure of their intentions. Ghosts generally never interact with humans, apart from the odd moving of things around. If they do it means they want something and you have no possible idea of what that could be until it's too late.'

'What does that mean?'

'Exactly as I said. Resist the urge, whatever urge you're getting. If you feel you cannot, you must let me know. Do you understand?' Penny nodded, she did understand. She was grateful that she wasn't alone in her thoughts, although she couldn't be sure she believed everything her aunt said. She contemplated telling Anita everything she had been feeling and seeing and her hands gripped tightly onto the tablet.

'Actually, there was something I think I should tell you…'

'Morning!' Her mother chirpily came into the room. 'You're both up early. How are you feeling, Pen?'

'Much better, although I haven't slept since I went to bed,' Penny replied.

'Oh no, what time is it now? Why haven't you slept?'

'I don't know, not tired I guess,' she let out a yawn, 'although I am now.'

'Did you still want to stay in today, love?'

Penny looked at Anita and considered her mother's question. Part of her wanted to go out and have a good time with her family, not wanting the apartment to win and keep her in, but the other part wanted to stay. She had confided in Anita and she felt that they had more they needed to discuss. She wanted help figuring out what was going on and part of her thought that if there were two of them to work it out, she'd be able to rid herself of the all-consuming dread and fear that was growing with each second that passed.

'Do you mind?' she asked her mother.

'Of course not, if that is what you want to do.'

'I think maybe if I got some sleep I might feel up to doing whatever you have planned for later?'

'How about you sleep now and get some rest? We'll text you a bit later and how about we all go out for a nice dinner later on? We haven't had a posh dinner at all since we got here, despite my plans!' she shot them a disapproving look.

'If you're sure that's ok by you?' Penny asked again, feeling guilty that she may have disappointed her.

'Of course I am. I'd rather you have a good day's rest. Go and get yourself off to bed, you look terrible.' Her mother took the cup out of Penny's hands which was now cold and gestured for her to leave the room.

Penny kissed her mother on the head and wished her a fun day. She reached the bedroom and slid beside her sister, who hadn't moved since she left earlier that morning. Penny thought about what Anita had said and was relieved to know that she wasn't as crazy as she was beginning to believe; thankful that someone else had also picked up on something unnatural lingering within the apartment. Being older and clearly more experienced in such matters, she thought she should listen to her when she said she ought to leave things alone. Penny definitely hadn't invited these things to her; if she had her choice she would happily un-see everything and revert to her normal little world where everything could be explained. She wished she could leave things be, however she couldn't shake the feeling that someone was trying to show her something. She let out a yawn and stretched out in bed. After an hour or so's sleep she'd be able to think clearer and she shut her eyes and settled into a deep sleep.

Seventeen

When she woke a few hours later she knew she hadn't had the comfortable nap she had intended. Her nightdress was clinging to her, her own heavy sweat weighing down the sheets where she had clearly been tossing and turning in her attempt to get some rest. She pushed herself upwards and felt her heart sink when she realised she felt just as unsettled as when she dragged herself out of bed earlier that morning.

A voice inside her head told her to curl up in the bed and stay there until the trip was over but the other voice shouted at her to jump straight up and find out what on earth was going on. She knew that the visions she had yesterday must have occurred for some reason but why? Why was she the only person within the apartment that saw the woman and the man and no one else? If anything, it should be Fiona or Anita who were seeing the things she didn't want to; they believed in such things after all.

As she forced her legs out of bed and touched the floor, she realised how still and silent the apartment was. She glanced to her right and noticed that her sister was up and out and she was relieved to see the bed was as it was when she went to sleep and hadn't changed once again. She realised that her mother and sister must have followed her instructions and left for the day without her.

She made her way into the kitchen after a speedy change of clothes and saw the kettle had recently boiled and English muffins were once again sitting on the table waiting to be eaten. Anita walked in the doorway and sat opposite her niece.

'I'm sorry you felt you had to stay in with me. Sorry for ruining your trip,' Penny said when she thought of the others spending their day without them.

'Don't be silly. I meant what I said yesterday, my legs are hurting a bit and it would be good for me to have a day in,' she took a sip from her tea, 'I'm not as young as I once was! How are you feeling?'

Penny breathed in and looked towards the window, tired of everyone asking how she was all the time. 'I am okay, but I feel terrible and feel like I've ruined everyone's break.'

'Your mother didn't mind, she would rather you rest and get fit and healthy for the last day. I am under strict instructions to look after you.' She pushed the tray of food in front of her. 'That includes getting food inside you.'

Penny looked at the food and knew she wasn't hungry. She was tired, restless and depressed in a way she had never felt before. The trip hadn't been kind to her and she noticed her face had become even greyer when she looked in the mirror earlier. Her jeans were now tighter than ever and the only thing Penny felt comfortable wearing was a loose flowery dress that hid her waist. The smell of the muffins made her stomach flip with queasiness and she had no desire to eat them. She pushed away the plate but saw Anita's wide smile and so she hesitantly picked one up and had a bite. Although she didn't want it to, her body thanked her for the fuel and she couldn't help but pick up another one as soon as she finished the first.

'I went to the local shop down the road this morning and picked up some papers. Here, have a read.' She tossed a tabloid in front of her.

'Thanks for leaving me on my own after what I told you earlier!' she mocked.

'Oh sssh, it was only for half an hour! You were sound asleep, I thought it best you sleep whatever it is off.'

Penny picked up the newspaper enthusiastically and scanned the news headlines. Finally, a chance for her to be sucked back into the real world. She felt her spirits lift as she held the rough paper in her hands. She skimmed the articles twice. Although she desperately wanted to read the news reports and feel normal again, she threw it down with a sigh, realising with annoyance that she wasn't absorbing any of the words. She folded the newspaper and placed it back on the table, taking another sip of her coffee as she sulked.

She glanced around and noticed that Anita was staring at her from over the top of her cup. Her eyes were fixed firmly on her niece and Penny wondered how long they had been sitting there like that; Penny trying to read the paper with her aunt staring solemnly at her.

'So, are we going to talk about it then?' she asked slowly.

'Talk about what? There was nothing in the paper that caught my attention,' she dismissed Anita's comment.

'You know I'm not talking about that; we need to discuss what has been going on with you,' Anita replied.

Knowing she couldn't avoid it any longer Penny said, 'Okay, well where do I start?'

'The beginning is always a good place...' Anita joked.

The start, Penny didn't know where the beginning was any more. Events flashed before her eyes in quick succession as she tried to pause them to establish what had come first.

'Well at first I saw someone upstairs in the window but just thought it was someone staying up there. There is a horrible chill in the bedroom and the bathroom appears dark when looking in from the outside. Have you noticed that?'

'No not really, although I haven't really looked.'

'Okay, well a couple of nights ago when I had a bad dream, I heard noises and thought they were you. When I went to look, the lights flickered off. Then the following night I ended up in the kitchen and saw a woman on the floor and a man standing by the doorway and I tried to move but I couldn't; I was glued to the spot. Part of me thinks that the man saw me. Oh, I went upstairs to check if anyone was there and I swear I saw someone move in the shadows but I guess that could have just been my imagination. My reflection changed when I looked in the mirror, but I'm not sure whether that was just the effect of the sleeping pills. Then I saw a woman crying, a woman in the bedroom and the man in the kitchen again.' Penny rushed through the events, hoping they didn't sound as far-fetched as they sounded to her as she said them.

'Wow, sounds like you have experienced a lot since being here. Why did you keep it all to yourself?'

'Well I thought there would have been an explanation, a logical reason. You know I don't believe in this stuff and seeing how spooked Fiona was getting, I didn't want to make it worse or add fuel to your stories.' As she was speaking she noticed her cheeks were wet from tears that were falling from her face as she recalled what had been happening, not having realised before now how scared she actually was. 'Do you think I'm crazy?'

'No, not at all. You are clearly distressed,' she reached over to wipe the tears from Penny's face, 'I don't believe for a second that you are fabricating what has happened.' She smiled at Penny but her eyes were cold, 'What did I tell you though? You should have resisted it! You have been incredibly stupid to let whatever it is in!'

'I don't think I really had much choice. I don't want to see these things! Is it bad?'

'Well this we do not know! We know nothing really about the history of the place and therefore have no idea what sort of spirits are residing here and what on earth they want from you.' She maintained strong eye contact with Penny. 'It could all be harmless; however, it could also be very sinister. Very sinister indeed!'

With this comment, Penny felt her back turn to ice. Anita had said something that Penny had not wanted to hear out loud. 'Well how do we find out? Do we want to find out? Maybe I will just resist it? Or maybe I can check myself into a hotel for the remainder of the trip?' Penny felt her stomach relax as the dread she had been hiding was slowly released.

Anita stood from her chair and moved to take the seat next to Penny, taking her hand in hers. 'From the look of you last night, I think we are past that stage, love.'

'How do you mean the way I looked last night?'

'My dear, you entered that doorway and stood frozen to the spot, face turning the whitest white I have ever seen. You seemed not to hear us as we were taking to you and made your way behind the table and stayed there, swaying on the spot until you suddenly dropped to the floor. I think it is safe to say we are beyond the point of resisting it.' She squeezed her hand slightly and when Penny looked down, she noticed it had lost all colour, her hands paler than she had ever seen.

'What should I do then? All I get is the odd random visions.'

'My experience, and there hasn't been too much, even in my many long years, is that you have to try and establish exactly what they want.'

'How do you know they want something?'

'If it were just a haunting, you would only see small visions and the odd thing moving here and there. I don't believe you would actually see a series of events. It is extremely uncommon that a spirit would look directly at you and start walking towards you.'

'How do you know all of this?' Penny asked.

Anita turned away and moved from her seat until she was standing looking out of the window.

'I've always thought I had a knack for these sorts of things. When I was younger I was always hearing noises and seeing things move around the house. Your grandmother used to say that she would often catch me looking absentmindedly into the distance, as if my eyes were following something across the room. One day your grandmother told your mother and me a story but your mum thought it was just another of her tall tales. Although the way Mum looked at me that day, in the eye, cold as ice, I knew she was telling the truth.' Anita took a deep breath.

Penny remembered her mother telling her how her grandmother used to try and scare them all the time. She wasn't surprised and had always thought that was probably where her aunt had got the scaring habit from.

Anita looked at Penny then continued.

'She told us that she had the 'gift', the ability to speak to the 'other side', see what was there, lingering in the shadows. We used to nod along, listen to her stories with interest. They were all pretty similar to be honest with you and nothing that we hadn't already heard in the playground. One day, when I asked her what was the worst thing she had ever seen, the question made her put down the dishes she was washing and turn to face us. I wasn't sure why, after so many years of telling us the typical ghost stories, she decided to tell this one; perhaps she couldn't keep it in anymore.'

'When she was a young girl, fifteen I believe she said, she told us that she had heard about séances. Not knowing exactly what they were, she decided to give it a go. She stole some candles from her mother's kitchen and began to call out to the spirits who might be hovering around her,' Anita turned and looked away.

Intrigued by this insight to her grandmother's life which she never knew existed, Penny asked, 'What happened?'

'She says she doesn't remember, not entirely at least. She had a recollection of calling out into the distance when suddenly, a pale figure with long black hair charged towards her. The mouth was forced open in a scream and her hands were outstretched, clawing at the air between them.'' Anita paused for a couple of seconds, capturing the scene in her mind. 'Mum said she couldn't remember exactly what happened next, but remembered waking up in hospital two weeks later. The doctors told her she had fallen over, but she wasn't convinced.'

Penny's mother had never told her this story, however she couldn't imagine her mother ever believing it was real.

'What happened after that?' Penny asked.

'Nothing! Grandma stopped suddenly and returned back to the dishes. I tried to ask her more but she closed off, refusing to be drawn back into the conversation. Your mother didn't believe her of course and put it down to another one of your grandma's elaborate stories.'

She looked at Penny solemnly. 'I believe there are good spirits living amongst us whom protect us to the best of their abilities, but as certain about that as I am, I am also certain that there are just as many bad spirits lingering around, waiting for us to be vulnerable before they take us victim.'

'Victim of what?' Penny asked, not liking the direction in which this conversation was heading.

'I'm not entirely sure. I like telling my stories and trying to scare you all, but if I thought something was real I'd leave well enough alone. I took what Mum said that day as some sort of warning; she'd seen the way I used to speak aloud to an empty room as though there was someone in there with me and I think she was telling me to leave things be.'

'Why do you carry on joking about it? If my mum told me that, I wouldn't ever mention it again!'

'Well, that's what I do! I guess I was never really sure that what she told me was real. I pushed it out of my mind as her trying to wind us up, the same way she always did and the same way I do with you.'

'But you think it is real now?'

'After what you've just told me, yes I do.'

'Why is it me then that is seeing stuff and not you? I've never seen anything before, why now? Why not Fiona, she believes in all this stuff?'

'They do say that the sixth sense runs in the family, so maybe you're the next one down the line? I don't know why I haven't seen anything though, that is quite bizarre.'

'You said that the bad spirits will take someone victim. Is that what is going to happen to me?' Penny asked nervously.

'That my dear, depends on what they want. I think we need to find out. Talk me through once again what has happened since coming here; the bathroom was black, you have been getting sick, the images have moved. Then you had the lights in the hallway turning off, whereabouts were you?' She moved away from the window and began walking down the hallway.

Penny followed her, the fear subsiding, being replaced with a small feeling of excitement. Almost as soon as she had started to tell Anita what she had been experiencing, she felt as though the huge weight which had been crushing down upon her had eased slightly. Someone believed her.

She stopped as she got to the door that opened onto the small terrace and reached out to her aunt to stop. 'It was here, the lights suddenly flicked off and on here.' Penny looked around.

'Okay, so… anything else happen here? Do you get any weird feelings when you stand in this spot?' she questioned.

Suddenly, a bolt of recognition shot through her. 'Here, the woman was crying here!' She nearly burst with excitement.

'A-ha that may mean something' Anita moved forward towards the old-fashioned desk and bent down to get a closer look. 'Let's open it up.'

Penny and Anita spent the next five minutes crouched down beside the bureau examining it carefully. Penny was surprised by how well looked after it appeared and how much it resembled what she had seen the previous evening. Fully standing, the bureau reached the top of her hips, four spindly but curved legs supported the weight of the oblong box that sat on top of them. They discovered that a triangle guarded the inside, a tiny key sticking out waiting to be turned. Penny twisted the key slowly, worried that it would disintegrate in her hand. It felt dirty and rusty and made her skin crawl as soon as her fingers clasped around it, already small fragments had flaked off into her hand after apparently not being touched for a long time.

The two women held their breath as they pulled the top down slowly. A strong, pungent smell came to their notice immediately. The lock felt as if it hadn't been turned in a while and from the smell that filled the room as the top came down, this was confirmed.

'Oh my, the smell!' Anita said, hand covering her nose. 'Let's look in quickly.'

Penny dipped her head in slightly, being extra careful not to allow it to hit anything as she peered in. Not wanting to touch anything for the fear of the dirt and grime, her eyes darted around until they landed on the only thing in there. Placed neatly on one of the shelves was a small blue book. Carefully, she reached towards it and pulled it out, blowing off the dust as she did.

She turned the pages slowly and her heart began to beat.

'What is it?' Anita asked, head still looking inside the bureau.

Penny glanced up, 'It's a diary!!'

Eighteen

'Well, I think this is what we may have been looking for,' Anita said, trying to peer over her shoulder.

'You think?' Penny replied. As she did, she began turning the pages of the book. The bureau was still in perfect condition, but the diary was not. As she turned the pages, they felt stiff in her hand and had discoloured due to age. It reminded Penny of a time when she made school projects at home, placing a used teabag on a bright white sheet of paper to create a rustic feel. Flipping through the pages quickly, she realised she had done a pretty good job at those pages back then as the pages in the diary bore a canny resemblance.

'Where did you say you saw her last night?' Anita asked.

'Sitting here, scribbling something before she started sobbing.' Her head jerked suddenly towards Anita, realising that she was holding that very thing that she must have been writing in. 'Then a different woman was peering around from in there!' She pointed to her bedroom.

'Well then, you need to read it and find out what she wrote it's been left for you, my dear.'

Penny opened the page, the first one was blank but as she turned to the second page she could see light scribbles stretching across the paper.

'I'm not so sure reading it is a good idea. She seemed so upset yesterday, I feel as though I would be intruding reading this,' she glanced nervously at Anita.

'Penelope, do you want to keep seeing these visions and being scared out of your wits or do you want to know exactly what happened?'

Penny considered this and realised Anita was right. Whatever it was that was trying to connect to her, she needed to know why and more importantly, she wanted it to stop. She cast her eyes over the page and began reading.

'Excuse me, I took a day off all of the fun family sightseeing so you best read it out to me too. I can't see any writing on there!' Once again, Anita peered over her shoulder.

May 21^{st,} 1801

Dear Diary,

I have not written to you in a while, I have been too consumed with arranging my thoughts to be able to put them down on paper. My mind is mixed, unable to think straight. I tried to recall the last time I could think clearly and realised it was whilst I was sitting here writing my last entry, telling you about my thoughts of John.

I cannot believe that this is happening to me and that this is now my life. What seemed so certain and so sure only yesterday has now become muddled and unclear. Every moment of my day, my mind is consumed with overriding thoughts about my future and whether I have made the right choices. I am trying not to question my actions, however as much as I try to fight it, I simply cannot.

You will recall my last entry about John was full of love and laughter. Each moment I longed to see him and often found myself being told off by Cook that I was standing still, eyes staring into the distance, imagining what it would be like the next time I saw him. Now I no longer feel that way. Now I wish I had never met him at all and resisted all those times when I would sneak out of my room at night to steal extra precious moments with him. Why did I allow myself to be so carried away?

I am certain that if news got back to my parents in London they would disown me, they had thought a life spent in a bustling town in the countryside would be good for me and I would be kept away from all the trouble in London. I am saddened to think I have brought shame on them and myself. Really, none of that matters any more. I have reached a point where I think nothing will ever matter again.

'Who do you think John is?' Penny asked her aunt. 'Is that the man I have been seeing, this woman's lover?'

'What are the entries before that?' Anita replied.

Penny flicked through the book, 'There aren't any more, it starts at this one.'

'Carry on reading it then, maybe we will find out more.' Anita urged her.

<u>May 24^{th,} 1801</u>

Dear Diary,

Each day it gets worse. Each day the fear grows inside me, I can feel it growing with strength each and every day. I don't have the courage to fight it any more despite my best effort.

I go to sleep at night thinking about it and wake with it being the first thing on my mind. Have I made the right choice?

I remember the look of disgust on John's face when I told him the news. Still giddy with love, I was excited when I found out and I was positive that he would feel the same. Instead he stabbed me directly through my heart, I could almost feel the blood drip out. My heart is heavy and full and I am constantly reminded of my stupidity and heartbreak every time I look down.

He said it would be the right thing to do, he told me it would save me. He told me it would...

'It would what?' Anita said, barely able to contain

herself.

'I don't know, look the writing trails off as though it was stopped suddenly,' Penny said, moving the diary towards Anita, who was now leaning so heavily over Penny's shoulder she almost toppled over under her weight.

Anita pushed the diary away, 'It's no use; I told you I cannot see any damned writing on the thing! Continue reading!' She pushed it back towards Penny.

'I told you that I thought she was pregnant? This John was probably the father, but when he found out he didn't want it.' Penny thought out loud and a wave of sadness filled her heart. She couldn't imagine being in this woman's position. She fully intended her first pregnancy to be planned, but she was sure that if it wasn't, Jason would support her whatever her decision. Penny tried to imagine how lonely and devastated this woman must have felt having been rejected at such a vulnerable time of her life.

She continued to read out loud,

June 2nd 1801

Dear Diary,

The day is getting closer. The day that will make it all better. That is what he says. He said it would be best for both of us although I am beginning to think it is more for them then it is for me.

I don't like him anymore. The way he looks at me, the way he stares. I thought he was my rescuer before; he would help me and protect my secret. He is not protective any more. He is mean, cold and cruel. Every maid and butler has now been sent home apart from me and he has told their family and friends that she has caught scarlet fever and is too ill to see anyone. When there is no one else around he doesn't have to pretend, he is the true reflection of himself. He comes to my room at night and hovers beneath the archway, staring at me. I pretend I don't notice him and pretend not to care, worried that doing so would give him what he wants.

At night, I get locked into this cold, dark room all alone and in the day, I am allowed access to the kitchen and servant's bathroom only. Everything else is out of bounds; everything he had promised I would receive has been taken away.

I want to go back on the promise I made; I want to run away. Whilst I will be shamed for the rest of my life, I am certain I can be happy again.

I know this is not possible though. Everywhere I turn he is there, every escape I try to make, he is a step ahead of me.

He's not going to let me go, he is going to keep me and make me...

'It stops again.' Penny looked up.

'The 'he' she mentions must be the man that you have been seeing,' Anita replied.

Penny read the passage again and thought back to the moment in the kitchen the night before. Maybe her aunt was right, she could tell that the woman was afraid of this man. Penny understood why she would be, she didn't know anything about him but the fear that bubbled inside her when he looked at her caused shivers to flow over every inch of her skin. She could only imagine what his presence must have been like in real life.

'But who is the 'she' she is referring to? And what did they do to her?' Penny asked.

She turned the page and begun to read out the next entry.

Dear Diary,

I visited her today, I didn't mean to but I had to go up and see for myself. She fears him, almost as much as me. I knew it from the way she cowered in bed. I hadn't seen her that much before, he always kept her locked in her room. The House said she was crazy and has been ever since her parents were alive.

She didn't seem crazy to me, well maybe she looked it but I hardly blame her. She has been kept in her room locked up with barely any light allowed in. She said she was unaware of his plan and that I must leave, run! Escape with the child growing in my stomach. He had a wicked plan, she said and I shouldn't trust him. That is it, I am going to escape, but before I do, I need to get her to come with me somehow.

I cannot leave her with him, not now I know what it was that he was planning...

A sharp screeching noise echoed in the background, forcing both the ladies to jump suddenly. In the shock, Penny's arms flew uncontrollably into the air, causing the book to escape from her hands. She listened as the book thumped loudly, hitting the floor beneath them. Once the noise had disappeared, Penny bent down to collect the diary and when she did, saw that the pages were now bare.

Nineteen

'What was that noise?' Anita asked, looking around, 'It made me jump!!'

'I don't know, but look, the pages are now empty, the writing has gone.' Penny pushed the diary towards her.

Anita took the diary from her niece's hands and flicked through it. Her gaze met Penny's as she said, 'This is strange; it's like whatever wanted you to read it, something else wanted you to stop.' She placed the diary back onto the bureau.

'Well, what should we do?'

'Have you heard that noise before?' Anita asked.

Penny knew that she hadn't. The sound the pair had heard seemed unworldly and unnerving. It had been so high-pitched that it made Penny's eyes water as the noise entered through her ears and travelled around her head. It was as though someone was dragging their sharp fingernails across a blackboard, however this description didn't do the sound justice. It was so much clearer and much more menacing. Although it only lasted a couple of seconds, it had done its job and diverted their attention away from the diary.

'I think we should take a look around the apartment and see if anything has changed, anything that wasn't here before that is now,' Anita said as she turned and started making her way towards the bathroom.

Penny reached out and touched her arm, 'There's no point, there will be nothing here. I think it was more of a warning.'

'How do you know?' Anita asked.

The truth was Penny didn't know; it was more of a feeling she had. Each encounter had been similar and while her fear and apprehension were growing, she also realised that she was feeling more and more in tune with the nature of the apartment; she could anticipate when something would be there and when it would not.

'I just know.'

'Okay, well that has put an end to that line of discovery,' Anita said looking around. 'So, we know that there was this woman, a pregnant woman, she had to make a choice and she didn't like a man. There was a crazy lady upstairs and a plan! I'm afraid that is not much to go on.'

'The choice seemed to be something to do with the baby. Why else would they send everyone away and lock her in her room?' Penny asked.

'We need to find out more about what happened here.' Anita looked puzzled and then suddenly smiled, 'I think we walked past a library on our first day, maybe we should go there to see if we can look up the history of this place. An old town like this has to have some sort of records lying around.'

'What about my "illness",' Penny moved her fingers into a speech mark expression. 'Won't Mum be upset if she comes home and sees we have gone out anyway?'

Anita thought about this, her teeth chewing her bottom lip as she considered their options, 'We'll say you were feeling a bit better, but bored, so we decided to have a trip down to the library to borrow a book. Therefore, we haven't technically lied.'

'Although you can't borrow a book if you're not a member of the library!' Penny corrected her.

Anita huffed, 'Stop complicating things and get your shoes on. This is getting interesting and I want to know what happened here. I'll deal with your mother!' She pushed past Penny and rushed down the hallway into her bedroom to get ready for their outing.

Penny smiled as she made her way into her bedroom. Anita was excited, she could tell from her reaction. Somehow, Penny felt the fear subsiding slightly knowing she was not on her own and instead her mind was filled with intrigue at what they were about to find out. Surely less harm could come to her if there were two of them aware of what was going on, although she wasn't entirely sure whether this was a good or bad thing. As much as she wanted someone to help her, she didn't want anyone else to experience the fear that was beginning to cripple her.

Knowing she couldn't face this alone, she hurriedly changed and met Anita back in the kitchen who was sitting at the table scribbling quickly on a piece of paper. 'Just writing a note to your mother so she knows where we are. Have you brought the diary with you? I think it may be best to hang onto it, we don't want it disappearing.'

Penny nodded and patted her bag; the two women had the same idea. The pair headed out of the door, in the direction of finding the library and getting nearer to the truth. Penny hoped that it wouldn't be a wasted trip. She agreed with Anita, assuming there would be public records about anything of interest that had occurred on their street, if the town really was as historic as it appeared. She remembered the old lady in the museum and thought they could take another trip to visit her if the library proved unsuccessful.

As she had reception on her phone, she also texted Fiona

to let her know they were out of the house. Fiona responded almost immediately, obviously clinging onto her phone while she could make contact with the outside world. They agreed they would meet back at the apartment later that evening. Penny was silently grateful for their separation, allowing them more time to complete their investigative work.

She also took this opportunity to contact Jason. Luckily it was a Saturday and he answered on the fourth ring. Penny almost cried when she heard his voice and realised again how much she was missing him. She decided to tell him everything, what was happening in the apartment, how she was feeling about it and what she and Anita were up to now. She held her breath after she finished talking, assuming he would tell her she was being silly. If he did, he didn't let her know. She could tell from the tone of his voice that he was sceptical, however it was clear that he had also noticed the panic and distress in Penny's voice.

He tried to calm her down, not by telling her that she was being stupid, but explaining that there could be a reasonable explanation. He asked her for the address of where they were staying and told her that he would do some of his own research to see if he could help. Penny immediately felt reassured after speaking to him and realised how lucky she was to have someone like him in her life. She had only been gone for a few nights and here she was calling him up like a crazy woman, talking about strange dreams and ghosts. She was grateful that he hadn't tried to tell her she was imagining things; she didn't think that she could have taken that on top of everything else.

Suddenly Penny began feeling optimistic. She now understood the true meaning of 'a problem shared is a problem halved'. Obviously she knew what this expression meant, however it was only when she felt the physical effects on her body that she really grasped what it actually felt like. Somehow she found breathing a little easier, she was no longer struggling to take deep breaths and she didn't feel like she was close to falling under the weight of the burden like she was the day before. She felt light and confident that they were able to tackle whatever they discovered. Although she still believed that she was the main player in this weird game, the thought of having two people she loved assisting her made her feel prepared and ready to take on the challenge.

The pair got off the bus and made their way to the library. Anita wasted no time and marched forwards in the direction of the building, pausing only a few times to check they were headed in the right direction. A few days ago when they had been walking down these very streets, Penny was preoccupied with taking everything in as they strolled leisurely through the city, enjoying the quaintness of the town. Now she couldn't care less about who she walked past and was focused instead only on her aunt's footsteps as they paced onwards in front of her. When Anita came to a stop, Penny raised her eyes from the ground to look at the building that hopefully held the answers she so desperately wanted.

Penny smiled as she looked up at the old building, finally seeing an end in sight. It was probably the optimistic feeling she had growing inside her that made it appear as though the arched entrance was an upside-down smile, welcoming her in.

'Let's start cracking the code!' Anita announced.

It turned out that the task itself wasn't as easy as they had anticipated. They went into the building and asked the woman at the main reception where they could find archived articles and the documented history of buildings. After wasting time getting lost in the large building, they finally reached the floor they wanted and an unusually friendly employee walked them to the end of a corridor lined with books until they reached a dark corner. The lady showed them how to work an ancient microfiche machine which allowed them to access old newspaper articles and how to locate the record of events in Charterville and Oakdene according to year.

Overwhelmed by the amount of work that had to be done, they decided to split the tasks. As Anita's eyesight was worse than Penny's, she appointed herself the task of trying to locate the old directories of the town as all it involved was looking through the spines of books on a shelf until the correct dates were located. Penny's task was to look on the old microfiche machine and scroll through endless newspaper reports until she found something of interest.

'What is the date we are looking for again, Pen?' Anita looked at her niece, small square reading glasses that didn't seem to make much difference perched on the end of her nose.

Penny picked out the diary from her bag and opened it again, hoping that the writing had magically reappeared. Her shoulders sunk as her suspicions were correct, the pages were bare. 'I can't remember, it was 1800's or something. I didn't pay much attention to the date though really.'

'Okay, well why don't we start on say 1795, something like that just to make sure?' Anita said.

'Okay, 1795,' Penny reiterated, moving her chair closer to the machine.

The library assistant had told her she had to go to a filing cabinet where articles were saved in date order. Once she had located the year she would have to bring the slide back to the machine and enter it into the bottom which would show them on a screen in front of her. If they found what they were looking for, they would need to put in a request for the information to be printed out, which they were advised would take up to two days. Penny was frustrated by this, much more used to the immediate results she got every time she searched for something on her phone.

An hour passed and Penny had covered years 1795—1798 but disappointingly she hadn't found anything of interest. She imagined what it would be like to have had lived in such an era; by the sound of the news it couldn't have been much fun. There were reports of the latest poem published, reports of prisoners that had been captured for allegations of treason and the strangest of advertisements. Penny giggled as she read them, pausing to read them out loud to Anita. One of them was called the 'Grand Restorer of Human Nature' for wind in the stomach, bowels, horrid thoughts and frightful dreams and other nervous complaints. She sniggered as she thought this was probably no different to what the everyday aspirin was now.

'Ah-ha, think I found something!' Anita shouted, her tone high-pitched as excitement filled her voice. Realising that she was in a place that was meant to be quiet, she reprimanded herself silently and whispered, '1803, this may be the year, Pen.' She moved to the table behind Penny and they both gathered around the book.

'Look, 1803, "*Oak Street, Oakdene in Charterville, deaths reported,*" Anita said, finger on the page, following the text as she read.

'Does it say anything else?' Penny asked impatiently.

'"*Mary Kelby, 1782—1801, body found, cause of death suspicious.*"' Anita looked up. 'How old does that make her then… 19? Is this the woman you've been seeing?'

Penny shuddered as she heard this information. She remembered the woman she had seen over the course of her stay and tried to put the name to the face she had seen. Although when she'd seen her, she had come to terms that she was not exactly real, seeing the word 'death' marked by her name made her heart feel heavy. Considering the fraught comments in her diary and seeing her death being regarded as 'suspicious' made Penny want to burst into tears. Seeing it in black and white made everything so real. She realised that a part of her had hoped the visit to the library would lead to a dead end; that nothing about her perfect little world had changed and she had imagined it all.

'Could be another Mary along the street maybe?' Penny asked, a hopeful tone to her voice.

'Could be, but somehow I doubt it.' Anita dismissed the idea, 'It's strange though, this is the book of record for 1803 yet her death has been confirmed as 1801.' Anita moved to the bookshelf and pulled another book from its resting place, causing a gust of dust to scatter in the air. She placed the second book on the table and flicked through it. 'See look, nothing in here for Oak Street in the book for 1801. Why?'

Penny didn't know, however she did know that she needed to find out more about this Mary Kelby. She took out her phone and sent a text to Jason, messaging him the name and asking him to include this in his research.

'Skip the rest of the years out love, search on that thingy magiggy for 1803 and see if there is anything on there, I'll carry on looking through here,' Anita said.

Penny nodded in agreement, there was no point wasting time looking through slides that she didn't need to, although annoyingly she realised she would have to as the slides that stored all the information came in batches. She was feeling agitated yet exhilarated. She knew she was close but was frustrated that she couldn't access the information instantly.

'Got something else!' Anita shouted, turning around. She quickly raised a finger to her mouth and blushed as she realised that, once again, she had acted inappropriately in the house of silence, 'I can't help it, I'm getting too excited!' She jumped, making Penny laugh out loud.

'Look, *"Oak Street – 2nd body found, Mrs Parks, formally Miss Peel of Oak Tree House. Death suspicious."'*

Penny let out a gasp and cupped her mouth with her hand. 'Oh my God! That is our house, isn't it? That old lady in the museum said that the house belonged to Lord and Lady Peel and they had a crazy daughter. Maybe she married a Mr Parks?'

Anita's eyes were wide, 'So they were both murdered then, these women; they must be the ones you are seeing.'

Penny shook her head as she tried to take in the information. She knew she had seen a younger woman and man more than once but also remembered that she had also seen an older woman fleetingly the previous night. They must have been the people in the reports. She returned to the machine, eager to find anything that had a bit more information. Anita looked at her watch and noticed that several hours had passed and the sun was beginning to go in. They were aware of the closing time of the library being 7pm and knew they only had a few more hours left to find out what they needed to know. Anita left Penny at the microfiche machine, telling her there was an urgent need for coffee.

Penny finally reached a year that held vital information. Irritatingly, the full report was no longer legible, meaning she was only able to determine the main points of the article.

1803 – October 5th

… Police were called to the respectable property at approximately 5pm in the evening due to reports from neighbours who grew concerned that there had been no activity in the house for some time. When they arrived, they saw the house was bare but were concerned when they noticed dried puddles of blood leading from the

bathroom into the kitchen... (illegible)... discovered a body beneath... (illegible)... a young woman, believed to be a maid... (illegible... circumstances suspicious... (illegible)... Doctor Parks is yet to be found... (illegible)...'

Penny re-read the article repeatedly, hoping to be able to make out some of the illegible text, but it was no use. Looking at the article, it was obvious that the document from which this originated had been folded up several times, meaning the text had not been transferred clearly.

She continued reading through the years, disappointed that the distortion of the text was the same on the other important slide she came across.

'1805 – January 21ˢᵗ

... following the discovery of the two bodies, the search continues for Doctor Parks. An autopsy of the younger of the two women discovered that she had been with child, however the baby has not been found. Suspicions of Doctor Parks involvement... the will and testament of the late Mr and Mrs Peel state that for the deeds of the house to be handed over to Doctor Parks there needed to be a ...'

Penny now knew the man's name, the man who was haunting her. His name was Doctor Parks and she now knew for certain that he had a part in both of these women's deaths. Although the reports mentioned 'suspicions', from the encounters she had with the man, there was no doubt about it. He was the one who killed these helpless women.

Penny looked away from the screen and stared into the space before her. Was the man ever found or was that the reason he was lingering in the apartment?

Twenty

Anita joined Penny and she showed her the screen as she hurriedly wrote the information she had found in her notebook. Realising time was against them, they quickly flicked through a few more dates in an attempt to find out more, before a short stocky man approached them, coughing as he walked forward to get their attention.

'Someone told me there were people up here. You's got to leave now I am afraid.' The man spoke with a thick, raspy West Country-like accent.

'Hang on, we're writing some stuff down.' Penny didn't glance up at the man to speak to him.

'You know that we has a printing service if you's write down the date and reference number? But I am afraid we have to process that Monday morning when we…'

'No thanks, we don't have the time to wait.' Anita snapped, also not looking at him.

'Not from around 'ere are you?' He had picked up on the differences in their accents and the unfriendly tone to their voices.

Realising that she was being rude, Penny begrudgingly put down her pen to look at the man, knowing her mother would be upset if she found out they had ignored someone who was just doing their job. When she looked up at him, she noticed his round face omitted a welcoming sense of warmth and she couldn't help but smile at him when he gazed at her. He had a big round belly that was struggling to be contained within the brown braces that secured his trousers and Penny couldn't help but laugh inside when she looked at him.

'We're staying in Oakdene for a few days. We just wanted to find out some more information on the history of the town,' she said as she smiled.

'Ah, I see's,' he nodded, 'I'm afraid these won't tell you's that much. You may want to consider popping down to see old Marjorie in the museum down the road, she knows everything about everything she does.'

'We have done already, thanks. Needed a bit more.'

'Well you's won't find out anything else, Marge knows everything there is to know about everything around here, past and present. Not much really to say about Oakdene apart from what happened in that house by the oak trees.'

Anita dropped her pen, her attention grabbed by his knowledge of their house. 'What do you know about that house?'

'Oak Tree House is what it's called. Heard they rented it for holiday lettings, not that I would stay there mind.'

'Why not?' The chill in Penny's spine was back.

'All those stories.'

'What stories?'

He eyed them suspiciously, 'You's aren't staying there are you? Don't want to scare you lasses on your trip away.'

Penny realised that this was an opportunity to find out more and could feel it slipping away rapidly if she told him the truth and so she lied, 'No, we're staying down the road. We met a man in the pub that told us a few stories, we wanted to find out a bit more. We like all of that stuff, you see.'

'Ah that's Oak Tree Tavern. Great pub, is that! Yes, it does the best steak and ale pies in Charterville. Have you tried 'em yet?'

Anita shook her head, annoyed by his pointless small talk, 'What stories?'

'Well there was those horrible, brutal murders years and years ago. Two women, I believes. They say the husband of the lady of the house killed 'em. Obsessed with women and wanted a child I think, for some inheritance. Anyway, they never found him and apparently, he is still there in the house, lingering around... waiting for someone to snatch.'

'How can he still be in the house, this article said it happened in the 1800's,' Penny commented. 'What do you mean "snatch"?'

'Well obviously he's not in the house, well not in the physical sense at least. A few stories have evolved over time you see. One that the man hid himself in there and then popped his clogs, the other that he came back after the story had died down and ended up dying there alone, his body left to rot so no one could find his remains. That old house was closed up for decades, you know. After them, there was no one left in the will. Typical village-type stories you know, I guess there is no way to ever know now.' Penny noticed that he hadn't answered the second part of her question.

'Well, why wouldn't you stay there? I'm sure lots of old houses have stories like that?' Anita was seducing him into telling them more information, the sort of information they needed to know which wasn't in the articles they had been researching.

'Eh, you're right there. But all the stories that happened after, people seeing things, people dying...'

'Dying?' The icy hand which gripped a hold of Penny's throat had returned once more, this time stabbing its sharp fingernails deep below the surface.

The man stopped what he was saying, realising he had been getting carried away with the story. 'You sure you's not staying there?' They shook their heads in response. 'Well, it matters not then does it? Anyway, we's be closing now, if there's nothing else?' He turned his back on them, his once friendly demeanour now stern. He refused to look them in the eye again and hushed them every time they tried to ask more.

They packed up their notebooks and walked towards the entrance, knowing that the man had given them all the information he was prepared to. Penny could feel excitement dancing around her body. She desperately wanted to speak to Anita but realised they couldn't say anything until they left the building, the man having insisted on escorting them all the way outside, as though they were criminals, incapable of being on their own. Instead, they threw knowing and worried glances at each other as they made their way down the spindly staircase and out through the door.

'Dying? What does that mean?' Penny grabbed hold of Anita's arm as they made their way to the bus stop. 'Snatching! Are they going to snatch me?'

'I wouldn't worry about it too much Pen, you know what happens over time, stories get built up and each generation adds a new layer to stop it from getting boring. It is obviously the town's ghost story.'

'Why did Mum bloody pick that apartment then? All that research she did you'd expect her to come across the famous ghost story of the town.'

'Yes well, like I said, your mother doesn't actually believe anything like that to be real. Here's our bus.'

They jumped on and as Penny sat down, a mixture of

emotions began to swim in different directions in the pit of her stomach. She was pleased that they had made progress with their research but was scared about what the man had said. She realised that Anita probably was right; she couldn't count the amount of times she had heard an urban legend, many of the times an alternate ending being given. Regardless, she was unable to shake the feeling of dread that was beginning to resurface in the pit of her stomach. Not having felt this emotion much in the past, Penny knew she hated it, hated how it made her feel and how vulnerable it made her.

When they got off the bus, Penny called her mother. It was later than she had thought and she was afraid she'd be worried about her. When they spoke, she told her that they had just sat down for some dinner, Anita having assured her that they should go ahead without them. Tired from the amount of reading they had done, the two women decided to grab some dinner in The Oak Tree Tavern.

As Penny and Anita settled into the pub, they took the librarian's advice and ordered two of the specialist pies and two large glasses of ale and the recommendation certainly didn't disappoint. As the barmaid came to the table with the two chilled glasses, they clinked them together tiredly, causing the foamy froth to fall from the sides.

'To a productive day,' Anita said, taking a sip of her drink.

Penny smiled; she was glad that her aunt was feeling positive about their trip and although she was also excited about what they had found out, she couldn't help but think back to what the man had said. Of course there was the potential that the story had been exaggerated, however she couldn't help but think of it as some sort of warning.

'Yes it was productive. I feel like we are a step closer to finding out what has happened, although I am even more confused now.'

Grateful for a bit of an insight into what happened in the apartment, she was angry they couldn't find out more. How was she supposed to know what she was meant to do if she couldn't find out any more information? She had spoken to Jason on the bus home, he had told her that he wasn't able to find out any more information on his basic internet search, but assured her that he would do more looking tomorrow when he had more time. Penny was aware that he was planning a night out and figured that he hadn't started looking yet, and as much as she wanted to scold him for not doing as he had promised, she didn't want to ruin one of the only times she had been able to speak to him.

'Okay, so let's go through what we know so far then,' Anita said as they were waiting for their food to arrive.

'Okay,' Penny agreed, 'so, we know that a Mary Kelby died in 1801 on Oak Street, but the death wasn't reported until 1803. That means that either the reporters were slow in catching up with the news or didn't think it was worth being printed?'

'The newspaper article you read said that the police "discovered" the body on that day. Her body and that of another woman,' Anita said, flicking through the notepad they had used to scribble their notes.

'So, the bodies were buried for two years unnoticed?' Penny felt saddened to know that such a young body could be left for such a long time without being discovered. 'How did no one come looking for her?'

'Didn't the diary mention something about that? Her mother and father sending her here to a respectable house? I doubt they had much communication, especially in those days,' Anita replied.

'Okay, so potentially they were buried somewhere,

presumably by the man. He obviously was married to the crazy woman. What happened to him do you think?'

'It's him I'm concerned about.' Anita replied. 'Spirits only come out when they are not at peace or if they are trying to warn you of something.'

The thought sent another shiver down Penny's spine. 'What happened to the baby do you think?'

'Yes, that is odd,' Anita said and then they sat in silence, thinking about what it meant before their food arrived and they went off topic, trying to push the strange apartment out of their thoughts.

*

They linked arms as they made the short walk home and maybe it was the three ales that she'd drunk, but Penny was once again beginning to feel better about things. The more they drunk and chatted, the more she forgot about the apartment and what they had spent the day doing. She had spoken to Jason and had a nice day with her aunt alone, which she hardly ever got to do these days. Penny told herself that tonight would be a good night and she was looking forward to seeing her mother and sister and finding out about their day.

As they opened the door, they heard music playing. She could see from the empty bottle on the table that her mother and sister had been enjoying some wine and they were sitting huddled together, laughing as they noticed their arrival. Her mother rushed up to give her a cuddle, before placing a full glass of wine in her hand. Penny was suddenly overwhelmed with love for her family. She realised that moments like these wouldn't come around as often as they were all getting older, and she resolved to spend the evening forgetting about what they had been researching earlier on in the day, deciding instead to focus on having a good evening with her family. She would leave thinking about what had happened until tomorrow.

'How are you feeling, love?' her mother asked. 'You look much better.'

'Tons better thanks, Mum. Having a lie-in and then getting some fresh air really helped,' she replied. 'What did you two get up to?'

'Oh, we didn't really do much, you didn't miss out on any fun.' Fiona said, not wanting to meet her eye.

'It's okay, I wanted you to have fun. I'd feel terrible if you told me that you actually didn't enjoy yourself,' Penny prompted, letting her know that she wanted to know more about what they had been up to.

With the response she had been hoping for, Fiona's face lit up, 'Ah Pen, it was a lovely day, although I don't think you two would really had liked it all that much, to be honest. We caught the first bus into Charterville and stopped off at a place that had really quirky little shops. I got this.' She rose from her chair and spun around in a circle, showing off a deep navy silk blouse which although very tight, suited her figure perfectly.

'Looks amazing as usual,' Penny said, taking her place next to her sister at the table.

'We literally spent the day going in and out of shops, stopping for food and then back to more shops. It was perfect,' she added, glowing from the excitement. Penny grinned, genuinely happy to see her sister so cheerful; she was after all, the reason behind the trip.

'We didn't forget you of course! We wanted to get something to make you feel better so we got you this.' Fiona placed an upmarket paper carrier bag into her lap. Penny rushed to open it, feeling like a little child again. When she pulled apart the bag, she picked out a gorgeous embellished silk scarf, exactly the same colour as the top her sister was wearing.

'I didn't think you'd like this top, but I loved the colour and the feel so much, I thought you had to have one, a scarf is more your style. Do you like it?' She looked at Penny nervously. Penny's heart once again felt like it was bursting, only this time it was out of love and not fear. She swooped her sister into her arms and gave her a massive kiss on her cheek.

'I love it!' she reassured her, trying not to notice Fiona wiping off her kiss the second she released her from her embrace. 'You shouldn't have!'

'What did you two do today?' Fiona asked.

'We went to the library and got a few books.'

'Where are they?' Her mother looked at their empty hands.

'Erm... well...' Penny considered telling her mother what they had actually been doing but decided against it, remembering the promise that tonight would be spent focusing on having fun and therefore lied, 'We couldn't actually take any out as we were not members so we just browsed around and read some in there.'

'That sounds nice, love. I was thinking you wouldn't be able to take any away with you.'

'Let's go to one of the bars in the city.' Fiona jumped up in her chair, her right arm holding her wine glass hovering above her head.

'I think we're too old for that, love,' Anita replied.

'Why don't you and Pen go now that she is feeling a bit better?' Her mother looked at Penny. The plan always was that they would be close enough to a town so the two younger women could go out if they wanted to. As they'd had such an active first few days, they had been too tired to even think about going back out. Penny looked at her sister, now very tipsy, and knew that she didn't want to move from where she was sitting. Feeling older than her years, the thought of having to put makeup on and try to fit into one of the two 'going out' outfits that she had packed made her feel tired at just the thought.

'I don't really fancy it.' She saw Fiona's face drop in disappointment.

'We can have a party here.' Anita tried to lighten the mood by filling up her drink. Fiona looked at her glass, shrugged her shoulders and took another sip. Penny figured that in a few hours she wouldn't mind much where they were and would have forgotten all about her suggestion to venture outside.

'Well I am glad you two still managed to have a good time. I was worried about you when we left,' her mother eyed Penny worriedly.

'I just needed the sleep that's all, Mum. Getting some rest and some fresh air helped.'

'Shall we tell some ghost stories?' Fiona swayed her body into Penny and started giggling, the alcohol obviously catching up with her first. 'This place is really weird.'

'No ghost stories tonight Fi,' Anita said and the words made the group stop in silence, all eyes looking at her. Penny was annoyed that she had acted so out of character, it was obviously going to arouse suspicion.

'What's got into you?' Even her mother was curious.

Anita looked between them. Seeing her eyes darting around the group, Penny knew she was trying to think on her feet. 'Penny is scared, she told me this morning, that is why she couldn't sleep.'

'Ooo, Mrs Sensible is Mrs Scaredy Pants is she?' Fiona

began to mock her. Penny shot her aunt an annoyed glare although she was grateful that she didn't reveal the truth. 'Ghost stories keeping you up?'

'No, I just don't like being somewhere new. I can take that wine glass off you if you're going to be annoying.'

'Oh ssshh; I am a mother you cannot tell me what to do. Pour one for yourself you grumpy mare.' Fiona poured her a drink, although most of it went over the side of the glass. Penny couldn't help but laugh. She enjoyed seeing her sister like this; she hadn't seen this side of her since they were in their early twenties going out to nightclubs with their group of friends. Penny took a long sip of her wine and enjoyed the sharpness of the bitter taste as it travelled down her throat, drowning the pessimistic thoughts she had with it.

For the remainder of the evening, a lot of wine was consumed and a lot of laughter was had. They recapped on family memories, jokes that only the four of them would understand and their plans for the future. For the whole evening, she didn't think about the strange goings-on in the apartment or about Mary or the strange man she had been seeing. It may have been the amount of wine that was being consumed or the nostalgia of spending time together, but Penny had almost forgotten that she was in a different apartment in a different city. The music was turned up loud and as the evening was drawing to an end, the four women were singing loudly from the top of their lungs, belting out the old classics that were playing from Anita's tablet. They even got up from their seats and danced around the kitchen, Penny and Fiona jumping between the chairs the same way they did when they were little.

Anita had given up smoking a long time ago but always kept a ten pack in her bag 'in case of emergencies'. Penny knew that this was for occasions where she felt stressed or had a lot to drink. 'Drinking and smoking go hand in hand,' she would tell her sister to stop her nagging in disapproval

184

whenever she tried to have a sneaky one. She reached into her bag and pulled out the pack, noticing the look in her sister's eye as she stumbled to the kitchen door to push it open. For some reason, they all huddled with Anita to go outside, walking like penguins behind her, not wanting to be separated as they were having such a good time.

As Anita pushed the door open, they saw that the night had been and gone and the sun was slowly beginning to rise; the birdsong light in the air as they were starting their business for the day. Penny's mother let out a gasp as she saw that it was no longer evening and scurried back inside to check the time.

'Goodness me, look at the time,' her words were slurred. 'It's nearly five in the morning! Can you believe it?'

'Well we haven't seen each other all day; let's have one more drink before bed.' Fiona turned to follow her mother inside but fell onto the floor as soon as she turned. She lay on the tiled floors while the others laughed hysterically at her normally composed self, sprawled in an undignified bundle on the floor.

'Maybe we shouldn't have any more. Come on, get up.' Their mother pulled her oldest child up from the ground and placed an arm under her shoulder.

Realising she wouldn't get her chance to have her sneaky smoke, Anita sighed as she pushed Penny back into the room and shut the door behind her.

'What's the plan for tomorrow, Mum?' Fiona asked as they made their way to the bedroom.

'Nursing these sore heads I would imagine,' Anita said, navigating them towards their beds by pushing them forward determinedly.

'Let's forget the plan and see where the wind takes us,' her mother replied, arm flying in the air causing the others

---

185

to succumb to another round of giggles at her sudden change in character.

As they stumbled into their room, Penny remembered collapsing into bed beside her sister, just about managing to take off her clothes to pull on a night shirt. As soon as their heads hit the pillow and the room stopped swaying, they both fell into an immediate sleep.

*

About an hour or so after they went to bed, Penny felt cold. The drunkenness was starting to wear off, being replaced by a slow thump in her head and a dryness in her throat. She placed her hand above her head and let out a groan, cursing her family for making her drink as much as she had. It was their fault obviously, not hers. She tossed and turned and pulled the covers over her shoulders, trying not to think about the sickness that was slowly rising in her throat. No matter where she turned, the coldness was staying on one exact part of her as if something was constantly blowing in her direction.

Drunkenly she opened her eyelids slowly. Suddenly they became alert.

She didn't need to blink to know that what she was seeing was real. A pair of eyes were staring directly into hers. They were open and wide, pupils dilated as if in shock. Penny screamed as she tried to move further into her bed. It was no use, there was nowhere to go.

In the second she screamed, she realised it wasn't just the eyes which were locked into her own. The face to which they belonged pushed down onto her, the cold nose resting upon hers, the firm forehead pushing her deeper into the bed, cementing her further into an unbreakable position.

She continued her plight to move backwards into the bed. The springs in the mattress allowed her to sink deeper and as she did, she felt a touch of hair which wasn't her own against her face.

No matter how hard she tried to struggle away, the second pair of eyes did not once blink and did not move away from Penny's own, keeping her firmly in their sight.

Twenty-One

The face still seemed locked against hers, unwilling to move. There was no point in looking away; Penny knew for certain she wasn't dreaming. She could feel the icy skin resting upon hers and she instantly knew that this level of intimacy had crossed a boundary that she wouldn't be able to come back from. She stared into the eyes that were glued onto hers. Unable to talk, she pleaded with her eyes, praying that no harm would come to her. The close proximity of the face meant that Penny was unable to make out if this was the woman she had seen earlier or another person altogether. The person seemed manic, panic stricken and most certainly not of this world. The limbs of the character spread out upon Penny's body as though they were not attached to its person, legs extended backwards over the arms that were holding Penny in place, as if the body was a crab and Penny was the sand it was using to walk along.

'Mary?' she whispered.

All at once the eyes flickered in recognition; the angry face seemed to soften ever so slightly with the call of the name. The figure released its firm grasp and jumped on the bed, standing upright and staring down at Penny. Fully standing, Penny could see that the thing before her was the same woman she had been seeing, although she looked as she never had done before. She was wearing a tatty, baggy white nightdress that hung from her shoulders and hips, showing the absence of the bump she had seen earlier.

Although she tried, the darkness of the room prevented

Penny from getting a clearer look at her visitor. It was the first time the woman had stared directly at her, eyes so wide it appeared as though they were permanently that way, as though they had no eyelids to protect them. They were cold and empty and as they kept their focus on Penny; she felt as though they were looking inside her, looking for something she didn't think they would find.

She wanted to run, push this creature away from her and head towards the door. Scared to move her head, she glanced over to the door to calculate how long it would take her to spring off the bed and reach it. Although she was lying down, she could feel all muscle strength had dissolved from her legs and she feared that she would collapse as soon as she made her desperate flight to escape.

'What do you want from me?' she whispered, her voice quivering as she pushed out the words.

Mary's face considered Penny's question and she cocked her head sideways the exact same way the man had done the previous evening, her un-brushed hair covering the side of her dirty face. She raised her arm but it didn't seem like an easy task for her; the movement sharp and jagged as though she had to force the arm out of its resting position to move upwards. Once the arm was up she left it there, elbow touching her body and she jerked forwards until her hands were either side of Penny's face, never moving her eyes away from Penny's own. She was straddling her once more in her crab-like impersonation, the head extended, touching her face.

'LEAVE THIS HOUSE... LEAVE THIS HOUSE NOW...' The woman screamed so loudly and the ancient breath smacked Penny in the face, causing her to shudder in revulsion.

When she opened her eyes, her hands still tightly clutching the sheet beneath her, she saw that Mary had disappeared. Almost scared to look around, Penny glanced backwards and forwards to check she had definitely left, preparing herself for another sudden movement. She continued to lie in the same position and although she still did not have the courage to move her head, she could see her chest rising in and out of view quickly beyond the tip of her nose and she took fast, rapid breaths as though someone was frantically trying to pump up her deflated body.

She tried to count numbers to get her breathing back to normal and to slow the pounding in her chest. Gradually, she loosened her grip on the sheet below her and looked around the room. When she was certain the woman had disappeared for good and she was alone, Penny pushed herself upwards into a sitting position and cautiously looked around. Thankfully she saw Fiona curled in a ball beside her the same way she was when they had fallen asleep. She knew that she should have felt a sense of relief that her sister was safe and seemingly undisturbed by the encounter, but she couldn't help but feel a strong sense of resentment that she had not even stirred during the noise or come to her sister's rescue. How could she not have heard her scream and feel the force of something else pressing down on the bed? She wanted to shake her sister hard and scream at her for not realising what had been going on. She raised her hand to shake her, the blood swimming around her head now at the forefront of her brain, but stopped as her hand touched her sleeping sister's shoulder. It wasn't her fault, Penny realised, she should let her sleep.

Penny grabbed her phone and saw that it was now 6am and she could see little trickles of morning trying to break through the darkness of the room. She really hadn't slept long, if at all, and she sure as hell felt the effects of the lack of sleep. Her mind was foggy and her eyelids pulled downwards heavily, although inside she was awake and alert. Gradually she pulled herself up out of the bed, her legs trembling beneath her with the effort. She was dizzy on her feet as she made her way down the hall and had to stop regularly to prop herself up against the wall to stop herself from falling, still not understanding what had just happened.

The walk was taking double the time it normally did as she tried to work out what the hell had just gone on. With each step, the dizziness began to get worse and Penny cursed herself for not waking up Fiona when she had the chance. Screw the apartment and screw whatever it wanted, limping down the hallway was enough to highlight to her the danger she was in. The thing had told her to leave and after seeing what she just had, she wasn't going to say no to that. Slumped against the wall, she tried to put mind over matter and forced herself to walk to her mother's room. She stood upright and marched forward purposefully, ignoring the banging in her head which was telling her to stop.

She pushed open the door and shook Anita gently on her arm. It didn't take long for her to stir and as soon as she saw the expression on her niece's face, she jumped straight out of bed and pushed Penny into the kitchen, silencing her when she saw she was about to explode with fear and closed the door behind her.

Penny didn't wait for Anita to enter the room fully to let loose the tears that had been building since she was so aggressively woken in the bedroom and told her the whole story, physically shaking as she recalled the memory of being trapped on her bed. Telling the story hadn't changed her mind about leaving, in fact, it only made her even more determined as she recalled the events in horror.

'Dear God, Penelope, you are shaking,' she placed a hand on Penny's. 'Sit down.'

'I don't want to sit down, I want to leave!' Penny snapped at her.

'Sit down.' Anita pushed Penny into a chair and pushed a glass of something under her nose. 'Drink this.'

Penny tasted the sugary drink on her lips and a few moments later she felt her shakiness reduce into a small vibration, the sugar seemingly going some way to settle her nerves.

'Sorry, I just need to leave. I don't want to be here anymore.'

'I know! It's scary, isn't it?'

'The whole thing is scary.' Penny looked at her, not believing she would state something so obvious.

'You don't look like you are going to go into any type of severe shock, so that's good.'

'Oh yeah, it's very good. I am not hospitalised like grandma just yet… yay!'

'I am going to ignore your tone because you're upset, but it would be good to remind yourself that I am only trying to help you.'

Penny saw her aunt's cheeks puffing as she turned her back away from her and moved towards the sink, and instantly Penny regretted the way she had spoken to her. She was right, she was only trying to help, but Penny was unable to think straight at that moment. She remembered Anita's story about her grandmother, about how she had been in a coma for some time after making contact with a spirit. Thinking about this only made her feel worse, what if she herself ended up in hospital? She shook her head; she wouldn't wait to find out.

'I think we need to leave… now…' Penny said, starting to make her way out of the room, words shaking as they came out of her mouth. 'I'll wake the others and…'

'Stop! Can you please stop storming up and down? My head is sore enough without you making me dizzy!' Anita said and Penny remembered the banging that had been going on in her own head, causing her to wake initially. She paused silently and tried to register if she too was feeling the effects of their heavy night. She knew she had a feeling deep down that something wasn't right but she was certain she wasn't suffering any drink related illness; she couldn't handle a hangover on top of everything else right now. She was sorry that she had woken Anita from a well needed sleep but she felt like being selfish right now, she needed help.

'Here, drink this.' Penny plonked a pint of water in front Anita the same way she had done to her, hoping it would clear her foggy head; she needed her to be able to think clearly.

Anita took the glass and downed it whole, 'Okay, I agree. We should leave.'

Penny let out a long, deep breath that she felt she had been holding since she opened her eyes, 'Really? Would Mum mind?'

'Let's talk to her when she gets up. I think it may be time to fill her in on what has happened. After you tell her about tonight, I'm sure she'll want to leave. Mind you, the amount we drunk last night, I can't imagine that she will be up for some time.'

Anita was right, Penny knew this. She looked across the table, taking in the sight of the night before and counted at least six bottles of wine discarded on the table. If she hadn't have been so rudely woken, Penny knew she wouldn't have been out of bed until at least noon. She tried, but failed, to be sympathetic and repeated impatiently that she wanted to leave straight away. She didn't think it was a good idea to wait until the others woke up naturally; if it were her she'd want to know right away. Besides, what if leaving them asleep was putting them in danger somehow?

Penny went to pick up her bag from where she had left

it the night before to show her that her mind was fully made up. Feeling aggressive, she yanked the bag away from the handles of the chair it had been hung against with such force that the handle snapped away in her hand, causing its contents to scatter across the floor. Amongst all the typical belongings that would be expected to be in a woman's handbag, the old blue diary toppled out and laid open in the middle of the floor, catching her attention immediately.

Although she wanted to ignore everything in the apartment that she couldn't explain, something inside pushed Penny forwards towards the diary, as though there were some sort of magnetic pull which was forcing her to walk towards the place where the book was lying. Penny picked it up and flicked through it again. She had to blink a few times to make sure she was seeing things clearly. The text in the pages had mysteriously reappeared.

'The writing is back,' Penny exclaimed.

Twenty-Two

'Read it while it's there!' Anita urged her.

Penny was unsure after what she had seen that night; she didn't know if she wanted to know any more. A moment ago she was adamant that she wanted nothing more to do with anything in the apartment, but now that she could see the faint traces of text appearing like a spider's crawl across the pages, she felt the pull once again and couldn't help but bring the diary closer to her face so she could read the writing.

'I don't know… That thing, person, whatever it was, really scared me. I'd rather just leave.' She was still hesitant.

'Nonsense!' Anita said, grabbing the diary off her. 'It is too much of a coincidence that the pages mysteriously reappear after you have seen her. Maybe it is another message.'

Penny had thought that the woman was trying to get her out of the apartment so why would she now be sending another message to her? The message had been received loud and clear, although she had to admit it was strange that the moment she wanted to leave, the writing reappeared, tempting her to stay.

Penny took the diary back from Anita, 'You're the one who said to leave things alone!'

'And I have told you,' Anita took the diary back, 'that it is far too late for that now. We have to see what happened.

I tell you what, when your mother gets up, we'll ask to leave a day earlier. Until then there is no harm in reading it.' She pushed the diary back to Penny to read.

Could any more harm be done by just reading the diary? Her head was telling her to keep the diary firmly shut but she couldn't help the curiosity slowly building. She drew a breath and turned the pages.

'The first entry is in February. Do you have the notebook there; how does that fit with the other dates?' Penny asked.

Anita went into the bedroom to fetch their notebook from the previous day and started flicking through it. 'Right, so I think that was before the other entries. I think June was the last one we read before we heard that noise.'

Penny began to read.

February 2nd[h] 1801

Dear Diary,

I was speaking with Doctor Parks and he has assured me that everything will be okay. When I found out the news that I was with child, he caught me crying as I took the luncheon up in the afternoon. Cook would have been so mad at me had she found out, sobbing miserably over the soup. I tried so hard to keep it in, but the pain was far too much. Thank goodness there was only Doctor Parks in the room at the time and no one else. All I ever see is the doctor lingering around. Mrs Parks is always in her room, she is constantly sick they say.

I always considered the doctor strange and was uncomfortable in his presence. He is always there, making his way into the servants' hall for unknown reasons, eyes lingering on the younger maids longer than I think is proper. The maids have all spoken about him, how he would seem to make an excuse to speak to us, especially the young ones. I am not one to gossip but I have seen the way some of the younger ones flutter their eyelids when he walks into the room and have often wondered where they have been when I hear some of them enter late at night and whether they had come from a visit upstairs. Such would be a scandal! Cook has told me to keep my eyes down and avoid attention, she said he wouldn't pay that much attention to me if I did that, although I am not entirely sure I know what she means.

Today he was a perfect gentleman, like something inside him changed. Of course, I felt uneasy when he noticed I was crying and asked me what had happened. I tried to act as a maid should act and hide my tears but I couldn't help it. He sat me down at the table and offered me a cup of tea from the tray I had just bought up! Can you believe that, I got to sit at a table and drink with those upstairs? How I wish it was under better circumstances! I couldn't help it, I let it all out as though someone had opened the gates to allow the tears to come pouring out. Being sent here by my parents, I often feel alone without anyone to speak to. The other maids are nice enough but I don't like the way they turn their backs and talk about people as they walk off. I thought it was different when I met John. Finally I felt I had someone to confide in and talk to. I have never been as happy as I was when I was with him.

'It's not just me who thinks he is weird then.' Penny paused from reading. The sun was now fully up and despite her earlier reservations, she wanted to read more to see what had happened to Mary to turn her into the thing that had woken her up in such a state.

Doctor Parks was ever so kind when I told him about the child, I thought he would be most displeased and furious that someone in his service had caused disgrace onto his family home and I was certain as soon as the words left my mouth that I would be thrown out on my ear without a day's further pay. Instead he was kind and gentle and pushed the hair out of my eyes and gave me his handkerchief to wipe my dampened cheeks. I felt bad taking it off him, it was nicely embroidered with neat little stitching across the side and I was sure that the thing would have cost me a whole year's pay. He told me that he had an idea and that he would come and find me later that evening to help me out.

I am sure that everything is going to be okay.

February 8th, 1801

Dear Diary,

Doctor Parks waited for me to leave for the evening two nights ago. He must have asked Cook for my staff pattern as he was waiting beneath the oak trees at the foot of the road when I left the house to head to the theatre. It was my first night off in two months and although I could not focus on anything other than what was growing inside of me, I was looking forward to being away from Oak Tree House and alone with my thoughts. I know that secretly I was planning on seeing John one more time to try to persuade him to accept me and my child. He loved me once, if I could convince him to do the proper thing and marry me, there would be no shame to fall upon us and we can be happy with our little family, we would make it work, I was sure of it.

I was startled as the doctor extended an arm through the trees and pulled me in. I must admit I was frightened for a moment, unsure as to why he needed to talk to me in such a manner. He said it was a secret and no one should know and that is why he was unable to talk to me about it in the house. I froze when he moved his arm around my waist and pulled me closer to him so that my body was touching his. John is the only man who has held me in such a way and as I felt the grip of his hand on the bodice of my dress, I knew his approach was improper. I was conscious as my chest rose and fell reflecting my rapid breathing and Doctor Parks shooting the occasional glance in that direction.

He whispered in my ear that he was there to help me, to tell me his plan and it was with this that my fearfulness subsided. Apparently, Mrs Parks had tried for many years to bear a child but nature had not been kind to her in that regard. He said that the years were not in her favour and he doubted they would have a chance to conceive naturally as she was rapidly exceeding child bearing age.

He said he was tired of the gossip within the town about her 'strangeness' and he didn't want to add to speculation as to why a couple did not have an heir. He promised that he would conceal my pregnancy if I agreed for them to have the baby after its birth and pass it on to them, Doctor and Mrs Parks. He has delivered babies before and he could deliver it here, in my very room in the back of the house. I would be comfortable, he said. Once it has been born I would hand it over to Mrs

Parks and they would register it as their own. No one would know, he has reassured me, and I would be paid to have two months' holiday after the birth! I have never had more than one day off ever in my life.

An absurd idea, I thought. I knew that what I was doing was wrong but there was no way I could give up the child I had become attached to growing inside of me. I gasped at his suggestion and tried to push myself out of his grasp but he held me firm. He told me to think about it and the life I could possibly give to the child if I kept it. He said he would throw me out, they cannot afford to have such a scandal occurring under their roof and it is almost a certainty that no other respectable house will take me in. What life would that be for me or the child? He says that I would have to end up working the street to get food and that would be a life of sin. He has assured me that the child will have a good life, one of luxury and good living. He pushed my hair away from my face and said that I had always been his favourite and he would look after me once it was done.

He has given me the night to think about it and I know he is waiting for me to go upstairs to tell him my answer. The more I think about it, the more I know I have not a choice in the matter. Even If the choice makes my heart break in the process.

Penny looked up, a small tear falling down her face as she considered how the young woman must have been feeling with the difficult choice she had to make. She noticed that Anita was also feeling the same, her face solemn and sad.

'Poor love, makes you grateful that we live in the day and age we do, doesn't it?' Anita said, moving to get a refill on her glass of water.

'So that is what he was after, her baby,' Anita said. 'In her latest entries, she must have changed her mind?'

'So, what? Were we meant to find her baby and give it back to her?' Penny shuddered, 'How on earth are we meant to do that?'

'I don't know, if that is even what they want,' Anita considered.

'What do you mean?'

'Well, let's get clear on what has happened so far. Young Mary got knocked up by a young lad who didn't want it, creepy Mister upstairs wanted the baby, and Mary decided she wanted to go back on the deal. We then know that a year later two bodies were discovered and the man is missing,' Anita said, reading through her notes.

'So, we need to know what happened from when she decided to go back on the deal to when she was murdered?' Penny asked.

'If you want to, although I think we have exhausted all lines of research. We've been to the library and we read the diary. Unless anything else happens, I can't see what else we can do!' Anita sounded defeated.

Penny picked up the diary and looked through the pages again which were now blank. She pulled the notebook from under her aunt's arm and began scribbling down what she had just read out loud, in case they needed it again.

'What is that you two are doing?' Her mother stood in the doorway, looking dishevelled, one hand rubbing her eyes as she entered the room.

'Just reading some of the literature that we picked up from the library yesterday,' Anita said, pushing the diary from the table onto her lap, hoping her sister didn't notice.

'What time is it?' she asked, pulling her dressing gown across her body. Her eyes squinted, still getting accustomed to the light and her short hair was sticking up on all ends. Penny could tell she had had a rough night's sleep, although she was certain it wasn't as bad as her own.

Penny drew out her phone from the pocket of her jumper

which she pulled on when she darted from her bed in the early hours. 'It's only eight, Mum; you haven't been asleep for very long. How are you feeling?'

'Being completely honest, I feel terrible!' She placed her head in her hands on the table as she sat down. 'Think we overdid it. Do you two feel okay?'

The pair eyed each other and then Anita said, 'We weren't feeling all that great first thing, but a strong coffee helps that, here,' she said, pushing a freshly brewed cup towards her sister.

'I doubt your sister is up yet, love?' she asked Penny.

Penny laughed at the thought of her sister last night, 'No, I can't imagine she'll be up any time soon, you know what she is like after a few drinks.' Fiona was well known for her terrible hangovers that seemed to last all day. She would either wake up still drunk from the night before, or dependent on how much sleep she had, woke up like the devil, angry and mean shouting demands at anyone who came into her sight. Penny was hoping that the version that greeted them this morning would be the former.

'Well at least we all let our hair down which is what this trip is all about, although I guess it is a shame we have ruined our last day; I can't imagine that we will want to do much today,' her mother said disappointingly, looking slightly ashamed that she had allowed herself to get carried away as much as she did.

She was right, Penny thought, last night was fun. They had laughed and sung until the sun came up and Penny had momentarily forgotten all her worries. She tried to cling onto that thought and not the one burning in her mind right now, deciding that last night would be the memory she'd take from the trip and not the one that crippled her with fear. As soon as they left the apartment she would push that thought firmly out of her mind and concentrate instead on the few happy memories they had made.

'Actually, about that, Mum. About it being our last night…' Penny said nervously, 'I kind of think that maybe we should…'

'Please. Someone. Give. Me. Water. Now. Why are you being so loud?' Fiona entered the room and Penny felt her heart drop as she realised the sister that emerged from the bedroom was the version she was dreading. Entering as though she was some sort of Hollywood A-Lister, gigantic sunglasses covering her face to hide her eyes that were most likely haggard from the over-drinking, she joined her mother and almost fell onto the table.

'Sore head?' Anita said, now getting up to place a glass of cold water underneath Fiona's face, which was also being cradled in her hands.

'Everything hurts. I'm too old for this,' she almost cried raising her head, 'I haven't had much sleep, I only managed a few hours!' She let out a dramatic cry and flopped her head back onto the table.

Penny sighed; she knew Fiona had slept well. She had slept through the most terrifying ordeal Penny had ever faced, so she felt no sympathy towards her and was secretly glad that she was in as much pain as she was.

'We had fun though eh? It wouldn't be a good party if the hostess didn't wake up with a sore head!' her mother said, trying to convince herself as well as Fiona.

'You're right, it was fun. Although I'm not sure I can function well today. Please don't tell me you have more plans for us today Mum, I can't bear to move,' Fiona moaned, head now firmly resting against the cold surface of the table.

'What were you going to say earlier, Pen? I know you didn't get a chance to get out and about yesterday. Is there something you want to do?'

Penny considered before answering to ensure she had made the right decision. More than anything she felt like getting up and leaving straight away, packing their bags and saying goodbye to the horrid apartment once and for all. She had almost decided that this was what she was going to say but when she looked over at her mother and sister looking dishevelled and sorry for themselves, Penny knew she didn't have the heart to get them to move more than they needed to know. Did they need to leave the apartment right now? Penny was unsure.

Strangely, as soon as her mother and sister joined Penny and Anita in the kitchen, Penny seemed to feel calmer, as though there had been no need for her to be as worried as she had been an hour ago. It was like they were an opening between two thick pockets of cloud that illuminated the path she was meant to take. The rationality that she had always considered to be her best asset had returned and she was able to see things for what they were. Why was she getting so worked up over everything? Yes, what had happened this morning had been strange and had scared the wits out of her, but how could she be sure that she wasn't still drunk and the image hadn't been a product of her over-active imagination playing tricks on her? They were due to leave tomorrow, what harm could one more day do? Everything that had seemed to happen so far had been one-off occurrences; surely she could put up with one more before she left, if anything happened at all.

'It's okay, Mum. It's Fiona's trip, so she can do what she likes. You've worked so hard on it too, you should spend your last day relaxing.' She stood from the table and put her arms around her mother and gave her a tight squeeze. Although she was upset that she was experiencing such horrible events, she was grateful that her mother and sister were not going through what she was. As far as they were concerned, they were having a fabulous trip away and that was all that mattered; Penny knew that she couldn't ruin this for them.

'In which case, I'm going to have a lie down I think.' Fiona rose from the table. 'There is no way I will function unless I get rid of this dire headache.'

'I may come and join you for an hour. Do you two mind?' Her mother looked at Penny and Anita.

Penny couldn't help but let out a yawn as she saw her mother and sister get up from the table. She remembered that she had next to no sleep herself and she started to feel sluggish, the effects of the alcohol starting to remind her of its existence within her body. Feeling more settled than she was when she first left her bed, she thought she would pass out as soon as her head hit the pillow if she had a lie down, hopefully not waking up until it was time to leave.

Her eyelids were drooping and she looked at Anita before saying, 'Actually, maybe I'll have a little nap too.'

'Are you sure, love?' Anita asked.

'Of course she is, look at the state of her!' Fiona rudely commented. Penny tried to ignore her, even more grateful now for her sister's pounding head.

'Yes Anita. I am tired and would quite like a little lie down.'

Anita looked nervous but thought it best not to question her niece's motives in front of the others. 'Well maybe Penny and I should share a bed in case we can't get to sleep, we'll give you two space to get your beauty sleep. God knows you need it right now.'

'Oi, I take offence at that comment, but I'm too tired to argue,' her mother replied, giving Penny a kiss on the cheek as she left the room.

Anita pulled Penny by the arm and whispered, 'That was your chance, you wanted to leave? Why didn't you say something?'

'I don't know, change of heart? I think I'm being silly. Maybe I didn't see what I saw, maybe I got it wrong? I'm so confused and possibly still drunk! More than anything I am tired.' Her eyelids were getting heavier and it was a struggle to keep them open. Although her pounding head had forgiven her for starving it of hydration the previous night, she could feel her back clamming up with sweat as the alcohol was trying to seep its way out of her body, punishing her in a puddle of moistness for over-indulging. 'I need to sleep. Let's rest for a bit and then speak to them when we get up, we'll still have time to leave before it gets dark.'

'Well if you're sure?' Anita still eyed her with suspicion.

'I'm not sure about anything at the moment but seeing them made me think rationally. I need a shower first; I'll come back in when I have washed and feel a bit more human!'

Penny walked towards the bathroom, taking a diversion into the cave-room to collect some clean clothes. Her sister and mother were cuddled up in the bed. She noticed they had fallen asleep quickly, almost instantaneously, their light snores filling the quietness of the room. Not wanting to be awake any longer than needed, she rushed into the bathroom, turned on the shower and ripped off her nightdress. As soon as she stepped beneath the water she immediately started lathering the shampoo into her hair, missing out the part of the process where she normally stood silently for a few moments, enjoying the first contact with the water.

Penny was feeling more hopeful and a part of her believed that if she rubbed her skin furiously, it would take away the feeling she had in the pit of her stomach and the nagging dread that was beginning to rear its ugly head, telling her she had made a mistake in not telling the others her concerns and leaving the apartment when she had the chance. As she was battling her dread demon, she realised she was also having a battle with her eyelids. She had closed them as she entered the shower but now was regretting it as she was struggling to push them back open. She thought of her aunt lying in the bed and was looking forward to getting tucked up beside her, knowing she would feel safer with her by her side. Although she wasn't sure she had washed all the shampoo out, she drew the curtain aside and stepped over the bathtub onto the tiled floor. Her eyes were stinging from her careless attempt to wash her hair properly and her hands fumbled around the space in front of her looking for a towel.

As she wiped her face with the rough towel, she had a strange feeling that she was being watched. She tried to shake off the feeling as she rubbed with a bit more force, but was unable to scrub it away. As she lowered her towel away from her face, she slowly turned around.

Standing by the edge of the bath where only moments ago her naked body had been searching for something to conceal it, she saw the man she now knew to be Doctor Parks standing.

He stood still and silent, watching as her mouth formed into a scream.

Twenty-Three

Penny blinked a few times, hoping that the soap was affecting her vision. She felt her heart plummet to the floor when she realised that there was no mistaking it. The doctor she read about in the news reports was standing directly opposite where she was, his eyes barely blinking as though he did not want to risk taking them off her. She felt exposed in her small towel that was barely covering her body and she wrapped it closer together and tried to tie it up in a knot, her hands clumsily moving across the fabric without risking looking away from the man. The way he was staring at her wet body caused her to jolt in panic. She felt her body start to shake, terror seeping through every vein she thought her body possessed. She was cold yet the pumping blood made her feel hot and uncomfortable, her breaths becoming shorter as her brain began to catch up with her eyes. She knew he was staring at her although it was hard to make it out by the way his eyebrows were scrunched together, looking at her with pleasure but also revulsion, his lip forming a firm line that didn't look like it was possible to move.

In a split second, Penny had to decide what to do. Her hands reached behind her, desperate to find the edge of the basin and potentially some object she could use to protect herself. Her fumbling hands behind her back didn't reach anything useful. Panicking, her glance darted towards the bathroom door and she tried to work out how quickly she could reach it; she thought she could make it in a few steps but didn't have the confidence to move. Her hesitation

---

sabotaged her opportunity to escape which allowed the doctor to realise her intentions and suddenly he was in front of her, hands on top of hers, forcing her to let go of her grasp on the towel. The movement had taken her by surprise, she hadn't realised he had moved he had been so fast; a sudden zoom and he was in front of her.

His grip was firm and the only instinct left inside her was survival. She wanted to shout in his face to leave her alone and push him off but as she opened her mouth, she was horrified that she could only muster a pathetic whimper in his direction, a hard lump wedged deep down in her throat which prevented any other sound coming out.

At the sound of her groan, he slithered his body closer towards her and tightened the grip on Penny's hand, causing her to flinch from the pain. The firm line drawn neatly across his face had turned upwards, although it was only the right-hand side of his mouth which had moved. His teeth were not visible through his lips but by the way his chin was firm and formed in a deep, ridged square, she knew he was gritting his teeth hard beneath his sadistic smile.

Penny felt a sharp pain in her chest as she noticed how tight her lungs had become; she was opening her mouth but was unable to take in enough oxygen to relieve the pain. Instead she heard herself take small raspy grasps. She was aware that she if she didn't breathe slowly soon she would pass out and end up in a ball on the floor the same way she had in the kitchen. Suddenly she thought this was not a bad idea and tried to hold her breath even more in the hope that she would faint and wake up away from this monster. Remembering that being unconscious around an unknown entity made her vulnerable, she fought against the part inside her that desperately wanted to give up. She opened her mouth and tried to soak in the air that had now become clammy, the moisture and steam from her shower still polluting the air. There was no way she was passing out now; electric bolts were shooting through her body as though someone had let off fireworks within her, causing her to be awake and alert.

He tightened his hand once more which finally pushed a sound out of Penny, a scream as she recoiled in pain, certain that he was close to snapping the bone with his force. She felt his long fingernails piercing through her skin and the sensation of blood leaving her body. Her left arm was still free and she used it to continue her desperate search of the basin behind her in a last-minute attempt for aid. He noticed what she was doing and quickly reached forward for her arm with his spare hand.

He now had control of both arms, moving them forward to the front of her body as though she was praying. Knowing there was no way to escape, fear began crippling her, freezing her body from her feet upwards and she began violently shaking in his hands, tears rushing from her as the terror of her situation kicked in. He had managed to control the shaking in her arms by his grip but not her legs and when Penny could not hold her own weight any more, she collapsed onto the floor.

The sudden movement of Penny hitting the ground was enough to take the man off guard; he released the hold he had on her arms and she brought them over herself to protect her body. Any braveness she once had completely evaporated and she lay still on the bathroom floor, hands over her head, violently sobbing, not able to even open her eyes to look for an escape route.

Her sobs were getting louder and more heart-breaking with each one that passed through her lips. Penny knew she had to control herself and try to make her way out of the room, towards the door in the kitchen and out of the apartment forever. She got control of her sobbing, but the crying continued. She realised the sobs were now not coming from her. Penny pulled herself up by clasping her hands on the basin, the task more physical than it should have been. Her legs had completely given way and without her arms to support her, she doubted she would have been able to get to her feet. She quickly looked around and was relieved to see the doctor had disappeared as quickly as he had arrived.

Not wanting to spend any more time in the room than necessary, Penny turned to run out as quickly as possible, but something made her stop before she began to run. She had glanced quickly in the mirror as she pushed herself away from the sink, but stopped to look back at the reflection as she neared the door. Had she seen it right? Slowly, Penny turned back to the mirror and gasped in shock, startled by the image that was reflecting back at her. She was not looking back at herself.

Mary was staring back at her, she was sure it was her. She remembered when she looked at herself the other day in the mirror when something hadn't seemed right, her eyes and hair colouring had seemed dissimilar but she had disregarded it as a sign of her need to rest. Those exact same features were staring back at her now, although this time the features were part of a face that filled the mirror, looking frantically into her own.

Anxiously, she raised her hand to her mouth to stop herself screaming in shock and saw her hand had returned to its previous shaky self. The reflection mirrored her gesture as she moved her hand and Penny sharply pulled away to survey the room to ensure there was no one else lurking in the steam ready to spring out at her. When she was confident she was alone, she returned to the mirror and was horrified to see that Mary's image was still staring back at her. She tried to figure out why her reflection had been replaced with the thin figure in front of her, belly not bulging from her waist the way Penny's had been recently. Penny looked into her eyes and saw that there was a glimmer of recognition staring back. This woman recognised Penny and the way she was staring at her indicated she needed her help. Penny felt her fear subside and instead she felt pity for the woman, looking so desperate.

Penny moved towards the mirror and bent forward, her stomach pressing against the basin, until she was close enough to reach out her hand and touch the glass. Mary's eyes were moving, watching Penny's movements in close detail. For a moment, Penny had wondered if she had somehow been replaced with Mary and that she was looking at herself through Mary's eyes, however as she moved forward and touched the glass, she saw that the reflection was no longer copying Penny's movements. She reached out her hand and moved her fingertips towards the glass, outlining Mary's body until she reached her face. Although all she could feel was the hardness of the glass, the rosiness in Mary's cheeks made Penny sense how soft and warm the real thing would be to touch.

'How can I help you?' she asked. Mary looked back at Penny and held the stare for a few moments, mouth twitching as though she was ready to talk to her, until her stare moved quickly into the distance, as though she had spotted something approaching.

Startled, Penny turned to see what she was looking at, expecting someone to be lingering within the steam. When she was certain she was alone, she turned back to look at the mirror. The desperate Mary had been replaced, the kindness in her eyes had vanished. The Mary who was looking back at her now was the same one who had visited her in the bedroom this morning, her desperate face filling every inch of the mirror. Gasping, Penny moved her hand quickly away as though the glass had shattered and was piercing her skin. The moment she pulled her hand away, the image disappeared and Penny was looking at her own dishevelled reflection staring back at her. She stared harder, willing Mary to come back but after a few moments of no movement, she splashed her face with cold water. Composing herself, she looked in the mirror once more, drew a breath and straightened out her hair. She had now accepted that there was no rational explanation behind what had been going on, but she knew she had no option but to face up to whatever it was that she was supposed to do.

Although the encounter with Mary had left her frightened, she felt a sense of emptiness when she had disappeared. The way she had looked when she asked her what she needed made Penny think there was something she had to do. Something about the way Mary had stared at her made her feel as though she wanted to burst into tears. Her eyes were rich with colour, but they also showed a darkness that made Penny think if she were to crawl inside them she would find nothing there, only emptiness. Breaking through her thoughts she heard gentle sobs echoing throughout the room. She turned around, this time expecting someone to be standing behind her, only to see that it was bare; only left-over steam from the shower filling the room like thick clouds covering the sky.

She heard a scream, 'Stop, don't, I'll do what you want. Please stop!!' The woman's voice was gentle and timid although the loudness of the voice shocked her. Penny could hear a tint of roughness, the syllables not clearly pronounced and there was a rasp in the throat that presented itself when the voice spoke.

'I'm not going to stop! You need to learn your lesson.' A man's rough, but well-spoken, voice echoed around the room. The very sound of the words made Penny shiver as they bounced off the walls. She looked around once more but still there was no one in the room with her.

'I've told you, I accept your offer. I won't change my mind again Sir, I promise. Please don't hurt me or the babe.'

The female voice was begging now, the voice quivering as she pushed the words out behind the sobs.

'Of course I am not going to hurt the child you stupid, pathetic girl. You on the other hand...'

Suddenly a grainy image appeared before her. It was slightly translucent in its appearance almost as though she was watching something which could not get into focus. The image was the doctor, hand raised holding onto a bunch of Mary's hair whose figure had now also appeared in the space before him.

'Stop it!' Penny shouted.

Although the image had not been in front of her for more than a few seconds, the way the doctor gripped onto Mary's head sent alarm bells ringing around her own. She remembered the emptiness in Mary's eyes in the reflection and the slight flicker of hope when Penny asked if she could help. Instinct took control and Penny darted forward. As she extended her hand and took grasp on his arm the same way he had done with hers only moments before, the image turned into something real as though she had pulled him out of whatever film-like state he was being shown in.

His arm stopped in the air and he turned to face Penny, his other hand still firmly holding onto the hair on Mary's head. He looked from his arm to Penny's and Penny was sure that she saw a flicker of shock pass over his features. He looked back again at her hand resting on his and he let go of his grasp on Mary, her head bouncing to the floor as he rose to his feet. Penny flinched when she heard Mary's head smacking the cold tiled floor and was panicked when she did not hear her make a further sound. Penny looked at her arm resting upon his and the realisation that she had tried, and succeeded, to connect to the man began to sink in, remembering the sinister encounter she had with him only moments before. Penny let go of his arm and began taking steps backwards.

'You touched me?' he asked Penny. Penny did not respond but her face gave her answer away. 'You touched me?'

The man turned and looked around. Penny noticed that Mary had vanished and that they were only two people in the room. The man took a deep breath inwards, held it for a few seconds and then let it out loudly, moving his back into a deep arch. He outstretched his arms as he looked up to ceiling and let out a long, horrifying, heaving laugh. The sound bounced off the walls of the bathroom and pierced through Penny's head, stabbing her deeply with each cackle. The noise made Penny close her eyes in pain and she covered her ears with her hands as she tried to block out the terrifying sound. He repeated this laugh three times, each time getting louder than the time before.

It was becoming manic now; he was wild with rage. He started darting towards her, hands outstretched, laughter continuing. Realising the impending danger she was in, she lowered her hands, turned her back on the man and ran as quickly as she could towards the door, slamming it shut behind her as she rushed through, almost throwing herself onto the floor with the force. She turned ready to run away from it but as she faced the hallway she saw a face peering out of the cave-room entrance. It was the older woman she had seen the other day, her hair still crazily wild in a nest around her head. She stepped out of the room and Penny could see that she was wearing a tight fitted bodice and a full skirt. Although it was dirty with holes in it, she knew that the clothing she was wearing was more expensive than the rags she had seen Mary in. The woman regarded her, one eyebrow raised high as she looked Penny up and down.

As Mary had done only moments before, the woman disappeared but then reappeared instantaneously in front of Penny, this time only inches away from her face. Penny

214

didn't feel the same fear she had felt when Mary had visited her in a similar way when she was sleeping, but she felt the temperature of the hallway suddenly plunge and saw the outline of her breath as she tried to breathe, the air in the room becoming tight again.

'Get out of my house.' The figure whispered so quietly that Penny almost didn't hear her. As soon as the last word was spoken, the woman disappeared.

Twenty-Four

After the woman vanished, Penny remained at the door, allowing herself a minute to catch her breath and consider what had just happened. So much had occurred in such a short amount of time; she could barely remember walking into the bathroom, it seemed like so long ago. She remembered the figure in the mirror and the doctor standing over her. Her heartbeat started increasing again as she recalled the fear she had experienced as the grip on her arm became tighter and the realisation that she might not escape started becoming more and more a possibility. Her thoughts were darting around her head in confused directions as if they were in a maze that they were urgently trying to escape. Penny felt a sharp aching sensation in her head as she tried to make sense of it all. She remembered Mary lying on the floor in pain and the doctor standing over her, ready to beat her as she lay vulnerable at his feet.

She wondered if she should go back in to try and help her but then reasoned that she wasn't alive and there was nothing she could do to help her even if she wanted to. She remembered the library and the articles, it was there in black and white; Mary had died within this apartment. Nothing she could do would change that fact; there was nothing she could do to help her. Penny realised that she needed to focus her attention on those who were living and breathing within the apartment and not on those haunting these four walls. Still, the thought of leaving the bathroom knowing that Mary could be left in trouble made her feel uneasy and she stood by the door and listened out for any indication of activity. When there was nothing forthcoming, and Penny's heart had returned to a more manageable rate, she decided she couldn't stand at the door any longer, for fear of the doctor returning to try to inflict more harm.

Once she was certain that she could walk without the risk of falling over, she ran quickly down the hall towards her aunt. She pushed open the bedroom door, expecting to see Anita fast asleep but instead she was at the foot of the bed, pacing up and down the room.

'What happened?' she asked Penny, rushing to her side.

Penny was panting as she said, 'I was in the shower and then... then... hang on, why aren't you in bed; how do you know something happened?'

'I got into bed and just as I was dozing off, I was woken by the bed sheet being dragged downwards. There was nothing in the room but I could sense something was here,' she replied.

Penny took in Anita's appearance before she continued her story, she had pulled on jeans and a jumper but had failed to brush her hair. She looked tired and the lines around her mouth were showing her age even more clearly now she was so worried. Penny didn't even register what Anita had said about the sheet being pulled down as being odd; after what she had just experienced, nothing surprised her any more. Penny filled Anita in on what had happened as quickly as she could, having no interest in recalling the events for longer than she needed, pulling on the nightdress she had managed to grab from the bathroom floor before running out.

'Let's go outside and talk,' she pushed Penny towards the door. Penny grabbed her jumper which was lying on the bed and threw it on as she walked.

Rather than going out towards the door in the kitchen,

her aunt navigated her sidewards and down through the hallway. They stopped when they reached the bureau and Anita opened the double doors that stood to the side of the old writing desk opening onto the small courtyard.

'Why have we come out here?' Penny asked, looking around. The courtyard, although small, was very pretty. Penny had a quick glance out of the windows when they had first arrived but didn't remember it looking as cute as it did right now. In the middle of a nightmare, it seemed to be a place of calm. It had little cobbled tiles scattering the squared floor and a small ornate cherub standing proudly in the middle. Although it looked quite unloved now, she imagined it in bloom and thought how quaint it could look when all the dead and decaying flowers that lined the courtyard were brought back to life.

'I figured that in the kitchen weird things have happened, along the street under those trees weird things happen, in the bathroom weird things happen. I thought we might talk out here; I don't think anything has happened here?' Anita asked hopelessly.

'How did you get it to open? I tried to a few times but it never budged?'

'I came out here when you were in the shower and the doors were open. I figured you might have opened them on your way to the shower?'

'Why would I do that?'

Anita looked at her sheepishly, 'Well now you say it like that, I don't actually know. I thought it was best to come out here for some reason.'

Penny wondered why it was open, but with all the other thoughts in her mind, she couldn't rustle up the energy to give this more thought. 'What shall we do? I'm scared Anita, I can't stand it here a moment longer.' Penny looked around and saw that the sun was now fully up. She thought of her mother and sister sleeping in the room behind them and was envious of their lack of knowledge of what had been going on.

'Well the good thing is that your mother and sister seem unaffected by all of these events. I checked on them when you were in the bathroom and they were sound asleep. I can't imagine that they will wake up and see what is really going on. We only have one more day here,' Anita said.

'Yes, but that means one more evening, I don't think I can stay here one more night. Each encounter gets worse,' Penny replied.

The thought of staying in the apartment made Penny's stomach crawl, she knew she wouldn't be able to handle one more evening of restless sleep and ghostly encounters. Each sighting was getting worse and worse and she was frightened about what would happen next. Although when she had seen Mary's reflection in the mirror she had been keen to help her and felt sad when she had disappeared before she was able to, she also remembered the fear she felt just seconds before when the doctor had grabbed her arm and his laughter like a mad man before she ran out. She suddenly had no desire to try to help Mary any longer.

'Okay, okay. We either leave the apartment now, or wait for the others to wake up and leave,' Anita suggested. Penny nodded in agreement, thinking the former idea to be best. She knew the other two were totally unaware of what had been going on, but she also knew they had to leave immediately.

'I saw the other woman, when I left the bathroom. She was calm unlike the other two. She whispered to me that we should leave the house. I think it was some sort of warning.'

'And you haven't seen this woman much have you? Maybe that was the second body they found, the wife?'

Penny was annoyed that she hadn't put this together herself. Of course, it made sense it would be the wife. She could tell by her appearance and the frantic look in her eyes that she wasn't all there; maybe she was as crazy as the stories they had been told.

'Okay, we need to leave. Come, let's get the others out. We'll tell them all about it when we leave the apartment.' Anita turned her niece around by the shoulders and pushed her back towards the opened doors.

Unexpectedly they heard a sound coming from somewhere in the courtyard. They stopped talking and looked around. The noise sounded familiar. Penny strained her ears to hear the noise more distinctively. She felt hopeful as she recognised the buzzing sound, something was vibrating. Confused they both looked at each other until Penny realised that the sound was coming from her. She patted herself down and realised that her phone was in the pocket of the jumper she had pulled on in a rush.

'Oh my God it's my phone!' she exclaimed. She pulled it out and saw a flash of light blinking from the top, indicating that she had received a notification. She glanced at the screen and saw several text messages and a few missed calls had been received.

'It's amazing, there's reception here! Why didn't we check earlier?' Penny was annoyed at herself for not checking this part of the apartment for reception sooner and thought of all the conversations she could have had with Jason before now, feeling suddenly elated that she had been given a chance to reconnect to the outside world.

She unlocked the screen hurriedly and scrolled through the notifications, trying to figure out what to check first. As she was reviewing the notification bar, the phone began to vibrate in her hand. The notification flashing on the screen showed that a voicemail had been left for her. Her heart began to somersault with hope. She pressed the button and placed the phone to her ear.

'Pen, it's me.'

'It's Jason,' Penny mouthed to Anita

'Listen, I've been doing some research on the place you are in. To be honest, I don't really like what I have found out, even if I don't believe in all that supernatural stuff. Well I guess you don't either, well not really, that's what made me look into it. Anyway, listen Pen, I don't really want to tell you this over a voicemail, so can you call me back please? Soon. Love you, bye.'

Penny replayed the message and looked at Anita, her heart racing as she wondered what Jason had discovered. The phone beeped again with a second voicemail. This time Penny put the phone on loudspeaker so her aunt could hear.

'Pen, it's me again. I know you don't have any reception in that place, but I really need you to call me. You're right about what you said, the legend is that place you're in is haunted, big time apparently. There are a lot of stories that don't end well. I'm sure it is all very superstitious and not real, but I really think you should leave… at least call me back…'

And then a third message.

'Penny, I called your landlady, the one who rented the apartment to you. The apartment is as advertised and was completely refurnished two years ago. I don't think you're in the right place. The woman hung up on me when I started asking questions. Anyway, I researched that woman, that Mary you texted me about, she was pregnant but that is where the story gets twisted… Listen Penny, I really think you should…'

The phone went dead.

Twenty-Five

She stared at the phone in frustration; it had run out of battery. She was really annoyed as she ran back into the apartment to charge it. She hadn't used the bloody thing the whole trip, how could it be out of battery the one moment when she needed it the most?

Running towards her bedroom to grab the charger, she had almost forgotten that her mother and sister were peacefully sleeping, oblivious about what was happening to her and Anita. She clambered noisily into the room, she didn't care at this point if she woke them now or in five minutes time, they were getting up and out of the apartment one way or another. She cursed herself for not taking the opportunity earlier to fill them in and get them out; if she had she wouldn't have had to experience the terrifying encounter in the bathroom.

Not caring to look at her family enjoying a peaceful sleep when she could no longer remember what that felt like, she looked around for her charger. She crouched down onto the floor to pick her bag up from underneath the bed where she remembered kicking it a few days previously. She hadn't turned on the lights when she rushed in and the darkness in the room meant she had to use her arms to navigate around. Outstretching her arm, she moved it back and forth under the bed in an attempt to touch her lumpy bag and push it out the other end. Despite her attempts, the bag didn't come flying out as she had hoped and the more her hands fumbled in the dark, getting caught up in cobwebs and dust that had been gathering over the years, the more frustrated she felt and had to consciously stop herself from exploding in rage, taking in deep breaths as she tried to compose herself.

Now fully aware that it wasn't under the bed, she needed to stop and think about where she would have put it, trying to push away her irritation about the level of thought she had to put into a simple task such as locating her bag. She stood up and looked around at where else it could be. As she was scanning the room, she stopped as she stared at the bed. She didn't have to look twice in astonishment this time; there was no doubt about what was in front of her.

There, standing proudly in the middle of the room, as if it was mocking her, was the single bed she had seen a few nights before. Her sleeping mother and sister had disappeared and the bed was empty and bare. Penny was no longer confused as she had been the first time the bed made an appearance. This time around she was livid, furious that everything kept changing in front of her eyes and that every time she came a step closer to finding some sort of normality, it was cruelly snatched away from her. It was as though someone was playing a game with her and enjoyed seeing her become more and more distressed with each minute that passed. There was no doubt in her mind now that what was happening was real. It was real and Penny was fed up.

She marched out of the room and ran back towards the courtyard where Anita was waiting. She had planned to grab her by the arm and lead her outside of the apartment where they would wait until the other women woke up, when they reappeared from wherever they had been moved to. Penny had had enough. She stopped as she reached the bureau in the hallway and looked to her left where she had just exited through the door moments earlier. She was expecting the doors to be wide open, Anita waiting for Penny's return in anticipation, eager to continue listening to the messages. Come to think of it, why didn't Anita chase after her when she ran out of the courtyard? She had seen how stressed she was, surely she would be just as keen as Penny was to hear what else Jason had to say. She took a step towards the door and saw that Anita wasn't waiting for her and had left the small courtyard empty.

Penny thought of looking around the apartment to see where she had disappeared to, but knew it would be no use; Anita hadn't followed her after all. Unsure what to do for the best, Penny stood in the hall helplessly. She felt overwhelmed and engulfed with emotions, no longer able to keep in what had been bottled inside for any longer. She felt her shoulders curve over as the weight of what she had been carrying began to cripple her. Everything around her was changing the way she thought about life, everything she had ever believed in. She had tried and tried to be rational but she could no longer force herself to believe in anything other than what she was seeing. Her family had disappeared in front of her eyes and she suddenly felt incredibly alone, as though she had been staying within the apartment for the whole duration of the trip totally by herself.

Her heart felt as though it had burst within her chest and what was pouring out of it was a sea of tears. The pain was hammering out of her in deep, heaving moans. She no longer felt that she had enough energy to stand and the weight of her misery pushed her onto the floor. She looked around again, hopeful that someone would step out and tell her what to do, she wanted this to be over and more importantly, she wanted to leave.

As she turned around from her seating position, she saw the door to the bathroom was open, lit by artificial lighting. Although only a few moments ago, the exposed windows filled the apartment with daylight, now it was dark and miserable with not a hint of natural light to be seen. Screams emerged from inside. Screams different to the ones she had heard before. These screams were screams of pain. Agonising, terrible pain.

Penny didn't know what on earth to do. She wanted desperately to stay sitting in the position she was in, consumed with her pain and self-pity, but she felt a strong urge inside her, trying to push her forwards towards the door. She stayed in her ball on the floor for a few moments longer, allowing her tears to run dry on her cheeks. Despite her head telling her to ignore it, she knew what she had to do. Reluctantly, she made her way to the bathroom, feet trembling as she went. She stood outside the room and moved her ear towards the door. She thought she ought to go in, but the voice inside her head was still yelling at her to stay put. The screams were getting louder, the shrill tone piercing through her ears.

Her trembling hands pushed open the door slowly, even though her mind willed them with all its might not to move. Looking through the crack in the door, Penny saw Mary lying in a puddle of blood, her back touching the floor and her legs open either side of her, soles of her feet firmly on the floor. She was wild with pain, sweat dripping from her tossing forehead, seeping through her dress which was now slowly turning a deep red as the blood from the floor began to spread upwards.

The screams were coming again, this time in shorter intervals. Penny could see that Mary was also panting and realised in horror that she was giving birth. Her wobbly hands reached her mouth to prevent her from shouting out, but then she took in the scene once more and realised that something about it didn't seem right. She had watched enough birthing television shows to know that the sounds she was hearing were not normal.

She saw the doctor emerge from the corner of the bathroom in front of Mary, covered in blood. Without seeming to notice the urgency of the situation, he glided slowly over to Mary and crouched down. He said some words into her ear quietly which Penny was unable to hear and with a final scream, a tiny bundle slipped into his arms.

The room became eerily silent.

Penny could see that Mary was frantically trying to catch her breath whilst trying, but failing, to push herself up from the bathroom floor which was covered in her seeping blood. Why hadn't the baby screamed? What was wrong? Penny anxiously threw a stare at Mary and could tell that she too was thinking the same, her eyes pleading to the doctor for some news, panic covering every inch of her face.

The doctor turned, the silent baby cradled in his arms, and marched towards the door. He zoomed past Penny as though she wasn't there. Mary was left alone in the room in a puddle of her own blood. Her eyes did not move from the spot the doctor had just left and she continued to try to pull herself upwards to follow him out of the door. In her desperate attempt to move, she slipped and ended up face down as she tried to crawl towards him. Her sobs were muffled as she breathed in her own blood which was like a swimming pool surrounding her.

Twenty-Six

As soon as Mary's face hit the bathroom floor, she disappeared. Penny turned around to see that the room had been restored to how it was before the horrific scene had occurred. The tiles on the floor were bright and shiny, not a trace of blood was left; natural light immersing the room in sunlight.

Penny was left horrified at what she had just seen. She felt anguish for poor Mary who had to deliver her child in such horrific conditions. She was aware that they were somewhat luckier now with the medical advances that had been made, but she was certain that Mary's delivery could not have been a normal birth. She had looked in so much pain and seemed so defenceless with no one around to offer her some much-needed support. Although she knew her actions were unable to change the past, she wished there was something she could have done for Mary and a part of her regretted not running straight through those doors to hold tightly onto her hand. The silence that had filled the room in the absence of the child's first cry was haunting her thoughts, telling her she should have done something.

Was it a coincidence that she had stumbled upon this scene? Somehow Penny didn't think it was. Mary had wanted her to see this, she was sure of it. She could no longer stay standing outside the bathroom, feeling claustrophobic from the crushing sadness that had engulfed the air. She ensured the door was firmly shut, desperate for the overpowering sadness captured within the room to stay there. Her mind recalled her first apprehension on looking into the room, seeing it so dark and miserable. Now she understood why the room appeared so dark to her, after witnessing the horrific event, the darkness of the room captured the mood perfectly.

She turned and began to make her way down the hallway, looking for Anita. She noted the hallway didn't look any different to every other time she had walked down it; at the same time, something about it seemed unnervingly dissimilar. The natural lighting had returned but she began to cough as she caught a whiff of the strong, pungent smell of mustiness swimming around her. Covering her mouth with her sleeve, she continued walking until she heard banging coming from her side as she approached the bureau and the glass patio doors. She stopped and saw Anita frantically knocking on the door and rattling the handle, her body pushed up against the glass.

Penny rushed forwards, grabbing at the door and looking at her aunt, tears rolling down her cheeks once more. She was elated that Anita was standing there, even though she looked panicked, frantically smashing her hand against the glass in an attempt to escape. Her face lit up when she saw Penny and she began to knock on the glass even harder. Penny pushed and pulled at the door with her body but despite using all her force, the doors would not open, the same way they hadn't all the other times she had tried. She pulled her gaze away from Anita and turned towards the desk, looking for an object to smash through the glass.

Without warning, the bright rays of sunshine which were warming the apartment disappeared and darkness occupied the space around her. She spun around and darted towards the doors, looking for Anita, but she was not there. Penny pressed her head against the glass and looked out onto the courtyard which was glistening in the moonlight. She let out another groan and slammed her feet on the floor beneath her in anger. Why, whenever she was so close, did something get snatched away from her?

With the moonlight, the smell had returned. Penny glanced back once more through the glass to double-check Anita was not standing there and when she saw no sign of life, she began to make her way towards the kitchen. This all started there, maybe it was where she could finish it. She was no longer the girl who only moments ago was sitting in a heap on the floor, flooded by her own tears. She walked with confidence towards the heart of the apartment. Finally she had had enough, she was sick and tired of whatever it was within the apartment bothering her and she needed to let it know.

The smell was getting stronger and more powerful the nearer she got to the kitchen. She tried to resist covering her mouth from the smell, which she saw as a sign of weakness, and instead pushed herself forwards, wading through the thick air until she reached the doorway. As she approached she could hear faint voices and stopped at the doorway trying to listen to what was being said before she barged in, trying to judge her safety and exactly what she was getting herself into.

'What did you do to him?' A woman's scream. 'What did you do to my Joseph?'

Penny peered around the side of the doorway. Mary was standing with her back to Penny, still wearing her bloodied robes, hands clutched onto the doctor's arm.

'Tell me what you did to him!!' Her voice got louder; she screamed the last sentence from the top of her lungs as if it were the last thing she would ever say.

Penny could tell that the doctor was not one who appreciated being spoken to with such venom and he pulled his arm violently away from Mary's grasp, shaking her hands off him and when they were free, brought them down firmly across her face. Penny heard his arm whistle as it travelled through the air towards Mary, as if warning her of its approach. It was a blow so forceful that it sent Mary flying across the room, landing her in a heap on the floor.

Out of nowhere, Penny felt a pull on her arm from behind.

'Penny,' a voice said.

Penny thought her body had exited her skin she jumped so high in surprise and fear that someone had grabbed her. She was so consumed in the voices she was hearing in the kitchen she hadn't been on alert for anything approaching her from behind. Protectively, she swung around and raised her arm to push away whatever it was that was holding her until the raised arm was also grabbed to stop the movement.

'Jesus, calm down, it's me.' Her hands were being lowered.

She let out a relieved sigh as she recognised the sound of the voice and felt her body retreat into its skin when she realised that it was Anita who had grabbed her. Pleased it was her aunt who had reappeared, she pulled her into her arms, engulfing her in the embrace.

'What happened? I couldn't get you out, then it turned into night.' Penny turned and once again saw that light was filling the room. The smell too had lifted and Penny found it easier to breath without the horrible stench polluting her lungs.

'When you darted out of the garden, the doors just slammed behind you as though someone was waiting for you to leave. I heard the sound of a click and I couldn't open the door. I rattled really loudly but no one came. Honestly, I was close to climbing up those walls to escape,' Anita said.

Penny almost laughed at the thought of Anita having to climb over the walls, but the severity of the situation prevented her from doing so. She suddenly thought of her mother and sister and began running towards the room they were sleeping in. Anita stood in her way to stop her.

'I checked on them first. They're okay, still sleeping. Soundly in fact. I thought of waking them but thought I ought to check on you first. I didn't think I could face telling your mother I lost you in pure daylight'

'But it wasn't daylight, it was night?' Penny said, looking around, confused by the sudden changes in time.

'Well I saw you come running out and trying to open the doors for me. Then all sudden you just disappeared. Like literally, you were there one minute and the next you were not!' Anita looked pale and shaken. Penny realised that she must have given her a fright. While she had been involved with what had been happening within the apartment, it was only because Penny had been dragging her in. She hadn't physically seen anything with her own eyes, yet.

'What happened?' Anita asked.

Penny told Anita what happened in the bathroom and what she had just seen in the kitchen.

'God!! So, the baby didn't survive? Is that what she wants you to do? Confirm her child died?' Anita queried.

Penny was trying to figure that one out herself; she hadn't had a moment to collect her thoughts to even consider it.

'I don't know. I mean, yes, the baby has some connection to it, but I'm not sure what. It seems there must be more to it.' She started pacing around the kitchen, 'It's him, I'm sure there is something I need to work out about him. What is it?'

She stopped as something caught her attention in her peripheral vision. The pictures she had seen when she first entered the apartment. Penny went running towards them and headed straight to the drawing of the two people by the unfinished house. She knew they had changed positions over the course of their stay; she wanted to know where they were now. Penny almost toppled over with fright as her eyes rested on the frame that was attached to the wall. The woman was no longer in the picture. Instead, the doctor's face filled the body of the sketch. His sinister grin wide; his eyes coloured in black.

She turned to speak to Anita. As she spun around, her head came face to face with another. She thought Anita had come too close to her but when she tried to back away, she realised it wasn't her aunt.

It was Mary. The version of Mary who had come to visit her last night, who had pinned her down on her bed and told her to leave.

As soon as she recognised the face, it zoomed closer to hers, so close that she felt the breeze of her breath hitting her skin. Without meaning to, Penny scrunched her nose as she tried to move away from the smell, realising now that it was the exact stench she detected earlier. She had been pushed backwards so vigorously that she was propelled against the wall and heard the shatter of glass as her back connected to the picture frame and knocked it to the floor.

'GET OUT. NOOOOOOOOW...' Mary screamed.

Twenty-Seven

'What was that?' Anita said, terror in her voice.

Penny looked around but Mary had disappeared.

'You saw that?' Penny asked. Anita nodded.

'Penny, I think we need to get the others up and leave. NOW!' She pulled on Penny's arm but Penny shrugged it off.

'No, we're so close now I can feel it. We need to know what it is they want.'

'Don't be so stupid! What makes you think that they want something, maybe they don't want anything? Maybe they just want you!!' Anita was angry, her voice was raised and she was shaking. Penny knew that she was talking sense, but she didn't care.

'I'm staying. Feel free to leave if you want to!' She turned her back on Anita, trying to figure out what to do next.

She walked back to where Mary was standing when she was thrown across the room. She suddenly felt confident and unafraid. Surprised by her sudden change in character, Penny felt empowered. Despite the warnings, Penny refused to leave. How dare this woman come in and out of Penny's visions, attack her and expect her to leave? Penny was angry that she had been manipulated this way and was determined to see it through till the end. Perhaps she was delirious from sleep deprivation but she was unwavering. She wasn't ready to leave yet, suddenly feeling as though she had enough courage to challenge whatever ghost was enticing her.

'What do you want, Mary? Doctor Parks? Can you hear me? You coward!' Penny screamed.

'Penny! Don't!' Anita said, pulling at her arm.

'Do you only mess with ghosts?' Penny ignored her aunt, shrugging her off. The smell was back, strong and pungent. Penny knew she was close to finding out what it was they wanted with her.

'Penny! Stop! I'm telling you! We need to leave, NOW!!' Anita was pleading with her but Penny was taking no notice, she was marching up and down the room, stopping only to turn in circles, willing something to reappear.

In a massive swoop, Penny's hair flew into the air and she felt her jumper sway away from her body as though someone had opened a door and let an almighty wind enter the apartment. Penny raised her hands to cover them from the effect of the sharp, strong breeze smacking her harshly across the face. When she opened them, she saw the older lady she had seen earlier in the day standing in front of Anita who was seemingly unaware of the apparition. The head was cocked to the side the same way it had been when she saw her earlier. Anita saw Penny's reaction and walked towards her, mouth open as though she was saying something but Penny could not hear the words she was speaking.

The woman glided over to where Penny was standing and grabbed her by the hand. She tried to pull away but couldn't escape the icy clasp.

'You need to leave the house now! You're not welcome here. If you don't leave now, bad things are going to happen,' she whispered into Penny's ear.

Penny tried to pull away but couldn't loosen her arm from the grip. Noticing Penny's resistance, the woman tightened her hold and as she did, Penny began to feel light-headed and woozy, the room swaying before her as she continued in her attempt to be free. She shook her head, trying to shake away the feeling but as her head began moving from side to side, she couldn't remember what she was doing or where she was. Her mind was in a daze and she struggled to remember what it was that she was supposed to do. Faintly she could see a woman in front of her, coming in and out of focus. She was aware that she was keeping her head straight but the room around her began to spin. Penny tried to pull her hand free but the sudden movement was enough to make wooziness accelerate and she felt herself descending onto the ground, hitting the floor hard as she reached the cold tiles.

*

Disoriented, Penny slowly opened her eyes expecting to be waking up in bed next to Jason. She thought she had been asleep for hours although as she tried to move her head, she realised it was heavy. She began to regain consciousness and little droplets of fear started to enter her mind, although she couldn't piece together why. A throbbing pain in the bottom of her back began to pound gently and she flinched as she tried to sit upright. Her hands moved to the space next to her to push herself upwards and she was alarmed to feel the coldness of tiles beneath her. Memories started flowing through her mind as though she were watching a montage of her trip and the reality of where she was and what had been happening pounded down upon her. Her peaceful wakefulness lasted only seconds before she was confronted with her harsh reality.

She jumped to her feet. Why was she on the floor and where was Anita? She remembered hitting the floor and the sharp pain in her neck as she fell awkwardly. She looked around and drew a breath when she saw where she was standing. She was unsteady on her feet but knew that she had not woken where she had fallen. There was no doubt that she was in the kitchen of the apartment and nothing obvious about it had changed, yet something seemed odd. To the side of the room was the massive fireplace with the old wooden table centred in the middle, however Penny saw that they no longer looked tired and overused. Instead they looked fresh and new. She had to adjust her eyes to the brightness filling the room, the brilliant white seeming unnatural.

'Here listen to this… I heard something earlier when I went up. Lady Peel has a plan to get rid of Agatha.'

Penny jumped as she heard the strong Cockney accent coming from her left. She turned and saw a woman, hair scraped back tightly in a bun on the top of her head, hand pushing a ladle around something that was bubbling away on the stove in front of her. The smell of whatever was in the pan travelled towards Penny, causing her stomach to rumble in hunger.

'What's that, then?' A younger woman wearing a maid's outfit brushed past Penny, not noticing she was there.

'They want to get rid of 'er don't they? She's driving 'em nearly as mad as she is herself. There's a doctor apparently, one that is prepared to marry 'er they say, although why someone would want to marry 'er, Gawd only knows.'

'Well, they're on their way out ain't they? Lord and Lady Peel; look at the size of this house, I think there's one good reason why 'e'd want to marry that crazy bat!'

'You should mind your mouth, she's not a bad woman is poor Agatha, just misunderstood. You two would be kind to mind your own business!' Another short, stocky woman entered the room. 'I've served the Peels for thirty years and seen her as a child; Agatha just needs some attention is all. The love of a young man may be all that is needed. Is that soup ready yet, Martha?'

The two women shut their mouths as soon as this woman came in, throwing mischievous glances at each other as the older lady scolded them. Martha poured some thick broth-like liquid into a bowl and handed it to the woman. The older lady gave the pair of gossiping women a disapproving look with the raise of an eyebrow and marched out of the room, broth in hand, towards Penny. Penny held her breath, not knowing what the woman would say to her, seeing her standing there in the middle of her kitchen. She needn't have worried, the woman walked straight past her and through the open black door by the fireplace, not noticing that she was there.

The black door was open. Finally, she was close to seeing what was behind the door that had been locked for the duration of their stay. Seeing her chance, she rushed forward to follow the woman up the stairs. The staircase was disappointing, Penny was ashamed to admit. Part of her was expecting Anita's tales to be true and anticipated cobwebs and skulls to be lingering in the shadows. Instead, a dusty plain staircase led to another open door. As she reached the top, the woman turned left. Penny walked out and was astounded by how elaborate and grand the upstairs was. The ceilings were high and airy, decorative chandeliers hung sporadically at intervals above her, the wood carvings on the wall shining vividly in the light that flooded the area.

Seeing that the woman had scurried off, Penny had to jog down the long hallway to catch up. She saw the woman standing in the doorway to a room at the far end of the corridor and she was startled to notice that the beige work dress she had been wearing only moments before had now changed to a black lace gown and she was no longer holding the steaming cup of broth she had handled so carefully as she walked up the stairs. The sounds of sobs travelled from inside the room and when Penny moved forward, still going unnoticed, she saw a woman in a heap on the bed, curled up in the foetal position.

'Now, now Agatha, you really must be getting up. Doctor Parks is coming back over this afternoon and we need to get you ready.' She marched towards the window and opened the curtains that had been drawn, puffing them outwards, causing dust to explode out into the stuffy room.

Penny followed her and looked out of the window. There was a door to the side of the glass and as she peered out she noticed black railings supported steps that led up to the bedroom from the floor below. Recognising the staircase, Penny knew it must be the same one she had reluctantly climbed up on her exploration to see if anyone was staying above them. She realised she was standing directly above the kitchen. She spun around the room and spotted the bed she had been able to make out when she had peered through the mouldy window.

'I know you have a sore heart with the death of your parents, but life must go on. You need to find a man to marry otherwise you'll be on your own and us staff will be out on our ear. You don't want that now, do you?'

The crying woman pushed herself out of bed and moved across to the dressing table adjacent to the bed. Penny recognised her immediately and although she appeared younger, there was no mistaking that this was the woman who had gripped her so hard it had resulted in her being transported to a different world. Her hair was no longer tangled in a knotty mess and she could tell from the fitted bodice she was wearing that she had a slim and youthful physique.

Agatha groaned and moved towards the maid, her feet heavy as though she had to drag them across the floor against their will. She stopped when she reached the centre of the room. Her face turned towards where Penny was standing. Startled that she appeared to be able to see her, Penny held her breath in an attempt to become invisible. The others hadn't seen her; there was a chance she couldn't either. She had been curious more than anything up until now but as Agatha turned slowly to face her, she felt her previously normal heartbeat picking up into a steady thump.

'Leave... NOW!!'

Twenty-Eight

'Penny?' Anita's voice brought her back to the present. 'Penny!'

'I'm okay.' Penny pulled herself up off the floor. She looked around the room and realised she had been transported back to the present. The rustiness of the kitchen was back and Anita was leaning over her, face frantic with worry.

'I saw her, the older lady, although she isn't really older, she is about my age, she lives up there, I went up the stairs.' Penny panted and pointed to the black door which was once again firmly locked.

'Penny, you're not making sense. Listen, we need to go. I'm getting your mother up.' Anita let go of her niece and started to walk towards the doorway.

'No, we can't. I saw something, I need to find out...'

'NO! This is enough, I'm scared and I don't like it. Accept what I'm saying, we are leaving. Get your things together at once!'

Penny opened her mouth to argue against Anita's comments but closed it again. She thought about the woman she had just seen. Part of her wanted to follow Anita out of the door and leave the apartment, she had been warned on more than one occasion by these people to leave and surely the warnings meant something. Penny knew deep down that she should listen to them, but she couldn't shake the feeling that there was something she needed to do. She remembered the feeling she had when in the woman's presence, whom she now knew to be Agatha. She hadn't felt fear like she had with Mary and the doctor. The encounters of the three people didn't make sense, they didn't add up and she couldn't figure out what had happened here in the apartment. But she also knew Anita was right, they needed to leave.

Anita left the room and Penny staggered after her, still slightly dizzy as confused thoughts somersaulted through her brain. When she was finally steady on her feet, she was almost knocked back over when a sudden gush of air blew in her face. She steadied herself and as her hair stopped blowing around her, she focused and saw the doctor had suddenly appeared in front of her, the shock of his sudden reappearance taking her off guard.

'Yes Penny, you should stop now Penny. We don't want any harm to come to you, my dear Penny.' His voice was quiet as he whispered the words but to Penny it seemed as though he was screaming; it was the only noise she could hear. The way he repeated her name showed her he was mocking her; his sideways smile was back, this time showing his yellowing teeth.

Penny could feel sweat forming at the top of her brow and the bottom of her back as she tried to piece together what was happening. She spun around the room in a pathetic attempt to look for a way to escape from him, although she knew the only exit out of the room was through the corridor to the bedrooms or out of the front door, and he was blocking both. As she finished her full turn, the doctor was in front of her once again, appearing in front of her as though he was floating around the room.

'You want to talk do you, Penny?' He emphasised the P of her name, dragging it out, making Penny squirm as she heard her name being repeated by this sadistic man.

'What do you want? Why am I seeing all of this? What did you do to Mary?' she whispered when she knew there was no getting away from him.

The doctor let out his shrill laugh one more time. 'You women are all so stupid. So serious, thinking you are important, but you're not. You're not worth anything. You are worthless.'

'All I wanted was a child and that stupid bitch was going to give me one. She couldn't even do that right; even the child did not want to be raised in existence when a thing like that was its mother. Then there was the other girl but she was too mad. And then... then... then you come along... well... that means...'

He was even closer now, she could smell his disgusting breath trickling across her face. The evil glint in his eye had lightened and Penny saw that he was enjoying himself, the smile across his face getting broader the closer he got to her. When he was within touching distance, he reached out and ran his icy, thin finger across her cheek. She felt his long fingernail scratch at her skin. Penny had to try with all her might to hold the bile that was pummelling upwards from the pit of her stomach, the revulsion of him touching her almost too much to bear.

'Well now I don't have to worry about Mary. Now... I have you,' he said as he moved his other hand to reach out and enclose her neck.

Penny managed to slither downwards and escape his grasp. She was on her knees and was trying to crawl away to the door. Her eyes searched the room for Anita and she kept them firmly on the doorway, willing her aunt to walk back in and help her. She thought about getting to her feet and running but she did not think she had enough strength in her and the time she wasted thinking about it was too late. Her head was yanked backwards as she was pulled upwards, forcing her to stand although she didn't want to. She felt her hair tug at her scalp as it was wrenched up, the excruciating pain causing her to scream out loud, her hands flapping around helplessly as she tried to free herself.

'Now now. Best to be a quiet little girl. You don't want to end up like that poor bitch. Women should not attempt to rise above their stations. She thought she could dishonour herself, dishonour this household and then deliver me a good for nothing child!!' His leg connected to her stomach and Penny doubled over in pain, clutching the spot where his knee smacked sharply against her abdomen. She was back on the floor now but his hands did not loosen the tight grip he had on her hair.

'In the end, she was worthless. So that is what I gave her. A death she deserved.'

The doctor moved his free hand across her face and Penny felt the swelling begin automatically, pain searing across the right side of her face. He pushed her away from him this time and Penny lay face down against the tiled floor. Her lips felt rubbery and she could taste the sharp, metallic bitterness of her own blood as she realised it was dripping onto the floor forming a puddle around her. Although the pain was something she had never felt before, she knew she had to get up. If she stayed on the floor like a helpless victim, she was vulnerable to whatever blow he would inflict upon on her next. She didn't have time to properly consider what he had just said to her but something about the words he spoke made her realise she was in danger of more than just physical harm.

She raised her head and saw the doctor gliding quickly back towards her, looking calm and unfazed by the brutality he had just inflicted and with that, Penny felt something inside her switch. She was angry. Angry that she had allowed herself to fall victim without giving him a fight. She had never been so fragile in her life and she would be damned if she allowed herself to be kicked about by a glorified ghost. She ignored every screaming vein in her body as she pushed herself off the floor, trying to tell herself it didn't really hurt, it wasn't real and she was able to stand upright, staring at him from a hunched position in the middle of the room.

Despite her bravery, her body doubled over when she took in the sudden, overpowering stench that had entered the room, poisoning her lungs. She tried to take in deep breaths but it was no use. Each intake she took just filled her body with more of the disgusting air, making her lethargic and nauseous. Hands resting on her knees, she fought against the smell and straightened her back.

'You shouldn't have fought against me,' the doctor came racing towards her.

The pain coming from Penny's stomach was so strong she couldn't move her body away from the man despite using all her will. Her only defence was her hands and she used them to wave them in front of her in rapid movements, frantically trying to attack the doctor on his approach. It was no use, her weakness prevented her from getting a good swing at him and he once again held her hands tightly in his clasp.

The doctor was no longer showing his wicked grin, instead he looked at her straight in the eyes, his own oozing danger. She saw that one of his hands was free and watched, almost in slow motion, him move it from behind his back. Something shiny reflected off the little light that entered the room and Penny realised that he was holding something sharp and he was aiming it at her.

The room suddenly became blurry and she no longer felt any pain. Everything was spinning and as she hit the floor, she heard the doctor's final laugh echoing in the background.

Twenty-Nine

'Hello Agatha.' Doctor Park's voice filled the room. Penny shuddered and tried to flee away from the danger, remembering the shiny object that had been travelling in her direction at speed. She expected to feel all-consuming pain as she rolled herself over and was surprised to notice she didn't even flinch as she moved onto her side. Her tongue felt the inside of her lip, expecting to come against a large rubbery cushion from where he had struck her, but there was nothing. Realising this was her chance, she jumped up and started to run in the direction of where she thought the door was.

'Hello,' a timid and gentle voice spoke from behind her, stopping Penny from reaching the doorway.

'It's been a year and still no child. What is wrong with you? I knew I shouldn't have married you.'

'I didn't want to marry you either. Why don't you just leave?'

She turned towards the voices and saw that she was back in Agatha's room. Agatha had seemed to have aged since she last saw her, her hair had become more tousled and deep, dark shadows were lining her drooping eyes. The doctor was standing with his back to Agatha and she could see from his broad shoulders that he spoke with confidence and ease. He spun around and ran towards her.

'I need a child. You're going to give me one.'

He had her pinned against the bed. She screamed as she

tried to wrestle him off, her body scrambling to free herself from his hold. He was stronger than her, overpowering her with his arms and the weight of his body now resting upon hers. Penny watched in horror as she saw the doctor rip off Agatha's clothes to expose her body before taking off his own. Despite the pain that the doctor had caused Penny and regardless of whether this was real, Penny knew she couldn't stand by and watch what she thought was going to happen next. She rushed forward as Agatha's screams became more and more hysterical.

As she reached the bed, the doctor disappeared and Agatha was perched on the end as though nothing had happened. She was fully clothed but she was sitting facing the window, looking out towards the trees that lined the path. Penny heard a noise from behind her and saw the older maid hurrying in with a tray held in her hands.

'The doctor said you need to take this, Miss. It will help you to sleep.'

'Where are all the other maids, Dorothy?' Agatha didn't turn to look at her when she spoke.

'Well the doctor has sent them all away, Miss. Said you need some space and time to get better and he can tend to you himself. He has paid everyone and even I am off today. Going to head down to see my nephew, he has a wife and a young child you see and... Oh. Sorry Miss, I didn't realise what I was saying.'

'So, I shall be left alone then?'

'Well yes, apart from Doctor Parks of course, and you will be safe with him. He knows how to look after you. He said you need to keep drinking this and you will get better. Oh, and young Mary is staying for a day or two, she is going to bring you up your food.'

'Mary?' Agatha's face turned towards the maid now.

'Yes Miss, the younger one. She hasn't got any family around here you see and she was keen to stay on and offer you her support. You'll be looked after, Miss. The doctor will send for us when you're healed.'

Agatha turned and stared directly at Penny. Penny rushed forward to ask her what she wanted from her, why she wanted her to leave the apartment. She knew she could see her and she'd had enough of playing games. She rushed forward and like so many times previously in the apartment, the figure disappeared in front of her just as she was within touching distance.

She was back in the kitchen now and she couldn't tell if she was relieved or disappointed. She heard noises in the background become louder as she allowed herself to fall back into the present.

*

'Are you bleeding? There is blood on your jumper' Anita's voice came into focus and she saw her standing in front of her, her arms underneath Penny's shoulders, trying to direct her towards a chair. 'Jesus, Penny. Can you walk? We need to get you out of here!'

'I can't leave now, I saw things…'

'One minute you were standing there, the next you were sent flying through the air!' Her voice was high-pitched. 'I can't wake the others, they won't wake up. We need to get you out of here.' She tried to pull on her arm but Penny wouldn't move, glued to the spot in the middle of the kitchen.

'I saw Agatha and the doctor and Mary. I think I know what happened, or I know some of it. I think…'

'It doesn't matter what you think. We need to get you out of here.'

'No, we need to solve this. We need to get back through the door. I need to get through, they want something from me.'

'Penny!'

'No Anita. I am doing this, either with or without your help.'

'Well you're on your own. This is a bad bad idea...' Anita's voice trailed off into the distance.

*

Penny saw a figure walk past her through the open doorway. It was Mary; she looked at Penny, 'We told you to leave. Now it's too late. It's too late for you and for your...' She was distracted and turned to look to her left.

Penny looked around the room and saw that Anita had disappeared and the kitchen was once again new and shiny. She followed Mary's gaze and saw the doctor standing by the stove, the smell of cooking now in the air, filling the room with its warm aroma.

'What are you doing, sir?' Mary asked as she walked past Penny, now seemingly unaware that she was standing there.

The doctor jumped at the sound of her voice and Penny saw that he placed his arm behind his back. He was hiding something, she thought, although she wasn't sure that Mary had noticed.

'Putting in the Lady's medicine. Be a good girl and take this up to her will you.' He walked towards her and stopped as he reached her standing point, hand reaching out to touch her protruding belly. 'Not long now until the baby arrives and then everything will go as planned.'

Penny saw the tears behind Mary's eyes that she was trying to conceal, although the doctor seemed not to notice.

She nodded politely at him and crossed the room to put the broth into a bowl and onto a tray. Her stomach had expanded even more and Penny wondered how her slight and petite frame was able to withstand the weight of the enormous bump that was protruding out of her. She realised that she must be nearly due and saw the discomfort in her face as she struggled to pick up the heavy tray. Of course, the doctor paid no regard to assist her in a duty which she clearly should not be doing in her condition. Penny watched him watch her as she stumbled up the stairs, the evil, wicked grin now spreading across his face.

Concerned that the weight of her stomach would cause her to topple over, Penny followed Mary from behind, up the stairs and into Agatha's room. Penny inhaled as she entered and saw how much Agatha had deteriorated since she last saw her. She was lying in her bed, covers drawn to just below her chin, the cheekbones that had once been clearly defined in beauty, now projected out from her face as though they were the only bones left in her skeleton body. Her skin showed a tint of grey and her hair fell in limp, coarse waves around her shoulders. Penny knew from the look of her fragile body that she didn't have much longer left.

Agatha watched Mary as she entered the room and placed the tray beside her on the cabinet. It was obvious from Mary's stiff body movements and darting eyes that she was uncomfortable being in her presence. She dipped into a courtesy and nodded her head before turning to leave. Something stopped her as she reached the doorway.

She turned and looked at Agatha for a second before saying, 'How are you feeling Miss? The doctor said this was meant to make you better?'

Agatha moved her gaze towards Mary, looked at her stomach and said, 'I fear I don't have long left. Thank you for your assistance, it is appreciated, especially in your condition. You could have left with the others.'

Mary walked back into the room, a confused look on her face. 'I wasn't allowed to, Lady Parks. The doctor said I must stay. It was all part of the plan, however if you're not getting better, I don't know what I am supposed to do.'

'What plan?'

'You don't know? But it was your idea?' Mary said confused. It was clear from the way her face was scrunched over in pain that standing was difficult for her. Agatha forced herself to sit upright and patted the space next to her on the bed, welcoming the young maid to sit down.

'Whatever are you talking about? I've been locked away in my room. He thinks I am crazy, they all think I am crazy. I don't get visitors, what plan could I possibly make?'

Mary started shaking her head as she tried to make sense of what was being said. 'No, it can't be.'

'Can't be what?'

'Well, you and the doctor were meant to be taking the child when it is born. He told me that you would look after it…'

Agatha rose from her lying position with such speed, Penny worried she might dislocate one of the frail bones sticking out from her skin. 'Child?'

'Yes, the babe growing inside me. I am not married you see.' She looked down at her belly in shame. 'So the doctor said you two would take it as your own. Although, if you're too ill then maybe I should…'

'Leave! You must leave!' Agatha grabbed Mary's arm. 'Before it is too late. You must leave. Now.'

'But I don't understand…'

'Leave… now,' Agatha whispered the words in the exact

250

way she had whispered them to Penny previously.

Thirty

Penny was now standing in the cave-room, although the room was no longer occupied by her sleeping mother and sister. Instead she saw the small wooden bed pushed to the side of the room looking crammed between three other identical beds which were sandwiched together. Penny glanced upwards and saw Mary bent over the bed shoving things into a small duffle-type bag. She saw that the effort was causing her stomach to kick back in protest as Mary continually scrunched her face in pain, cradling her belly with her spare hand. She tried to reach out to Mary, to ask her why she was seeing what she was seeing, but she realised that she had been cocooned back into her invisible bubble, unable to make a sound, despite her efforts.

Although she was pleased she had gained a bit of an insight into Mary and Agatha's lives, she couldn't understand why she had. It had been like she was looking at them from the outside in, as though she was sitting in the back seat of a cinema watching a series of events pan out. She recalled the violent encounter she had with the doctor and remembered the throbbing pain in her face as he was beating her mercilessly in the kitchen. She knew she had passed the point of no return. The words Agatha said to Mary haunted her mind. They were the exact same words she had whispered to Penny which she had foolishly decided to ignore. A feeling in the pit of her stomach told her that somehow the fate of Mary would be connected to her own.

Mary startled as she heard a sound in the background. She quickly pushed her bag under the bed and walked out of the door. Penny hurried after her; she had a strong sense that Mary walking out of the door would mean she would never walk back through it again. Mary rushed towards the kitchen just as the doctor entered the room, brushing off the cold of the winter's day as he shut the door behind him.

'I was just about to bring up the Lady her supper. I thought you deserved some too.' She turned her back on him. Penny thought she could see Mary's hands move to add something to the cup but the pregnancy had caused her back to swell out, and so she couldn't be sure.

'Is this the soup I made? Because Lady Parks has her medicine in that one.' He eyed the cup cautiously as she placed it into his hands.

'No, I'm afraid I burnt that lot. I became tired and had to lie down. I'm so sorry, perhaps you can give her the medicine later? I have just cooked this the way Cook had instructed me before she left.'

'Very well. Pass it to me.' Penny watched as the cup reached his mouth and he took a gulp of the liquid. Licking his lips, he said, 'Good job.'

Penny realised that Mary wasn't leaving. She was waiting to watch the doctor. Penny felt uncomfortable in the silence. They both stood staring at each other, daring the other to say something first. After a few seconds, Penny saw the doctor was beginning to lose his focus and that he was slowly swaying on his feet. Mary rushed forward and gently helped him into a chair. She moved the cup out of his hands but still continued to stand on her feet beside him, watching his face become redder and redder until it looked as though his tight collar was causing him to choke. He loosened it just as beads of sweat began swimming down his face.

'What did you put in here?' he coughed. 'You... you...

you…' His head dropped onto the table with a loud bang, causing both women to jump in surprise at the sudden movement.

Mary ran into the bedroom but Penny couldn't follow after her. She walked cautiously over to the doctor. He was still and silent. Penny did not know if he was sleeping or if Mary had killed him. Maybe that is why they didn't find the body, she thought. Perhaps they killed him and hid his body, scared of what would happen to them if anyone found out. Inside she jumped with victory. Mary had done it! She had defeated this evil man and would be free of his violent ways. As she was celebrating to herself, she was caught off guard when he suddenly reached for her arm. Penny jumped backwards and pushed him off her.

The pregnant maid came running into the kitchen, past Penny and up the stairs. She had dropped the bag Penny had seen her packing by the front door, but failed to look back at the doctor to check that whatever she had given him had done its job. If she had done she would have realised that his eyes were still moving and his arm twitching as he was trying to get it to move. She opened her mouth to warn her but the words wouldn't leave her throat. All at once she forgot about her own safety and what she had read in the library and thought of the pregnant young woman who had so bravely run up the stairs to help an invalid who was quickly travelling towards death.

Penny raced up the stairs and entered Agatha's room just as Mary was helping her get to her feet. She had placed one of her arms around her shoulder and was tugging her off the bed.

'I couldn't leave you with him. I found what he had been putting into your soup. It's arsenic. We must leave. Leave now. You need to get up.'

It seemed as though Agatha had lost the ability to speak

but she recognised the words Mary was saying. She seemed to find a strength that Penny believed took even her by surprise and suddenly she was on her feet and limping towards the door.

'We'll go out the main door. I put something in his tea, he's passed out on the table below. Try to hurry, we may not have long.'

The movements of the pair were painfully slow. Their capabilities to move anywhere fast had been hindered by their individual medical conditions slowing them down. Penny was jumping up and down on the spot, waving her hands in gestures to hurry them along. She went alongside Agatha and tried to pull on her second arm in the hope of moving her faster but as she reached out to touch her skin, she saw that her hands passed through Agatha's frail body. They needed to hurry. Penny's heart was racing in anticipation that they wouldn't get to where Mary was leading them. They needed to be faster.

They managed to make it to the staircase that connected them with the downstairs, passing it only seconds before they heard, 'Where do you think you are going?'

Her heart sank. At that moment, Penny knew that it was all over. They had tried, but they failed, to succeed. Penny almost cried as she saw the look on Mary's face as she turned to face the doctor and realised it too. It was too late; her heroic gesture had been pointless.

'She needs a doctor Sir. Another doctor I mean. I don't think she is getting better, I am worried about her.' Mary was thinking on her feet, 'If we can just get her perhaps to the hospital in Charterville, I heard they have excellent facilities there that...'

'You stupid bitches. You're all the same,' he roared at them. 'All you had to do you stupid, stupid, pathetic girl was give me that child. That is all I wanted. I don't care about you, about her, about anyone. I probably would have been good to you after the child, although you're just a cheap, dirty whore. But now you have ruined that plan. You wouldn't play nicely, would you? Now you need to be punished.'

'No!!!' Mary had let go of Agatha's arm. She turned to run but a sharp pain from her stomach made her double over. She tried again but it was no use, Penny saw that it would be impossible for her to move any further forward, fearing the baby was on its way.

The doctor was moving forwards and was now only inches away from the women, standing at the top of the stairs that lead to kitchen.

'You just had to do what I said,' the doctor growled.

He reached out his hand, threw it across his chest and with an almighty force swung it forward. Agatha noticed the impending danger and threw herself in front of Mary. The blow was so powerful it knocked the already weak woman off her feet, causing her to topple down the stairs head first.

An unearthly crack echoed up the stairway followed by Mary's shrill scream.

Penny rushed over to the stairs and saw Agatha lying at the bottom, her legs positioned up by the side of her head, which was unrecognisable as it lay in pieces within a pool of blood.

Thirty-One

'NOOOO!!' Mary screamed, rushing down the stairs after Agatha. She screamed once more when she reached the body. Penny was following from behind and retched at the sight of the mangled body and the smell that was suddenly filling the room.

Mary was sobbing uncontrollably and ran towards the door, not stopping to notice that the doctor was fast behind her.

'I didn't need her anyway. It is you that I need. Well not even you, the child.'

He grabbed her from behind and raised his hand to hit her. Knowing what was coming, she turned to move but as she did, his blow connected to her stomach, causing her to fall onto the floor. Concern spread across the doctor's face as he realised what he had just done. Urgently, he grabbed her arms and pulled her across the floor. Mary kicked and screamed until they reached the bathroom, attempting but failing to halt the process by gripping onto the woodwork of the corridor as she was pulled.

As they entered the bathroom he pushed her into the middle. He pulled her legs apart and said, 'It is time. The child will be mine.'

Penny couldn't stand the sight any longer. She knew what had happened next, she had seen it. She rushed out of the room and began screaming her family's names at the top of her lungs between desperate sobs. They needed to leave.

She needed to get out. Why hadn't she listened? She was well aware of the fate of the two women; she had read it in black and white. She ran in and out of the rooms, bashing around frantically to try and get back to the present. Why wasn't she going back? She continued to scream as she ran into each room twice. She would have to leave without them; she couldn't stay there a minute later. She ran towards the door but something made her stop. She heard footsteps getting louder behind her. She turned and saw the doctor with his back to her, cradling something in his arms.

'My child, my babe, what did you do to him?'

Mary flung herself at the doctor, covered in her own blood. She was hysterical with rage. She began punching and kicking at the man, pushing him towards the wall. Penny couldn't move. She was traumatised by the sight and frozen to the spot, shaking and crying as though she were a little child. Mary continued to kick and scream at the man until suddenly the room was silent once more. Penny saw Mary's body had become eerily still. She backed away from the doctor and Penny saw that she had a metal fire poker sticking out from her chest, glistening in the light which was bouncing through the window. The poker was pushed deep into her skin, red circling the edge where the sharp point had penetrated her skin. The doctor moved forward, noticing the recognition in Mary's eyes as he edged closer. In one swift movement, he yanked the poker out of her skin and threw it onto the floor. Mary had just enough energy to move her hands up to the big gaping hole before taking her final, raspy breath and she fell to the floor in a heap beside Agatha.

That was it. Penny knew she needed to move. She swallowed the tears which were now flowing down her face and flung open the door and sprinted outwards. She pushed herself forwards as fast as her legs would take her. She was grateful for the extra exercise she had been doing, despite her weight gain she was still fast on her feet. The path of trees was in front of her and if she could only get herself out beyond them, she knew she'd be safe. A sharp burning sensation from her muscles protested as she pushed them past the point where she knew she should stop. Finally, she reached the thin, leafless, spindly trees but she continued running. She needed to get out past the oak trees. Why weren't they getting any nearer? She continued forward yet the gap between her and the trees was not shortening. Having used all the breath left in her lungs she had to stop. Bent over, hands on her knees, she took deep breaths and quickly looked around.

In the time she had been running the air seemed to change. It was as though she were running inside a greenhouse, the temperature hot and humid, her hair literally sticking to her face. There was no sunlight, yet no moon, just a grey misty glow. She turned in a circle but her sight was not changing. Everywhere she looked she saw the path of trees grinning down at her. The more she looked the taller they became, as though they were engulfing her underneath them. She fell to the floor, hands covering her ears, trying make sense of what was happening. She thought this was what lunacy must feel like, trapped in her own mind.

A grunting noise broke her out of her trance and she turned to see the doctor pulling the bodies of both women, one after the other towards the trees. She couldn't move. All she could do was sit and scream. She watched as the doctor dug two deep graves and threw the pair in with such a roughness, she doubted he had any regret over what he had just done. When he was finished, he straightened his back and spat disgustingly into the graves. Penny couldn't help it, she was violently sick on the ground beneath her. He heard her heaving and gagging as her revulsion poured out of her body and suddenly she came into his focus.

He marched towards her and pulled what looked like a

blade from his pocket. Penny tried to get to her feet but the ground beneath her was wet and she was unable to get good purchase, causing her to fall flat on her face. She could taste the gritty moist soil entering her mouth as she tried to breath and move her head out of the dirt, tasting what it would be like to be thrown into her own muddy grave. Suddenly a sharp tug on her leg moved her backwards and she knew the doctor was dragging her bruised body over to where he had thrown the other women. She screamed out in burbled sobs, desperately trying to stop her descent as her fingernails pierced deep through the mud in her frantic attempt to stop this terrible destiny.

He rolled her over and pinned down her knees with his own. Penny felt the weight of his strong body overpowering hers and with one hand, he brought her arms above her head and threw his body down onto her so she was unable to move. Despite Penny wiggling furiously with every effort she had left, she wasn't strong enough to beat him and with his free hand, he lifted her jumper and placed the cold blade against her stomach. Penny couldn't move. He held the blade there for a few moments, seemingly enjoying seeing her stomach move back and forth as it matched her pounding heart. She felt the pain before she realised what he was doing, the blade was scratching upon her skin and she could feel her blood begin to seep out.

This was not how it was supposed to end for her. There had to be more than this. She closed her eyes and with all the energy she had left, kicked the doctor swiftly between his legs causing him to double over in pain. She pushed his body away from her and began running towards the house, falling once more as she tried to steady her feet.

He wasn't down for long and was running behind her, laughing his evil laugh as he was closing the distance between them. She daren't look back in case it slowed her down but she sensed he was getting closer, the same way prey in the wilderness would know it was being hunted. She could feel his eyes on her back as though they were burning a hole, marking the spot where he would finally push the blade in. Penny knew she had to speed up. Unlike the oak trees, the house was becoming closer. The adrenaline was keeping her going; she could feel it on the tip of her tongue as she neared, the excitement of being so close yet the frightfulness that she would not make it mixing together like a dangerous cocktail.

Finally she reached the door and tried to slam it shut. She scrambled through the doorway, almost falling over as she threw herself in so aggressively. The doctor had caught up and slammed his hand on the door, preventing it from closing, causing Penny to fly backwards across the floor.

He was upon her once more. Her head was dangerously close to where the two women had died, the smell of death still lingering in the air. He ran towards her with the knife and fell on top of her. This time the weight was too much for her to move. Her hands were running over the floor in a last attempt to find something to help her. His body was pressing down harder and she could hear from the grunting in his voice that he wasn't expecting such a fight. As his hands tried to still her thrashing arms, it spurred Penny on more. He grabbed her by the neck and tightened his fingers. Penny could feel her throat close and her eyes become tighter in her face but she wasn't going to stop. Finally her hand rested upon something, a glimmer of hope. It was sharp and heavy and she grabbed it and swung it hard into the doctor's body and did not let go until she felt him go limp.

Thirty-Two

Penny lay there for a few moments in shock as she tried to get air into her closed throat. When she realised the doctor wasn't going to retaliate, she tried to push him off her but she needn't have worried. Slowly the man vanished before her eyes, from the bottom up. The last thing she saw was his horrific face as the pieces of his body disappeared. She felt her body vibrate and realised that to an observer, it would have seemed as though she was having a fit; her body shaking in a way she was unable to control. Tears continued to run down her face but this time it was out of relief. She looked at her hands and saw them trembling as she held the metal poker and, realising it was the same instrument the doctor had used to kill Mary, Penny threw it across the floor and heard the echo as it bounced away.

She managed to get to her feet and walk towards the window, still cautiously looking around the room as though she didn't quite trust that she had made him disappear for good. She peered down at the pathway lined with trees that only moments ago had been teasing her so cruelly. They didn't look menacing now, just sad. Their bare branches pointed towards the one by their side, seemingly leaning that way for comfort, desperately seeking to share some of the burden of what had lain beneath them for so long. Penny now understood why they would never bloom, knowing that the fate of two desperate women lay miserably beneath them. A single tear rolled down her cheek as she remembered the horrific scene of the doctor disposing of their bodies and the two women that were controlled and manipulated by that horrible man.

Out of the corner of her eye Penny saw Agatha and Mary, walking hand in hand towards the oak trees down the path. They walked as though no one was watching and walked with purpose and with speed. Penny rushed out of the door to catch up with them; she wanted to know they were okay. As if sensing her approach, they stopped and turned to face her. They stood silently for a few moments, no gestures needed or words spoken. The memory of what had just happened was holding them together like a thread, sealing the gap between the past and the present. Finally, Penny felt free and noticed the wind was blowing in her hair as she raised her hand in recognition. They responded with a nod before they turned back and continued their walk past the spindly trees and out beyond the oak trees. Penny knew they were at peace and realised that this was why she was there, she had done what they had needed her to do. Content, she watched them walk towards the oak trees until the sun that shone vibrantly from beyond blinded her to the view.

Penny returned into the kitchen and saw that it had returned to how she remembered it. Nothing looked new and out of place and the old rusty fixtures had returned. Anita was pacing up and down the kitchen, looking as though she was muttering to herself. She jumped when she saw Penny walk through the opened door and pulled her into her arms, holding her tightly as she continued to mutter to herself. Penny felt herself relax as she allowed herself to sink into her aunt's arms. She enjoyed the embrace and found herself reaching around her back to pull her closer. Anita moved her away to arm's length and started straightening her hair the same way she used to do when she was a child.

'What happened?' she asked gently. Penny wasn't sure what she had been witness to but by the lack of urgency in her voice, she thought she had seen enough.

'It's okay. It's over now; we don't have to be scared anymore.'

'But that doctor? I saw him attack you but I couldn't do anything; it was as though I was glued to the spot.'

'He's gone now, he won't bother anyone again.'

'Did you find the child? Is that what they wanted?'

Penny looked out of the window and at the trees in front of the path. 'No I didn't, but I think they are at peace now.' Penny truly believed that. She had no anxiety and no strange feelings bubbling away in her stomach, she felt free.

'Goodness, is that the time?' her mother made her way into the kitchen. Penny smiled as she saw her nurturing figure enter the room. In a good mood, she ran over to her and enveloped her mother in her arms, 'Gosh, hello to you too.' She was taken by surprise but didn't push her loving daughter away.

Penny almost didn't want to let go. Having witnessed what the two poor women had encountered she now had a greater appreciation of how lucky she was to have such a kind and supportive mother in her life. She considered all the things her mother had unselfishly done for her and she thanked her silently inside for every single one.

'You're looking a lot better,' Anita said. It was true, her mother was fresh-faced and dressed, no longer looking so tired. She had a spring in her step and it seemed the sleep had done her good.

Her mother smiled and glanced at her watch, 'Oh my, its 5pm, I can't believe I slept all day. I was only planning on a little nap, seems all the excitement was too much for me. We've wasted the day, haven't we?' She looked disappointed.

Penny and Anita looked at each other and laughed.

'We've been keeping ourselves busy!' Anita mocked.

'Oh yeah... What have you been doing?'

'MORNING, or afternoon I guess.' Fiona marched through the door, also looking renewed and fresh, no longer looking like she would attack the first person who came into her path. 'I had the best sleep, I feel amazing. Ouch, you two; don't!'

'Well some of us haven't been sleeping all day,' Penny said, suddenly panicking that her clothes were showing signs of the trauma she had just been through. She thought that one day she might share the story with them, but not now, she had no energy left to answer the barrage of questions that would come her way if she did. Relieved, she saw no signs of trauma on her clothes or her face; it was as though it never happened.

'So, it's our last night. What shall we do?' Penny said, keen to make the most of feeling free.

'Well our train is first thing in the morning, so maybe an early night, although I doubt I will be able to sleep. I don't know what came over us; I have never slept that long in my life!' Her mother said.

Penny wondered why the two hadn't woken up with all the commotion going on around them. She vaguely remembered Anita saying that she tried to wake them but they wouldn't move. Agatha and Mary had tried to warn Penny away from what was inviting her in, perhaps it was their way of protecting some of them. Although Penny had freed them, she thanked them for this small favour.

'Why don't we go out and get some food in the pub down the road and then come back to sleep?' Fiona asked. 'You'd be surprised, Mum; I bet you could sleep again, I know I sure could.'

'Actually, what do you think about catching a train

tonight and heading back now?' Anita asked, eyeing Penny cautiously as she did, aware that hours ago she wanted to leave.

'Why ever would we do that? We'd have to pay double, I didn't get transferable tickets.' Penny's mother seemed offended even at the suggestion.

Anita continued looking at Penny, waiting for her reaction, willing her to speak out. This time she didn't need any time to consider her answer, she knew that they would be okay. She could feel it in the air, it was light and calm. She found herself standing a bit taller than before and she no longer felt as though someone was holding her heart trying to squeeze it shut.

'Just something we were talking about earlier,' Penny said, 'but thinking about it I don't think it's a good idea. I think staying for one final night will be absolutely fine.' She smiled with confidence, this time she was not pretending.

'Well if you're sure?' Anita gave Penny her final chance to object.

'I'm sure,' she squeezed Anita's arm as she walked towards the bedrooms.

They each returned to their rooms to freshen up for the evening ahead. Although feeling strangely content with what had happened, Penny was still keen to rid herself of the clothes she was wearing, stuffing them at the bottom of her bag which she found tucked away at the bottom of her bed. She made a mental plan to bin them as soon as she got home, not wanting to be reminded of what had happened. They didn't spend long getting ready and the foursome left the apartment for their final night out. They linked arms as they made their way to the oak trees. Penny couldn't help but shudder as she walked past the line of skinny trees and tried her hardest not to look back at them. Instead, she tried to remain focused on the path in front of her, enjoying the light air blowing against her skin.

They reached the pub and all ordered way too much food; none of them had eaten a thing since their meal the previous night, making them ravenous. Perhaps Penny allowed herself to drink a bit too much wine, partially congratulating herself on setting the two desperate women's spirits free, but also to try and savour some precious moments of the trip that she had missed out on. They talked and laughed and for the first time that holiday, Penny allowed herself to be fully immersed in what was going on around her, her mind no longer distracted and fearful about returning to Oak Tree House and anticipating what misery it would bring.

As they staggered back at around midnight they headed straight to their rooms. Penny felt relaxed as she pulled the duvet up around her shoulders and was looking forward to having a peaceful, uninterrupted night's sleep. For the first time in the entirety of her stay within the haunted house, she got what she wanted.

Thirty-Three

Penny woke naturally as the sun was coming up and stretched out her arms as she opened her eyes. She looked to her side and saw that everything was as it should be; her sister was lying beside her stirring, as she too was beginning to wake. Penny nestled herself back into the bed and enjoyed how peaceful she felt. She heard her aunt and mother walking up and down the apartment and could hear their natterings about how long they had left to pack. She smiled at the normality of it all; they were always panicking and fussing about something.

Not wanting to disturb her sister, she moved out of the bed quietly and moved towards the bathroom, waving at her mother who was standing at the bottom of the corridor looking stressed and flapping in her normal fashion. She paused as she stood outside the doorway and smiled as she saw the large amount of natural light pouring out from the cracks in the door. The bathroom was black no more.

She enjoyed a leisurely shower, appreciating the feeling of her body heating up from the almost boiling water. She thought she would use up all the water and there wouldn't be enough left for the others, but she cared not. She needed this shower more than them. As she returned to the bedroom she saw Fiona was out of bed and walked out of the room without saying hello; she had never been one for pleasantries in the morning. Penny collected the few belongings she had with her and stuffed them into her overnight bag. Once done, she rolled it into the hallway and sat down at the kitchen table to eat some of the breakfast spread that her mother had laid out.

The remainder of the morning was rather chaotic for everyone apart from Penny. She remained at the kitchen table as she saw the others flapping around. Her sister had realised that she had left a shopping bag in every room and was running around trying to ensure that she had packed up all the expensive items she had purchased over her stay. The volume of purchases surprised Penny; she hadn't noticed Fiona had returned with so many bags. Part of her felt guilty that she hadn't bought Jason a small souvenir the way they normally did, although she reasoned that this trip was not one that she wanted to be permanently reminded of every time she opened the fridge door. Her mother was also running around, worried that she hadn't packed everything and ensuring that nothing in the house description had been broken 'I don't want to lose the deposit,' she kept saying under her breath. Anita was mainly running between the two women, nearly giving herself a heart attack in the process of trying to get them to calm down. Penny loved watching her family. Only a few days ago she knew she would have found this tiresome and unbearable to watch, but now she looked at them with admiration, thankful that she had been given the opportunity to spend this time with them.

Finally they managed to pack everything and have something to eat before heading for the door. Anita was the first one out, clearly not wanting to stay in there a moment longer than absolutely necessary.

'Goodbye apartment, you have been fun,' her mother said as she placed the set of keys in the middle of the table.

Penny was the last to leave. As she was closing the door, she gave one final look around the kitchen and remembered what had happened the night before. The last thing she looked at was the black door, still locked, looking untouched.

269

'Rest in Peace, Mary and Agatha,' Penny whispered under her breath as she closed the door behind her.

They made their way down to the end of the road, under the oak trees until they reached the street.

'Hey, look at that,' Fiona said, stopping them in their tracks. Her face turned backwards as she looked at the path they had just walked down. 'The trees look different today.'

Penny turned to see what her sister was talking about. The trees did look different. Before they had formed an archway, framing a path that led to Oak Street. Now there was no arch, the trees stood very separate and were no longer touching, as if they'd had a fight and were refusing to touch branches in an act of defiance. Whereas before you could barely see past them, they now gave a clear view of the main house from the street.

Her mother shrugged, 'Maybe it was that big wind that came a few nights back, pushed them back a bit?'

Penny looked at the trees, puzzled by the contrast in their appearance, while the others walked on. When she could no longer hear her family walking in the distance, Penny decided she had spent enough of her time worrying about what was going on down Oak Street, turned her back to the trees and ran to catch up with her family.

They boarded the train and Penny chose to sit next to her sister by the window, linking arms and sharing a bag of chocolate as the train left the station. She was aware of her sister talking to her about what she had missed on the days she was 'unwell' but couldn't focus on what she was saying. The rocking sensation of the journey made Penny realise how exhausted she was. She closed her eyes and was woken five minutes before the train pulled into the station near home.

'So, Jason called me while you were asleep. I think your

phone is still out of battery. He sounded quite worried about you. I told him that we were on our way back and he said that he would leave work a few hours early to meet you back at the flat,' Fiona said. 'It sounded liked he missed you.' She gave her sister a wink.

Poor Jason, she thought. Once again she had failed to check in and let him know she was safe. She felt her stomach fill with butterflies at the thought of seeing him. All she wanted was to get back to her own flat and cuddle beside him where she could be sure of being safe. As he was planning on returning to their flat earlier than anticipated, Penny passed on the offer of going back to her mother's house for a quick cup of tea. She hugged the others in turn as she queued for her taxi. She thanked her mother for organising the trip and told her sister that they would arrange a night out soon. Anita stood before her and cuddled her a bit longer than the others.

'Are you sure you're going to be okay tonight?' she asked.

'Of course, I'm home now. Nothing can happen to me there; besides, I sorted everything out. Sorry you had to go through that too.'

Anita looked at Penny as though she was unconvinced by her response before hugging her once more. 'You let me know when you get home and call me if… well, if you need me.'

Penny gave Anita a kiss on the forehead and jumped in the nearest taxi. She couldn't wait to get home and could feel the butterflies begin to take flight in her belly. She threw the driver the money as she reached her road and felt immediate relief as she took in the familiar scent of her own home as she pushed open the door.

She placed her keys down by the side of the door and saw the note she had left for Jason still sitting on the table next to the phone. She smiled as she remembered writing it. The first thing she needed to do was charge her phone so she could tell Jason she was home. She found a spare charger lying on the kitchen counter and plugged it in. While she was waiting, she opened the fridge and found a bottle of wine chilling. She felt her jeans rubbing against her stomach and debated whether she should have the extra calories. Deciding she deserved it, she poured herself a large glass and changed into comfortable clothes, finally settling down on the sofa and pulling a throw over her curled up legs. As she was enjoying being in her own home, she saw out of the corner of her eye the landline was blinking with messages. She stretched out her arm and pressed play.

'Penny, it's me. Fi told me that you were on your way back. I have a meeting that I can't get out of but I am going to leave as soon as I can. See you soon.' It was Jason's voice. Penny smiled at the thought of him coming home early; she couldn't wait to see him. She wondered whether to tell him everything that had happened. Although she had shared a little of her troubles when she called him while she was away, she wasn't sure filling him in on the whole story was wise. She wasn't sure he would believe her; she was struggling to believe it herself.

She glanced around the flat to try and find something to occupy her time before he came home. She noticed on the small dining table under the window, there was a stack of papers sprawled out. Walking over, she moved her hands across them, not taking much notice until she saw one paper which had **OAK STREET** in big bold letters displayed across the top. This must have been the research Jason had done for her, she thought. She smiled as she saw the amount of effort that he had clearly gone to; grateful that he was prepared to do that for her even though he may have initially thought she was foolish for suggesting the apartment could be haunted.

The first article she picked up she had already seen, it was the print-out of the advertisement for the apartment her mother had disappointedly showed her when they realised they had not been given what they had paid for. This advert showed a brand new, refurnished apartment that was completely different to the one they had stayed in. She put that aside and picked up another.

LEGEND OF OAK STREET

The legend of Oak Tree House situated at the end of a path lined with trees is one which is puzzling and a mystery yet to be unravelled. In the 1800's the house was owned by Lord and Lady Peel, intelligent socialites who were landed gentry, having inherited most of their huge fortune and estate. They spent the majority of their days idly entertaining their fashionable friends or travelling the world. They had one child, Agatha, born to them late in life and who, by all accounts, was considered a strange child.

Lord and Lady Peel tried their best to instil in Agatha the traditional ways but stories have revealed that Agatha throughout her life was 'odd', almost verging on insane. Although they tried their best to include her in their activities, Agatha would often appear out of place amongst the fashionable crowd.

Concern grew for her future when she was unable to choose a husband from the many suitable men her parents introduced her to. Lord and Lady Peel became increasingly concerned when they realised her 'health' conditions could easily be taken advantage of when they were no longer around to protect her. To this end they wrote a condition in their will that the total control of their estate would be passed down only to Agatha and or any children she produced. In the event of Agatha's death, if there were no surviving children, the estate would be left to charity.

Tragedy struck one day when Lord and Lady Peel were travelling back from a three-month holiday. The carriage they were travelling in hit a bump in the road and overturned. They did not die instantly but a friend of the family, Doctor Parks, who was working nearby, was able to offer them some comfort in their final moments. It is recorded in the Parish Records that Doctor Parks married Agatha quietly in the local church soon after their death.

Legend has it that the old house under the oak trees is haunted by two ghosts, that of a young maid and her evil killer Agatha, the lady of the house. The story goes that Agatha was jealous of the young maid's beauty and pushed her down the stairs in a fit of rage. There have been a handful of sightings...

Penny put the article to one side. Yes, the place was haunted but not for the reasons stated in the report.

She picked up another;

In 2006, Cosy Holiday Rentals purchased the house, supposedly haunted, and have spent a significant sum on refurnishing the apartments. The owners are aware of the history of the house, and the apparent ghosts that have been seen but are keen to put the past behind them. Prior to the refurbishment, a young girl who had been renting the apartment with a group of friends was found dead one morning after an evening meal back in 2005. The police report states that the female, Emma Greene, was found in the kitchen lying in a puddle of blood, after having slipped and hit her head in the middle of the night. Unbeknownst to her friends, Emma was pregnant and the trip killed both mother and child. Cosy Holiday Rentals have updated the house to make this dreaded place into something modern to attract new visitors...

Penny's hand shook as she read this article. Although she didn't know anything further about this other woman, she thought that it was too much of a coincidence that she was found dead in the very spot where Doctor Parks had tried to kill her. She very much doubted that this was a coincidence. She realised how lucky she had been; Penny could have easily had been another news report of a tragic death in the apartment.

The voicemail beep went off again and this time a woman's voice spoke.

'Hi, this is Claire from Cosy Holiday Rentals returning a call for Jason. I don't really know what to say… to be honest I shouldn't really be calling you but your message sounded urgent. I'm not meant to say anything if anything happened, in case what happened before happened again. All I can say is that your suspicions are correct. Something bad has happened and probably is happening within that apartment. As much as I wanted to go there, there was nothing I can do…'

'Hello?' Penny picked up the phone.

There was no response.

'Claire, this is Penny. I believe we met on our first day. Anyway, we are home now,' Penny said.

'Oh… well… that's… that's great. I hope you enjoyed your stay; bye…'

'Hang on.' Penny interrupted her. 'You were saying something to my boyfriend about the apartment?'

Silence.

'Listen, I saw and experienced things in there that I shouldn't have. If you know anything about that, I would be grateful if you could tell me?'

There was a long pause before Claire said, 'I'm really not supposed to be calling. Jason, I take it he is your boyfriend? He called after he got some worrying phone calls from you. I hung up because I didn't know what to do. The truth is I never wanted to be put onto that horrible house. I grew up around here you see and I heard the stories. But I had no choice. The thing is, I never actually believed the tales until you walked through the door.'

'What do you mean? What tales?' she asked.

'Well, legend has it that a man killed a young, pregnant woman. Or a woman who had given birth. Anyway, the baby was meant to be his and he didn't get it. This made him angry. Their spirits both live within the house. Well I tried not to believe that but as soon as you stepped foot into the apartment, everything changed quickly. My boss spent a fortune removing any trace of previous decorations and features. When you stepped in the door, that all changed. The apartment changed within seconds. I was no longer standing in a modern kitchen but one that looked exactly as it did when that poor girl died. And when I looked at you in the shop. You… well… you… you were covered in blood.'

'What? That is ridiculous,' Penny laughed, not believing what Claire was telling her.

'But that means, if you were covered in blood… Hang on, let me think of the story.' She paused for a few seconds as Penny held her breath. 'Well if you were covered in blood but made it out… Oh God… are you pregnant? I've got to go…'

The phone disconnected.

Penny stared at the phone in her hand in disbelief. What was she talking about? Pregnant? Why would that matter? She pulled her laptop out from where she kept it under the sofa and powered it up. When the screen lit up she saw that Jason had left his last internet page open. It was another archived news article. Penny shuddered as she scrolled down and saw a grainy black and white drawing of the doctor. Instinctively she slammed the laptop shut, not wanting to look at his face. Her hands trembled as she remembered what Claire had just told her and reluctantly she opened it back up.

THE DISAPPEARANCE OF DOCTOR PARKS

Over the years there have been many stories surrounding the mysterious goings-on at Oak Tree House and of the ghosts that haunt it.

Nobody knows exactly what happened to cause the tragic deaths of the two women, or of Dr Parks' involvement in them.

One legend has it that the man was so angry that his plan was thwarted that he pledged to spend the rest of eternity haunting the apartment until a pregnant woman entered.

Stories are that his ghost wanders around the apartment making noises and scaring the inhabitants until he makes a connection with someone. Although there have been reports of strange things happening within Oak Tree House, no one has actually communicated with the ghost apart from one group of 'ghost hunters' who spent a weekend wandering around the house.

During a séance, the doctor made contact and told them that he would only be seen by 'a woman with child'. The test was then for the woman to get through a 'locked door'. Once this door was opened, the man would no longer inhabit the house but instead inhabit the woman's mind until the baby was born and he would take it away...

Penny shut the laptop quickly and pushed it off the sofa. No, that can't be right. At least she wasn't pregnant. Suddenly, a hundred memories came flooding back through her brain that were desperately trying to be placed in a logical order. She remembered the feeling of bloating she had before she left, how she was annoyed that she was putting on extra pounds despite her healthy eating and daily exercise. A feeling of dread hit her hard as she recalled the continued sickness she experienced in the mornings recently. Surely she couldn't be pregnant. How could she not have realised? Everything started to make sense and Penny had knots in her stomach as she tried to figure out if it could be possible. She was so certain she didn't want to have a child yet in a few short seconds, everything in her life could potentially change.

She rushed to the bathroom and opened the cupboard doors, pushing everything out onto the floor. Although she was normally careful, she kept a pregnancy kit in the back. She had bought it a while back when one of her friends had found herself in need. They had gone together to buy the test and this was the second one that came in the pack. Penny had stored it safely away in case of any other such emergencies. She sat on the toilet, anxiously biting her nails and waiting for the blue lines to show on the screen. She read and reread the instructions to make sure there was no room for error. When she realised it was time, she turned the stick over. She refused to open her eyes for a few moments as she knew what it was going to say. Her heart stopped when she eventually turned the little stick over and saw the lines confirming her fate. She was pregnant.

She didn't know what to think, she wasn't ready for a child. She thought of Jason and knew it would be okay. Her memories turned to Mary and how her lover had abandoned her when she told him the news. Jason wouldn't do that to her, she was sure of it. All she had to do was wait for him to come home and they would talk about this, talk about their options. Placing all the items she had practically thrown onto the floor back neatly into the cupboard, she thought that maybe having a child wouldn't be the worst thing in the world. She and Jason had been together for some time; it was surely the next logical step forward in their relationship.

Regaining her breath, she opened the door of the bathroom and made her way outside. Her phone would be charged now; she would grab it and find out where Jason was and how long it would be until he got home.

Penny stepped into the hall, the stick still clutched tightly in her hand. She saw the outline of Jason's figure standing by the door, his back to her. Penny gulped as she looked at his familiar broad shoulders and tried to push away the fear that was slowly building when she thought about telling him her news. Knowing she had no reason to be fearful, she swallowed her dread, took a deep breath and moved towards him.

She tried not to notice that the hallway had suddenly turned cold and that the familiar broad shoulders were becoming less so the closer she walked towards him. The temperature plummeted further as her steps neared the silhouette.

She stopped walking.

Dropping the stick out of her trembling hands, she tried to turn away but she was frozen to the spot.

Slowly, the man turned around and Penny screamed.

Doctor Parks was standing directly in front of her, his arms outstretched, beckoning her forward, an evil grin spread menacingly across his face.

Acknowledgements

There are a number of people whom I would like to thank, for without their unwavering love and support, this book would not have made it to publication stage.

Firstly, thank you to Lizzie Gardner for creating my Paperback and Digital cover. You took an idea from my head and transformed it into my perfect debut cover and I couldn't be happier with how it turned out. A huge thank you needs to be given to my wonderful editor, Loma Halden who worked on giving my novel a 'professional polish' ahead of the second edition rerelease.

In March 2016, my mother organised a girly trip away for my sisters 30th birthday. We didn't travel to my fictional world of Charterville or Oakdene, but visited the beautiful city of Bath. Excited about our weekend away, we enthusiastically dropped our bags off into our beautiful apartment just outside the city. Whilst the old apartment was without a doubt beautiful, there were certain aspects of it that were strange. There was a locked door tucked away in the corner, strange pictures on the wall and a freezing cold cave-like room at the back where my sister and I stayed. It didn't take long for us to make up stories after a few bottles of wine and we tried to ignore our fear when we heard bumps coming from the vacant floor above and noticed cupboard doors opening mysteriously on their own. Whilst we all allowed our imagination to get carried away with us on that wonderful trip, *my* imagination was planning my very first novel and The House Beneath the Oak Trees was born. Thank you to my mother, sister and Aunty Ann for creating a trip I will remember forever!

I would like to say thank you to my sister for all her

support and encouragement in helping me finish this book. Thank you for reading my many drafts and spending hours in the library critiquing and giving me your opinion (although I didn't always listen). Your support and encouragement has meant the world to me and without my number one cheerleader keeping me motivated, I doubt I would have remained positive at times. To my father, who has always been the person who has encouraged me to write, from poems when I was younger up until now. Over the years you have always asked, 'you written that book yet?' and been the one person who believed I would actually do it one day. You have always believed in me and I thank you from the bottom of my heart for all your love and support, not only whilst writing this book but always.

To my partner Dave, for everything you do for me. Thank you for funding part of this project, listening to me talk about it for hours on end, calming me down when I have found the process a little overwhelming and always telling me that I could do it. You have refused to be a 'dream stealer' and you have pushed me further when I felt like giving up. From writing silly annotations in the margins of my early drafts, to sending me funny pictures whilst in a writing haze, you have never failed to make me laugh! Having you by my side supporting me has made me feel as though anything is possible and there is no way I would be writing these acknowledgements without you in my life.

The biggest thank you I need to give is to my personal editor, my mother. Not only being the reason why I fell in love with books when I was a little girl, you have held my hand at every single part of this writing journey. From the original idea, the first draft, the editing, read throughs, and more editing, you have been amazing! You have put nearly as many hours as I have into this book and there are no words to express the level of gratitude I feel for your unconditional love and support. Thank you for never giving up and ensuring that I didn't either. Sorry for the late-night phone calls, endless days of reading and holiday days spent crouching over the countless drafts, rearranging and editing. I'm glad we got to share this experience together and I hope I have put enough hyphens in for you!

Finally, thank you to whoever is reading this, thank you for purchasing my book. It has been a long journey to get to this stage and I really hope you enjoy reading The House Beneath the Oak Trees as much as I have enjoyed writing it!

About the Author

Faye Belle is a British author and the House Beneath the Oak Trees is her debut novel.

For more information about Faye, visit her website www.fayebelle.org

Printed in Poland
by Amazon Fulfillment
Poland Sp. z o.o., Wrocław